TWO MOONS OVER C

"YOU KILLED HER!"

"That ain't the way of it. We gotta go back." Salter's eyes darted from the boy's face to his grip on the stick and he could feel the boy digging deep for the level of hatred it would take him to carry out the deed. Salter's voice rose at the same time he tried to rise from his knees.

"I gotta go back, Jack. I gotta let them know where I buried it."

He had time to protect himself, but he did not. He could have ducked a half-dozen times as, in a leisurely pace and close up, the knotty pine stick in Jack's white knuckled grip rushed toward his temple and found its mark. Salter had no desire to save himself. Somehow, he had known all along that this was how it would end. There was no place on earth he could have found to make a home for himself and Grace as man and wife.

Sofie Couch

TWO MOONS OVER CEDAR HILL

Sofie Couch

Copyright © 2013 by Annette Couch-Jareb. All rights reserved. No part of this book may be used or reproduced in any manner whatsoever without written permission, except in the case of brief quotations embodied in critical articles and reviews. For information, write to Sofie Couch at sofie@sofiecouch.com

Manufactured in the United States of America

International Standard Book Numbers
ISBN-13: 978-1492893356
ISBN-10: 1492893358

This book is a work of fiction. Names, characters, and incidents are the product of the author's imagination. Any resemblance to actual events, places, or persons, living or dead, is entirely coincidental.

TWO MOONS OVER CEDAR HILL

In Memory of
Ann Elizabeth Crump Couch

Who never showed frustration with a houseful of unruly grandchildren, but rather, told us to go outside and search for the lost family treasure.

Sofie Couch

TWO MOONS OVER CEDAR HILL

By Sofie Couch

Sofie Couch

"...the distinction between past, present, and future is only a stubbornly persistent illusion."
– Albert Einstein

TWO MOONS OVER CEDAR HILL

Chapter 1

Cedar Hill, 10 years ago

It was pitch dark, but that made little difference to Stewart, who tapped a red-tipped cane along the fence. There were sixty-six fence posts between the house and the road, fifty-four cedar trees along the way, one 'chuck hole, three boulders that were too big for Jorgé to move with the tractor, and a pothole at the end of the drive where he used to wait for the school bus. Stewart couldn't see any of those hazards, but at eighteen, he had memorized every hazard his home had to offer. He knew this farm better than most sighted people.

Before he touched the third of the sixty-six fence posts, he heard the pick-up truck's engine. Jorgé would not be able to stop him this time. He was determined to leave.

The truck idled beside him and he turned his ear, rather than his eyes, toward the sound.

"Need a ride?"

Christina. "Go home."

"I don't know about you, Stewart, but this hasn't felt much like 'home' for a while now."

"I've already called a cab. It's pickin' me up at the end of the drive."

Stewart kept moving and Christina played a balancing act with the clutch to find a speed slow enough to stay alongside her brother.

"And how long do you think your savings is going to last if you throw it away on expensive cabs? It'll cost $40 just to get to the bus station."

"I'm taking the train."

"Think we can get a group discount?"

"Go - home," he enunciated his words. Only Christina could tell he was working hard to keep his voice from going quavery. Twins knew things about one another that other people did not notice. Stewart knew more about his twin sister than nearly anyone else. *Nearly*.

"I'm going with you."

He stopped walking and Christina stopped the truck.

"I'm not going back," he challenged.

"I'm not asking you to, Stewart. What Mama did - is unforgivable – sending Annabelle away, but she must have had cause…"

"She paid Annabelle to leave. She wasn't sent. She *chose* the money over me."

." Now her voice went quavery, so she cleared her throat. "I… can't stay here any longer either."

Her voice grew faint, and Stewart could tell she was looking over her shoulder, away from him, as she spoke.

"And what about… you and Jorgé?"

TWO MOONS OVER CEDAR HILL

No one had ever said it out loud before. It had been silly of Christina to think no one had noticed.

"He's made his choice too. He's gonna stay here with Mama… and the farm."

"You told him you, we, were leaving?"

Christina nodded, knowing full well her twin brother couldn't see her. "Yes."

"And he didn't try to stop you?"

"No." Her voice caught. "Will you just get in the truck already?"

Stewart let go the fence and tapped his cane on the ground until it clunked against the tire, then with his hand on the fender, then the hood, then the opposite fender, he rounded the truck to the passenger-side door and climbed in. He stuffed his backpack at his feet and both he and his sister, drove away from the only home either had ever known.

"Where to?" he asked.

"You didn't have a plan?"

"I had a plan… to get as far as the train station."

Christina looked both ways at the end of the driveway, then with decisiveness, she turned out onto the road, in the direction that would take them to the interstate.

"Where're you driving us?"

Christina swallowed hard. "The only *other* place we have any right to go."

Sofie Couch

Stewart leaned toward her, put his hand on her head, and then kissed her cheek. It was wet.

TWO MOONS OVER CEDAR HILL

Chapter 2

Cedar Hill, 1864

We are all slaves to someone… or something… and Salter Lyons was both.

The blade preceded his hand and a curl of wood wound up over his knuckles, the shadow cast by the candle, moving away at an angle like chimney smoke as Salter finished carving the initials and the date into a beam, "G.T. + S.L. 1864", high up enough that no one would notice for a very long time. He thought, maybe if he just drove the knife blade down into the wood deep enough he might have been able to lodge there, digging in and never having to leave his home, this place of enslavement.

But the task was done, his initials and the initials of the woman he loved, carved into the beam and into the center of his heart.

He climbed down from the loft and picked up a piece of fatwood from the corner beside the fire, then lit it from his own hearth. It flared bright.

Salter silently opened the hinged tin door on the lantern above the mantle and lit the stub of candle in it. Lantern in hand, he opened the wood batten door, its leather hinges creaked softly. The dewy chill from outside crept in around his ankles. Salter looked at the log house one last time. His mother's ghost sat at the hearth weeping over the children who never made it to full grown and wept for the only child who did survive - him. He closed the door and, like most people, never saw the vision of his mother.

Outside, a wooden trunk with metal straps stood against the split pile of firewood. Salter hefted the trunk to his shoulder, then with his free hand, picked up a spade and the lantern. As with everything in his life, it was just a matter of finding a balance that he could live with.

With store-bought, leather shod footsteps that sunk into the moss, Salter made his way into the woods and the weight of the trunk lifted with increments equal to the distance he put between himself and those who would call him property.

This mountain was as much his as anyone who claimed ownership. Here it did not matter if the color of your skin was butter white or bark brown. If there was a wild dog, mountain cat or bear hungry enough, they would eat you. This was his home and it would take more than oppression to see him driven from it. Trees creaked above him. Small animals scurried away from him and twinkling "peek-a-boo" moss winked back at him.

The ground slowly rose with the thickening of trees until it was too dark to navigate even with a lantern, or it would have been if Salter did not know this hillside better than his own backside.

He came out of the woods into a clearing and the lantern lit a circle that touched the edge of his own brother's grave. This place, marked at its four corners by four young cedar trees, was where he intended to bury the trunk.

Lowering the trunk from his shoulder, he moved to a spot a good number of yards from the other grave stones, simple shards of slate that jutted up from the ground. The clay was hard, but Salter's muscle was harder and he turned his back on the dead, then carefully put the lantern on a piece of flat stone.

He cleared the ground of underbrush, pulling back the sheet of antler moss to expose the rich black, pungent dirt. Not more than an inch below that was nothing but rock hard red clay and shale.

He dug with the spade and his calloused hands never smarted from the exertion, yet the deeper he dug, the more tears he shed, the shovel gnawing at the wound in the earth like it was his own liver pecked by crows. He tried to tell himself that he would find a new and better home. One where he and Grace could live together, marry, raise a family. Then he would come back for her.

He drew the task out, digging the hole deeper than was strictly necessary for hiding a trunk, a full five feet. Then he dug out the hole at both ends so that it was six feet long and more closely resembled a fresh dug human grave. Not even a Yankee would dig up a fresh turned grave.

Sofie Couch

When the hole was finished he stood in the wound and put his arms on the earth's surface and laid his head on his folded arms. The dirt mounded on both sides of the hole resembling the dark loins that bore him as a babe. The similarity was not lost to him. It protected him, but like his mother's body twenty-odd years ago, it would eject him.

Birds began to twitter in the trees. A glow seeped up from the east. When his shoulders were wet with dew, he raised his head and climbed out of the womb.

A snap and two buckles released the lid on the trunk and Salter put his arm in and pulled out an oil cloth. As careful as if it was a new baby, he wrapped the trunk in its oil hide, then slipped the swaddled trunk into its earthen nest. The clang of metal inside the trunk, poorly cushioned in a blanket, was absorbed by the hard packed red clay tomb.

Salter clenched his teeth. The dirt mounded easily, just like a fresh grave and after patting it down with the back side of the spade, he dropped to his knees to say a prayer. This prayer was not for the salvation of any soul other than his own.

Behind him a twig snapped. He lifted his head.

"Salter? What're you doing up here?"

Still on his knees, Salter blinked, waking from whatever fantasy he had concocted that would see him safely out of this place. He squinted through the

TWO MOONS OVER CEDAR HILL

dark trees, although he knew the voice as well as his own. He hastily wiped his eyes on the arm of his shirt.

"Jack? That you?" Salter's voice was stale from disuse and the white boy's name came out slurred.

Jack Lyons stepped out of the trees into the circle of light. "Somebody die?"

Salter looked down at the mound of dirt beneath him. "One the dogs over to Cedar Hill… Ain't nobody else had time to bury him and… he starting to stink. So I told Mrs. Thompson I take care of it." He lied poorly, a virtue at any other time, but a curse at present. He did not think the boy was fooled.

The boy looked around nervously. "Anybody else up here to help you?"

To the boy's credit he did not ask Salter if he was there in the indecent hours of the morning with Grace.

"Don't take but one person to bury a old dog."

Jack's eyes moved from the foot of the grave, up its full six feet in length and Salter watched as something in the boy snapped.

Jack Lyons looked around, saw a stick, a piece of pine the size of a healthy ax handle, and snatched it up.

Sofie Couch

Salter had taught this boy everything there was for a young man to convey to a boy, from brick making to peeing on target. He called the boy, "sweetie" and "sugar", and the boy called him "Uncle" and used to mean it in the familial sense, but as he had grown up, he felt the weight of the title as it was intended – to distance young folks from marrying outside their own skin color. When the boy, Jack, was little, it was Salter who was assigned the task of taking the boy out back to beat him with a switch when he disobeyed his mother. Salter wept more than the boy on those occasions and the boy never held that against him. Now it would be the boy's turn to beat him for lying and Salter knew he could never allow that. They used to share their thoughts about the on-going War Between the States, but with the rising separation of neighbors, the boy and man had also grown apart. As if the boy had been saving up every ounce of his racial prejudice, hatred and condemnation of the war, in Jack's eyes, Salter had become the cause of his every hurt - just some half animal nigger who raped and murdered white girls.

Salter read the boy's thoughts as clearly as if he had voiced them aloud.

Salter, still on his knees, looked up at the boy.

"Sweetie, I see what you're thinking. But that ain't the way of it. I come out here to bury something. Something *else*." He shook his head. "I'd deserve more than that look you're giving me now if I'd been guilty of what you're thinking."

Jack shook his head, his bottom lip beginning to tremble. "Why'd you do it?" His eyes filled with tears. "She loved you. I saw it. Saw the two of you… earlier." He looked over his shoulder as though he could see the spot where she and Salter had lain just a few hours ago, her white skin in the moonlight and the absence of color in the shape of his dark silhouette on top of her. There had been no violence there, only consent, acceptance, and love.

Jack's eyes spilled over. He turned back to face Salter. "I wasn't close enough to see proper." He took on a cornered animal look. "That must'a been it. You forced her?" His voice broke. "You forced her and I was standing right there all the time? I could'a… could'a helped her?" His eyes fell to the fresh grave. "You might as well be buryin' me alive."

"That ain't the way of it. We gotta go back." Salter's eyes darted from the boy's face to his grip on the stick and he could feel the boy digging deep for the level of hatred it would take him to carry out the deed. Salter's voice rose at the same time he tried to rise from his knees.

"I gotta go back, Jack. I gotta let them know where I buried it."

He had time to protect himself, but he did not. He could have ducked a half-dozen times as, in a leisurely pace and close up, the knotty pine stick in Jack's white knuckled grip rushed toward his temple and found its mark. Salter had no desire to save himself. Somehow, he had known all along that this was how it would end. There was no place on earth he could have found to make a home for himself and Grace as man and wife.

Instead, he reached to his throat to clasp the necklace that had always lain there against his heart. It was gone.

Thwack.

The stick snapped in half. Salter's body unfolded from its half kneeling position and fell to a flat sprawl, his lips and nose smashed into the fresh dug dirt. His last breath was of that piece of ground he loved best in the world.

In the first instant, Salter might have held on to life, but he found that he had lost his taste for living and he rose up.

Looking down on the vessel that used to hold Salter, he never felt the repeated blows, then kicks to his head. His spirit rose and turned toward a brighter place – a place full of the smell of sweet sweat and bright sunshine and warm mud.

On earth, everything was inequitable and weighted against him. Here was the balance of things.

TWO MOONS OVER CEDAR HILL

On earth, the boy continued to strike at the body with the stick, then the broken end of the stick until the flame of the lantern's candle was blown out. Then he kicked him about the head and body until the boy was exhausted and stood panting over him. Then he wept.

The boy rolled Salter's body over onto its back. He stroked the dark cheeks, kissed his lips and wept some more.

With as much tenderness as the boy had shown fury, he caressed Salter's face and chest, willing him to be drawn back into the vessel… too late.

Tidewater, present day

Christina woke tasting her own tears… and slowly, she remembered where she was, not at home. Home was ten years and three hundred miles away. She reached to her head expecting to touch blood and a concave dent in her skull. What she felt was her hair, wild from sleep, and tears hot on her face and salty in her mouth, but there was no blood. No bashed in skull. She ran her hands down her face, over her breasts, then down one arm until her hands were extended. She looked at her hands. Her skin was a white half-shade darker than the rest of her family's, darker even than her twin brother's skin, but not the sun baked black of the man in her… dream? He looked so familiar.

Sofie Couch

Or was it mental illness, the result of too much inbreeding?

TWO MOONS OVER CEDAR HILL

Chapter 3

Cedar Hill, present day

October 25th...
Dear Christina,
> *I have many regrets in my life, but of those, my greatest regret is having allowed this divide to come between me and my children. I am sorry and hope that soon you might come to know and understand me a little better. I love you, something I have admitted but twice in my life.*

Your Mother — Mayella Thompson

Words came easy when they flowed from the tip of her pen. Words spoken had the annoying habit of tripping over her teeth. She was vain in her satisfaction that she had been able to retain most of her original teeth, although the rest of her body was falling apart. Mayella folded the lined note paper and placed it inside the front cover of her journal and slipped it to follow the other two journals, a transcription of her life, between the mattress and box spring. The effort caused her the loss of much of the strength she had been holding in reserve. She shoved the marble composition notebook under the mattress so only a corner of it protruded, then she sat up too quickly and had to steady herself with twisted hands on the edge of the bed. After a moment to recover she took the phone from the bedside table, then leaned back against her pillows. Again, she had to pause to summon the courage to dial the number she had long since committed to a central spot in her memory from which every other thought was spun.

"Damn coward," she muttered to herself, then dialed before she could think of an excuse not to make the call.

A voice on the other end of the line answered.

"Hope Chest. Can I help you?"

Mayella went dumb, the words slipping around behind her stubbornly permanent teeth.

"Hello? Can I help you?"

Mayella cleared her throat. "Christina. It's me."

Then there was silence on Christina's end of the line.

"Christina? You there?" In her agitation, Mayella practically rubbed a hole into the wrinkled head of the old dog that lay beside her on the bed.

"I'm here. Is that you?... Mama?"

Mayella was a brittle old apple tree, afraid she might snap if ever she tried to bend. Her limbs creaked as she melted back into the pillows. "It's me."

"What's wrong?"

The older woman took her hand off of the dog's head and held the receiver with two hands to steady the shaking. She funneled her every reserve into her voice, speaking with more strength than she had in a month. "I suppose you know it would have to be death or dismemberment for me to up and call you after all these years."

"So which is it?" There was no forgiveness in Christina's voice.

Mayella wondered if her daughter looked as bitter as she sounded. Her regrets doubled.

"Death."

Christina's sharp inhale was audible through the phone line, having been lulled into a dormant stupor, then recoiled and sprung 300 miles and ten years back on herself.

"No... not...."

"No. *He's* fine." And then Mayella laughed, an indication of her own taut wires. She never laughed and she quickly capped the hysterical flow lest it should bubble right out and her very insides spill all over the bed on which she sat. "It's me. I'm about to kick the bucket." Her voice quavered, but to someone on the other end of the phone line, and separated by ten years of estrangement, it might have been interpreted as a crackle in the line. "You know me. Selfish to the end - I thought I should make peace with you and your brother before I go to meet my maker."

Her voice was too loud and her heart hammered while she waited for the verdict from her jury of one. Mayella pinched her temples hard between the thumb and fingers of one hand and gripped the black, spit smelly phone receiver with the other, until her knuckles turned beyond white to gray.

When she answered, Christina's voice was cold. "What do you mean, 'kick the bucket.' You're not about to do something foolish, are you?"

Mayella heard herself in her daughter's voice and smiled. They were more alike than one of them cared to admit. And Christina was perceptive.

"'Something foolish'? Like suicide? Hmmm." She snorted. "I'll leave this earth shortly, one way or the other."

"How can you be sure? What's wrong?" Christina asked, dismissing suicide as one of the options.

"Oh, don't let's get into the boring details. Suffice it to say it's terminal."

"And you choose now to call? Now that it's too late to do anything about it? You haven't changed a bit, Mama."

The Christina of old would have forgiven first and asked questions later. This was the embittered tone of a girl grown into a woman who might pass as Mayella's twin rather than her daughter.

"And the fruit don't fall far from the tree." Mayella sighed and softened. "Actually, I've changed a great deal or I wouldn't be calling now, would I?"

TWO MOONS OVER CEDAR HILL

Her daughter was silent a moment and Mayella could feel her struggle against an emotive response that would forgive without too much penance.

On Mayella's end of the universe, sunlight streamed in through dusty white cotton curtains and was absorbed by the dark wood floor. The golden retriever that took up more than his fair share of an old woman's death bed gnawed his ass in pursuit of a flea. She tried to put her own nausea and regret out of her mind for the moment.

"What more do you want from me?" Christina's voice cracked on "more."

"I want you to come home."

Again, Christina was silent a long while before answering.

"I've got no home."

"Don't be silly. Of course you have a home. Cedar Hill is your home."

"I belong there about as much as I…." She trailed off. "You made it pretty clear, ten years ago, what you'd do if I came back… under the same conditions. Has anything changed I should know about?"

Mayella felt her gut twist like pulled taffy. It only made her more firm in her resolve. "Well, it should have been pretty obvious that was an empty threat. George – Jorgé – he's still living here, ain't he? I didn't fire him… And I've swallowed my pride, what little I have left, to call and ask you to come back."

"And Stewart?" Christina left the question hanging between them. "We've built a life here now. I have a job – a business to run. I've tried to make this exile a good thing."

"That's why I want you to come home. It was… wrong of me to ask you to carry the burden of your father's sins – to help me keep *his* secret from your brother. I want to make amends."

"Amends with Stewart too?"

"Yes, your brother too." Thinking on the fly, Mayella tacked on, "I don't care how you get him here. Tell him his inheritance is a condition of your return." She winced and swore under her breath.

"As if your money ever mattered to him." And Christina's bottled up resentment came through loud and clear. "It was your money that put us here in the first place."

"It was a lie of omission that ran Stewart off. Did you… did you ever tell your brother the truth?" She could feel her child on the other end of the line as she took the sucker punch with little more than a sharp intake of breath.

"You know as well as I do he won't come back, not for an inheritance, and especially not if he learns the truth now."

"Hears the truth, or learns that you helped keep it from him?"

TWO MOONS OVER CEDAR HILL

There was a pause, assuring Mayella she had struck a chord.

"I'm all he's got now, Mama. I won't come back if it's your intention to take that away from him too." She took a deep breath. "Mama, why don't you ask him... and me to come home without attaching conditions to everything?"

"Would you come?"

Again, long silence was her answer.

"Would you?"

"I'll come home... this weekend."

Mayella slumped back onto her pillows, her hand going so suddenly limp she nearly dropped the heavy black phone. As it was, she knocked over a half dozen amber colored pill bottles on her bedside table which clattered to the hardwood floor and rolled around in arcs.

She could not expect more. On the one hand this weekend was an unbearably long time to hold off dying. On the other hand, this weekend didn't leave much time for living. Before she spoke again, Mayella straightened, unsettling the dog that had just settled down with his head in her lap.

"Good. You come on home, Christina. Try to talk Stewart into coming with you." Nervously, she fondled the baubles on the chenille bed spread over her legs. Out in the hallway she heard the housekeeper's footfalls as she came to check on her and the commotion from the pill bottles. Quickly, she tacked on, "promise me, you won't change your mind?"

"I'll come, but Mama?"

"Yes?"

"It's sad that you won't know if he's coming because of the conditions you've placed on him or because he's forgiven you for what you did."

"You just come. Stewart'll follow." Mayella's voice, always vibrant, was suddenly soft and uncharacteristically tired and emotional. "This weekend," then like a sledge hammer, because it was not in her nature to leave well enough alone, she added, "it'll be a big ol' happy family reunion – you and your brother… and me… and George."

"You okay, Mayella?"

Mayella quickly hung up the phone and lay back against the pillows. The housekeeper poked her head around the door facing and looked in wonder from Mayella to the phone.

"No, I'm not 'okay.'" She shoved the old golden retriever off of the bed and tried to re-settle herself in the bedcovers. "I hurt like hell. But don't look so damn smug just 'cause I have to admit it. Go ahead." She pointed toward the door. "Get that home health nurse to come and plug me into that drug pumping octopus. Looks like you're all gonna get your way and I'll have to die tethered to the drip."

TWO MOONS OVER CEDAR HILL

Treeny, who had been keeping house for Mayella since the twins ran off ten years ago, only gave her a look that said, "I told you so." Mayella knew, once hooked up to a regulated morphine drip, her hours were numbered. She was ready for release, but as everything else in her life, she meant it to be on her own terms.

Chapter 4

1864

 How can one regret doing what has to be done? Jack Lyons wept over Salter's still, bloodied body until he had no more tears.

 It was morning now and just as his family would start to wonder where he was, he knew that Grace's family would be even more frantic – a woman missing from her bed in the morning. He had to go to her home and tell them.

 Jack picked himself up. He turned one more time to look at Salter's body. What, he wondered, had that bastard done to Grace before killing her? He had seen them kissing before – had seen them lay together too, but he pushed that image out of his mind. He gave Salter's body one last kick before he stumbled away, nearly falling over his own hurried footsteps, down the hill.

 He imagined the scene shortly to unfold. Grace's father was away – a prisoner of war. He was a state legislator and having disgraced his family by voting against secession, as self-inflicted penance, he joined the cause with his body only to be captured by the Yankees and currently held prisoner, a victim of irony.

 The women were in the house alone. Aunt Flossy, a house Negro, would probably be the first to discover the girl's disappearance. She would make inquiries. It would be slowly revealed that Grace had not been seen since the night before.

He, Jack, would have to be there to support the family in their time of mourning... and disgrace. They could not be spared the details and he prepared the story he would have to tell – that he saw Grace with Salter the night before – that he had, in his innocence, thought it consensual. Perhaps he could omit that ghastly bit. After all, Mrs. Thompson was of a delicate constitution.

It was common knowledge that Grace was far too free with her attention to the Negroes. The family was at fault for seeing a woman so highly educated. Yet Jack had been well able to overlook those flaws. Grace would have made a wife of exception. With their marriage, the two estates, River's Edge and Cedar Hill, would have been joined to form a formidable farm – virtually a state unto itself. Let the Yanks be damned. There, they would have conducted their lives as they always had. Free enterprise was the backbone of this nation and a war would not change that.

As he stumbled out of the woods, Jack looked down on the house with its fine out buildings. It was to have been the home where he and Grace would have lived. Every brick in this house had come from the brick kiln on his land. It was practically his already. The impressive columns that support the porch roof were made of brick, covered in a thick limestone wash. Everyone thought Llewellyn Thompson, Grace's father, was mad for painting over the brick work on the body of the house. He always had been an extravagant man – in the treatment of his house, the women in his care, and his Negroes.

But this was no time for recriminations. Grace was dead – murdered and raped – and he, Jack Lyons, was to be the one to have to break that news to the family. He, whose own heart was broken almost beyond repair, would have to be strong for them all.

The double front doors at Cedar Hill blotted out the scandal the new morning would bring. He had lost that span of time it took him to walk down the hill. Without knocking, Jack barged through the front door. Mrs. Thompson was already up and threw her hand to her breast when he barged in.

"Jack. You fairly scared the life…." She trailed off, recognizing something in his affect that intimated the dread news to follow. "It's the Yankees, isn't it? They're on the way?" Mrs. Thompson's voice was shrill with sudden fear.

Jack could do no more than shake his head.

"Salter said we should open our doors and welcome them in as honored guests if they should raid this farm. My husband's disgrace may even be our salvation if we are given a chance to explain."

Jack shook his head again.

TWO MOONS OVER CEDAR HILL

"Jack, you don't look well. What has happened, Son?"

The worry returned to Mrs. Thompson's face and something like embarrassment, as if she perhaps already had a hint of her own daughter's disgrace.

"I just come from...." He moved across the room and took the older woman's hands into his own. "It has to do with Grace... and Salter."

The woman pulled her hands out of his and laughed nervously. "Jack Lyons, I'm sure I don't understand a solitary word you're saying."

He re-launched his effort to take her hands, closing the space between them. Tears erupted from his eyes. "I had hoped, in a few month's time, to call you 'Mama' and that you might call me your son with every right under the eyes of God and society." His voice cracked. "I could not imagine the circumstances that might make that impossible... until now."

Mrs. Thompson jerked her hands away from him, her angry, lace covered bosom rising and falling.

"You are mistaken, Mr. Lyons. My only child has ever conducted herself as a lady should. This brief disciplinary action on the part of the lady's school is a sign of their weakness – in deed – a sign of the weakness of this whole southern cause. It is impossible to fight a war when the state's leaders are so divided in their convictions. I applaud Grace for her temerity. You should too. A strong Southern man needs an equally strong wife at his side."

But Jack was still shaking his head in anguish. "No. I was proud of Grace. I could over look any unwomanly flaws." He plowed his fists into his eyes. "I'm false hearted even to suggest that there might be flaw in the woman I declare, to this day, to love beyond all things. There is no flaw in her. She is perfection. Yet, she is beyond my reach now." He searched Mrs. Thompson's cornflower blue eyes for understanding, because now that it had come to it, he did not know how to tell her.

Still with poorly concealed anger in her voice, the matriarch attempted to comfort the distraught neighbor.

"I am about to break fast. You will come in and calm yourself. You are over excited. You have witnessed something you cannot make sense and you need a fresh view of things." She turned to lead the way to the dining room, but Jack did not follow.

"I'm sayin' it all poorly, Mrs. Thompson." A tear escaped the corner of his eye and he scraped it away with the back of his hand. "I mean to comfort you when I reveal to you what I have just found," and he pointed in roughly the direction of the tallest hill this side of the Piedmonts.

But Evelyn Thompson snatched his hand out of the air and held that hand to her heart.

TWO MOONS OVER CEDAR HILL

"I promise you, Mr. Lyons, no matter what you may have discovered, it can be of little concern to me. I love my daughter. I might have had an earlier hope that this farm would be passed down to my Jamie, but God and a Yankee's bullet saw fit to take him from us early. I am comforted by the thought that it is you who will someday inherit Cedar Hill – when you marry Grace and I pass from this earth. Indeed, my husband and I have every intention of giving you full reign over the farm from your wedding day. Nothing you could possibly say to me could sway me in this conviction. My first concern is with the perpetuation of this farm and I see in you a worthy steward.

"Grace is nervous now. You'll see. She'll come 'round and show the affection that is your due." Her tone softened and she spoke to Jack in motherly tones meant to soothe and comfort. "All young girls get like this before their wedding. And what with the war, and that unfortunate episode at her school, she is naturally not herself."

"Mama. Don't make excuses on my behalf."

The blood drained from Jack's face before he looked up from the mother to see the daughter at the top of the stairs.

The railings and risers were painted white, the walls, a pale buttermilk yellow, and the low morning sun came in through the arched window over the front doors, flooding the foyer with an ethereal glow. Grace stood at the top of the stairs, still in her white nightgown and in that first instant, Jack was able to half convince himself that he looked at Grace in her angelic form. Then she started down the stairs.

The sun that lit her and the room shifted from her face as she descended, reclaiming her earthly form.

"My behavior does not warrant excuses. Jack knows of what I am capable. I do not intend to alter my behavior for his or any other man's benefit."

"Grace." He croaked out her name.

"Now is as good a time as any for me to inform Mr. Lyons that I have no intention of accepting his offer of marriage." Turning on her mother she added, "And Daddy would be most displeased with you if he knew the pressure you were trying to exert on his behalf in his absence."

Jack pulled away from Mrs. Thompson and first, backed toward the door, then turned and ran, leaving it open behind him. Half way down the porch steps, he fell, but quickly picked himself up at the bottom and kept running. Inside the foyer, Mrs. Thompson wrung her hands and Grace Thompson clutched the necklace that was hidden beneath the lacey neck of her nightgown. It was the last time Grace or her mother would see Jack Lyons.

TWO MOONS OVER CEDAR HILL

Chapter 5

Tidewater, present day

Christina folded the phone and returned it to the top of the showcase. Her hands shook and like a sedative, her first response to stress was to reach for the terracotta pendant that was always warm against her skin under her dress, her "tell".

"You are pitiful, woman," she scolded herself aloud and recognized the muted southern accent that always came through in times of distress, labeling her a foreigner in this small, dispirited coastal town.

The shop door opened and she jerked her hand away from her traitorous neckline, causing her to bump the showcase. A line of kitschy nodders, velvety dogs, a kissing Dutch couple, a bobble headed Pinocchio, all stood watch across the top of the antique cash register and nodded in agreement. A hula dancer doll waggled her fanny at her.

"Oh, shut up, you."

"Her lips say 'shut up. Go away', but her eyes say, come in and show me what you've got in that bag." Richard greeted from the doorway.

"Sorry. Not you." Christina looked across the showroom and caught her own reflection for the second time in one morning, causing her to take pause. Wasn't it just yesterday she had been a teenager and her biggest problems were of the algebraic variety. The woman in the mirror was starting to prune on the vine, untasted. What would Jorgé, George, as her Mama still called him, think of her now? The thought came into her head like some sneak-thief, without invitation and taking with it a small piece of the old Christina. She turned away from the woman in the mirror.

Richard, carrying two coffees and a white bag, crossed the showroom and set the gift on the counter. Christina struggled to dredge up the smile that should have come easy after years of practicing the rehearsed sentiment. This time, her sunshine must have come out more warmly than she intended.

"Good morning." Richard leaned across the counter and gave her a peck on the cheek.

She tensed the muscle in that cheek as a subversive effort to brush away his kiss. "Morning, Richard." She struggled to drag her thoughts back 300 miles. Richard usually required the full use of her faculties.

Picking up the cup of coffee before it was cool enough to drink, she put it to her mouth and burned the tip of her tongue. She winced, then ran her tongue across her lips. Richard moved around the counter and took her gesture as an invitation to give her a more intimate kiss on the mouth.

TWO MOONS OVER CEDAR HILL

Christina inhaled sharply from surprise. He tasted of some exotic spice, probably the residue of his aftershave mixed with the coffee.

"Burn yourself?" He asked as he pulled back. A smile flickered at the corner of his mouth. He stood so close, his eyes had to dart from side to side to focus on first her one cornflower blue eye, then her brown eye before he pulled back slowly.

"Yeah." She put her hand to her mouth, forestalling a repeat. She was hemmed in by several boxes and the amount of available air in this corner was limited.

He tilted his head and in that moment reminded her of some beautiful golden show dog.

"You look pale." His eyes traveled down her front and he wore his opinion of her dress on his arched brow.

Richard bore a handsome face and, like the vague memory of her daddy, the clean scent of a man who was ready to be admired, but not ready to do anything admirable.

Richard liked dressing like an advert for whiskey, turtle necks and pee coats, and it suited him. Christina dressed like packing material with hair that hung down her back with the same color and repetitious wave as corrugated cardboard.

She ran hands down the front of her flour sack jumper to pull out some of the wrinkles.

Sofie Couch

"Yes. I…." She pointed to the phone, but glanced at the nodders who were still jeering at her. "I just got a call… from my mother."

Richard pulled in his angular jaw and dimpled chin. "Your Mother? Really?"

She pointedly never spoke about her family, and Richard, not so subtly, always wanted to ask more on the subject, but never had. Theirs was an odd sort of working relationship that only one of them wanted to make less professional and more familial.

Christina nodded. "She's ill." Even that simple admission cost her something and highlighted the distance at which she had kept everyone. The velvet dachshund was the only one still nodding as if he had known it all along. She put her finger tip to his nose to stop him giving her away.

"Nothing serious, I hope." With what seemed like vacuous indifference, Richard picked up the stack of mail that was on the front counter and started rummaging through it.

He held an envelope up to the light before passing that one to her. She smacked his hand and slid it under the phone.

"It is, actually. She's asked that I come home." At least that was her story, but Christina knew from past experience, her mother, Mayella, had a way of skewing the details to suit her own needs.

TWO MOONS OVER CEDAR HILL

"Really?" He looked around for a seat, then sat back on a box that looked sturdy enough. They both had their backs to the wall so to speak, him literally, her figuratively. "When?"

Christina, with more caution this time, pulled the lid off of the cup of coffee and blew it, hiding her trembly bottom lip against the Styrofoam. She drank until she had it under control. "This weekend."

"Festival weekend? You know, I need all the help I can get here in the shop."

Christina winced. She had forgotten about the sidewalk sale scheduled for Festival weekend.

Richard waved it aside. "So, now, I finally get to hear about 'home', this mysterious place you and Stewart ran away from, but never talk about."

"Cedar Hill's not our home anymore."

"Sounds like a quaint little town."

"It's not a town. It's a farm."

He lifted his eyebrows. "You're heir to a farm? Lucky you." Richard still held some resentment over Christina and Stewart having turned up unannounced ten years ago to take possession of their late father's beach property. Richard claimed it had been promised to him when their father had been alive, but conceded a compromise, retaining control of the business below and moving himself out of the apartment above to make room for the runaway teens.

Christina always felt guilty about what Richard had given up in the absence of a will to convey the promised ownership. To this day, she felt the inconvenience they must be to Richard and her brow puckered. Then because just that morning in the bathroom mirror she had noticed the crease that was marking with permanence the asymmetry of her eyes, she made an effort to relax. "Stewart and I grew up on a farm."

"Big?"

"Yeah."

"Probably full of antiques?"

She looked at him in disbelief. "My mother just told me she may be dying."

He winced. "Sorry. Tactless." He shook his head as if to clear it from the fog of his obsession, then reached out and took her hand. "Sorry. You know me," and he nodded toward the newspaper he would later read for obituaries and potential estate treasure steals. "Of course you'll want to go to her. I can handle this weekend."

"You're certain I'm going?"

"To see your aged, frail mother? Yeah."

"Yes."

"Wait. I'll come with you."

"You'll do no such thing." She rose from the stool and did not like that she had to brush so close past him to get out from behind the oak and glass display counter. Again, she felt boxed in by stuff in a shop that had taken on the look of something from a Dickens novel, and like her, ten year's worth of accumulation and dust and limbo.

"Don't you want to introduce me to your family?"

"No." She tried to pretend she did not know how badly Richard wanted to familiarize himself with her family. He was starved for family, probably the reason he had taken in Christina and Stewart ten years ago.

"No?" He followed her around the counter.

"You wouldn't like them. They're weird."

"You forget. I've already met your brother."

She stopped and Richard nearly careened into her. "Stewart. I almost forgot Stewart."

"That would be a first."

Christina spun around. "Can you look in on him this weekend if I go away?"

Richard shook his head. "Your brother is twenty-eight years old. Don't you think he can take care of himself by now?"

"Yes. And he'd be plenty pissed if he knew I had asked you to look in on him, but it would just make me feel better."

Richard assented with a nod, but it was grudgingly. "But it'll cost you."

Christina laughed, but found herself backing, and being backed, into another type of corner.

"Get ready for it. I'm gonna ask you again," he warned as he followed her through the shop.

"Richard. You promised…."

"But I'm not going to go down on one knee again. New khakis." He pointed at the crisp crease on the front of his trousers. "I'm just gonna say it." He held on to the now familiar words. "Marry me."

"No."

He shrugged, giving up easily. "Someday you're going to say 'yes'."

"No."

"Then at least let me drive you home this weekend."

"No. You've got the street festival this weekend or did you forget that you own a business with weekend hours? Besides, I don't want to impose."

"You mean, you don't want to feel indebted."

"I didn't say that."

"You didn't say that, but that's what you're feeling right now." In a characteristic gesture, Richard tossed his head and his thick sandy blonde hair out of his eyes. "Better yet, we could ask Stewart to mind the shop, take me with you to meet my future mother-in-law,…"

Christina gasped.

Richard laughed at his own suggestion.

When he laughed casually like that, even Christina had to admit that he posed a striking picture. Any other woman would be flattered by her own ability to draw his attention and Richard seemed to be genuinely fond of her. But still….

"Silly, I know," he chided himself. "Leaving your brother in charge would be like leaving the clowns to run the circus."

Christina put up her arm, elbow locked, and held it out against his chest to safeguard her bubble. Richard was a momentary weakness that she always later regretted.

"Mama asked that he come home too. That alone should make me suspici…," but she caught herself before the thought and sentence were complete.

Richard was shaking his head. "You've never mentioned a family beyond your brother and now, all of a sudden, you have a 'Mama'." He exaggerated her southern accent. "…And a farm called 'Cedar Hill.' Any other secrets?"

"No," but again, her traitorous hand shot to the necklace under her dress. She tried to cover it with a laugh and upon seeing her awkward reflection in the gilded mirror hanging on a lattice covered wall, she hastily pulled her hand from her neckline. "My mother and I simply had a parting of the ways. I've kept in touch… regularly." She chided herself for feeling guilty. "She just never chose to reciprocate. This is the first time she's called *me* in… years."

"Really? An exile?"

Christina sighed. "She did something very hurtful to Stewart. He left. She left me no choice, but to go with him."

Unable to stop herself fidgeting, she folded her arms across her chest and pressed her hands under her armpits, but her chin she raised an inch in a vain attempt to achieve a height advantage over Richard who rang in at a daunting six-three.

Richard let out a descending whistle. "What'd you do to earn an exile?"

This was more than she was prepared to go into with the man who was, for all intents and purposes, her boss. It was only in the past couple of months that he had begun to broaden the boundaries of a more friendly relationship – a cup of coffee and bagels in the morning, the occasional peck on the cheek, the singular buss on the lips this morning. His proposals of marriage were always clownish. He treated her like an ugly cousin who needed to have her ego inflated by his attentions. This flirtation had developed almost without her knowledge and certainly without her conscious encouragement.

"My mother can be very controlling. She had certain expectations of her children that Stewart and I were unable to fulfill."

TWO MOONS OVER CEDAR HILL

Richard laughed. "I can well imagine Stewart falling short of… <u>any</u> mark, but you? What'd she ask of you that you couldn't deliver?"

She held back a moment before throwing caution to the wind. "Mama took issue with my choice in men."

Richard's smile – the one that gained him deference from complete strangers, especially female strangers – melted. He found it as quickly and contrary to her desired result, he took a step closer and planted a hand on each side of her boney hips, trying to draw her closer. It was an awkward embrace with Richard having to bend at the knee and lean back to see her face properly. "That's actually rather comforting to hear."

Christina stepped back until the backs of her knees were pressed against the arm of a gooseneck rocker. She put her hands up between them.

"I don't get you, Richard."

"Christina, I've tried every maneuver I can think of to get your attention and quite frankly, I was beginning to think, maybe you didn't care for men."

Her vanity was pinched and she pushed him away, at the same time laughing light heartedly. She had no delusions about her appearance. Compared to Richard, she was frumpy and she made no effort to improve her looks for his benefit on principle. Men who looked like Richard were not attracted to women who looked like her unless they had some ulterior motive. Mama taught her that... and Jorgé reinforced the lesson.

"You ego maniac." She turned and grabbed the white bagel bag on the front counter and peered inside in an attempt to put things on a more casual footing.

"So, it's not men in general. Just me in particular."

Christina fished for a bagel and the cup of cream cheese and started slathering it with a plastic knife. She could feel him and a dozen mirrored reflections from various points in the crowded shop still watching her, so with a sigh she looked up, offering him half of the bagel.

"You know, in some circuits I'm considered a pretty good catch. No physical deformities, no vices."

She shoved the bagel at him when he didn't take it. She thought Richard had always envied her metabolism, thus he made a habit of tempting her with fattening foods to see if he could find her Achilles heel. She wouldn't give him that kind of power. She wouldn't give anyone insight into her weaknesses ever again.

"And because of your own lack of deformity and my lack of attribute I should swoon at your feet?" That was the embittered Christina talking.

TWO MOONS OVER CEDAR HILL

"Nah, nah, nah. Don't you try to put words in my mouth." He wagged his finger. "I see beyond your sack cloth and ashes routine."

"I don't put on any kind of sack cloth...."

But to prove his point, Richard reached out and swiped the side of her nose. He held up his finger, now smudged with dirt.

"...And ashes."

She stepped around the rocker and backed into an oak hoosier, the surface of which was covered with green depression ware. The whole thing trembled and chattered like a jeering crowd. "I'm not putting on any kind of sack cloth routine."

He pointed to the bib of her dress with its Gold Medal Flour label.

"You try to keep me and everyone else at a distance." She was about to protest, but he gestured between them. "Don't deny it. Look at you. You've backed yourself into a corner again, pulling all this semi-precious crap between us. You throw up blocks, I side-step them and you throw up more." He wagged the bagel in her face. "You don't take me serious."

"Were you being serious?"

He scowled. "Do I really need to go down on one knee to prove it?"

"I guess that just goes to prove another point, Richard. I don't know you. I can't even tell if you're being serious." She pulled up a box of junk from the last auction.

He pointed down at the box. "More barriers?" He sat down on the box. "Until this morning I thought I knew *you*."

"I'm sorry, Richard."

"What is it, Christina? Why can't I get you to take this relationship to the next level? If it's not me, then what?"

On a sigh of defeat, she admitted, "Maybe it's... someone else."

"Ouch."

"It's not." She waved a hand, aiming for a casual gesture, but managing to hit the cup of coffee and spilling it all over the showcase. She scrambled to mop up the mess with a roll of paper towels that she kept stowed behind the front counter. "That ended... years ago. Maybe it never even started. It's just — I can't think of you in that way."

"Double ouch."

"It's not personal, Richard. It's just that... I'm happy with my life just as it is." She could hear Mama preaching in her head. *Girl, you tell a lie often enough and you'll start to believe it.*

Richard roughly bit her abandoned half bagel and moved away, speaking through the bite. "You're committed to taking care of your little brother."

She could breathe again with each step Richard took away making the room feel slightly less claustrophobic. She produced glass cleaner and moved around the nerve center of the shop to the customer side of the antique cash register that was covered with bric-a-brac. "Number one, he's only my "little" brother by a handful of minutes and number two, you don't give Stewart credit."

"Stewart's like one of Peter Pan's lost boys. He'll never grow up."

"That's part of his charm."

"And why should he? He's got you to look out for him." Richard dropped sullenly into an art deco cloud chair and pulled out his newspaper. Christina felt mild annoyance at his putting up barriers before she realized this is what he had accused her of… and it was true. She was the hold-up.

"I'm sorry, Richard."

"And this man that 'Mama' didn't approve of?"

Richard watched over the top of his newspaper with an expression she couldn't decipher. Annoyance? She didn't think it was jealousy.

"I never said she didn't approve of him. I said she had "issues" with him." There. She'd let him stew on that. She turned toward the back stairs that led to the upstairs apartment. "And now, if you'll excuse me, Richard, I've got a date with some sleeping dogs."

Chapter 6

Cedar Hill, 1864

Jack Lyons stumbled into the woods, nearly blind with his own self-hate. He could not reconcile his having committed the heinous crime he had accused Salter of perpetrating. At the gravesite, he fell on his knees beside Salter's body. A green bottle fly had already found the body and buzzed over his dark lips showing particular interest in the soft pink crescent of flesh to the inside of his open mouth.

Jack screamed at the fly and lifted Salter's shoulders and held him to his breast.

"But you *did* do it. There ain't no dog buried there." He put Salter away from him and turned, unable to look any longer.

Maybe more than half crazy, Jack threw himself at the grave and with his bare fingers, he dug at the ground. He dug straight down into the center, the heart of the matter, and it did not take long before his fingers bled. Looking around, he spied the spade, then took it up and dug through the pain in his tender hands until the shovel's blade hit the metal side of a trunk.

"No!" He cried out. "Cain't be. Cain't be. Cain't be...." He repeated in a moan, while clearing the side of the trunk of dirt, digging his fingers in along the edge and pulling with all his strength. His strength was double what it used to be, half of what

TWO MOONS OVER CEDAR HILL

Salter's used to be. He pulled up the trunk and the oil cloth wrapping fell away from it. It rattled with metal. On the end of the trunk was a painted label: *Evelyn Thompson, Cedar Hill, Poropotank, Virginia.*

He opened the lid and pulled back the corner of a blanket and his eyes widened.

"You stealing from my soon-to-be family? You stealing my inheritance?" He threw the accusation at Salter's body.

Then partial sanity returned. "No. No, you didn't." He wept and let his nose run unchecked. "You were hiding it for them – because of the Yankees – because of the way Grace brought all that trouble on her family, because of her behavior at school."

He stayed there until the sun was nearly midway in the sky, then he turned back to the grave and dug it out the rest of the way. At first, he stopped to shoo flies away from Salter's body, then they were too many, so he turned to his task with devotion and kept digging, beyond the point where his already bloody fingers screamed. When the spade broke he used the same stick he used to kill Salter, and he dug the hole deeper until he stood in the hole and the surface of the earth was at the height of his forehead.

He climbed out with difficulty and opened the trunk. Taking out the quilt, he used it as a shroud, rolling Salter's body over on to it, wrapping him in it like a baby doll. He held the trunk by its end handle and gently lowered it back into the hole and pulled the oil cloth back over its top. The coin and silver rattled and clanged until they finally settled into their last resting place. With reverence, he cradled Salter's shrouded body, then stepped down, into the hole, pulling the body in with him. There, he folded Salter's form around the trunk – the guardian of Grace's dowry and her family's fortune.

By the time he covered the grave, raking the dirt into the hole with the broken spade, then dragging handfuls of dirt, mounding it over the entire site, Jack had no more tears to cry. He knew he would have to endure hell *on* earth and after. But he would make Grace pay for her part in all this too. It was because of her behavior that he jumped to the conclusions he had. It was easy for him to believe that Salter's death was as much her fault as his own and she would have to pay with her family's fortune. The insanity in him convinced him that Grace deserved to lose it.

TWO MOONS OVER CEDAR HILL

Chapter 7

Cedar Hill, present day

"Gone out for a smoke. Back in fifteen. – Treeny."

    Which meant she had had to make a run to the country market to buy more cigarettes. It was less than a mile away, but Mayella was not supposed to be left alone until the home health nurse arrived. It was only by chance Jorgé had come in from the orchard to lunch early.

    His days were measured by trips back and forth from field to house. Not his field. Not his house… not his family. Not really.

    A pot of soup was on the stove, still simmering. Jorgé switched off the burner, ladled some into a cup, sawed a slice of bread from the loaf and filled a glass with sweet tea and plenty of ice. She wouldn't eat it, but he would try to persuade her.

    Upstairs Mayella appeared to be asleep. Jorgé put the bed tray on the foot of her bed, then moved to straighten the covers over her. She smacked his hand when it came close to her breast.

    "Where's that nurse?"

    "She'll be here shortly. Treeny had to step out for a minute."

    "No doubt buying more of those damn cancer sticks. You'd think I'd be a wake-up call to her." She smacked Jorgé's hand again as he tidied the bottles on her night stand. "Stop fussing, will you? You're worse than an old woman... and I should know. Leave that," and she snatched a pill bottle from his hand. "That's the nurse's job."

"You're right. Her job is to see to your medical needs. Mine is to make sure you eat your lunch." He put the back of his hand to her brow and she melted back into her pillow. Her shriveled body waged a losing battle against itself. And that was so unlike Mayella - to lose a battle, skirmish, or argument.

Mayella waved him away. "I don't want any lunch... thank you," she tacked on in a softer tone, closing her eyes and absorbing strength from his touch. "I can't bear even the smell of it."

Jorgé hesitated then set the tray on the floor at the foot of the bed. He recalled when he first came to live here, how it had been difficult getting used to the smells - lavender, cooked butter beans and moth balls. He barely noticed anymore, so acculturated were his senses. He never realized that his own scent had become a part of the structure – the smell of wood, soil, and patience.

"You seem strong today." He lifted a side chair with one hand and placed it silently beside her bed. He put a dark muscled hand over one of Mayella's frail, white and blue veined hands. "Treeny told me you were sitting up earlier."

TWO MOONS OVER CEDAR HILL

"I'm ready to run a damn marathon."

It was not Jorgé's habit to linger at her bedside over lunch, but he knew her days were drawing to a close. Soon it would be too late. She eyed him suspiciously through one open eye.

"Go ahead. Ask me... for the two thousandth time."

"I thought it was more than that."

"Probably."

"Then why ask?"

"'Cause you know I'm about to snuff it and the secret of their whereabouts will die with me if I don't tell you."

"I'm not prepared to see you off just yet..., but... I do want you to tell me, Mayella. Where are Chita and Stewart?"

"So, she's still your Chita, eh? Haven't heard you use that particular endearment in a while."

"Where are they?"

She pressed her lips tight together and it reminded him of a determined child.

"They should be with you - now – of all times. Don't you want to have those who love you with you now?" One skill he had never acquired was the ability to read Mayella Breeden. Behind her weathered, wrinkled face, her eyes had a light that was beyond his color spectrum. Her daughter inherited at least one of those blue eyes. The last time he had seen Chita he couldn't read her either.

"There's no preamble with you, is there? No sweet talk. No sugar. You just come right out and say what you want."

"Now is not a time for…." He hesitated, "'sweet talk', Mayella. You're dying." His expression did not falter. He watched her for some sign of surprise. He saw none. "Chita and Stewart would want to be here with you. Don't deprive them of that."

"It's about time somebody started talking about it instead of tiptoeing around the topic." Her tone softened. "And I could always depend on you for plain talk, George."

She raised her hand. It hovered between them about to bridge some prejudicial gap, but she let it drop to rest on the bed beside her again.

Over their heads, the ceiling creaked.

"There's that sound. Did you hear it this time?"

Jorgé turned to look up at the ceiling too, but only lifted his eyebrows like a shrug. "The roof settling. I'll go up and check later."

"No, damn it. Let the whole house fall in around us. I don't care."

"You'll excuse me if I do. I sleep across the hall. I don't want to wake up one morning under a pile of rubble."

"This house is a curse."

"Just ghosts."

TWO MOONS OVER CEDAR HILL

"I'll be joining them soon enough."

He glanced at the ceiling again, then turned his attention back to her. "Only if you have unresolved business here on earth."

"It's *my* business."

"Tell me where they are, Mayella. Let me call them for you."

"And what makes you think they'd wanna come home again?"

"You are their family... their mother. They will feel cheated if you leave this earth before they've had a chance to settle their differences with you."

Mayella rolled her head against her pillow. Her short gray, frightened hair, flat on the back, jutted out at the sides. Illness had robbed her of the extra pounds that her lack of physical vanity had never been able to shed. Her loose skin was transparent.

"You know my way with the boy. I've never favored him. Too much like his daddy: pretty, flighty. And Christina," she held Jorgé's gaze for a moment before looking away, "you know how headstrong she is."

Jorgé arched one eyebrow. "Aren't you the pot talking about the cauldron."

"It's 'kettle.' Pot calling the *kettle* black.' You speak the language better than I do. Stop screwin' it up, damn it."

He ignored her outburst other than taking note that her short-lived annoyance zapped her of strength. "You have it within your power to make amends with Chita…" he pressed his lips together. "…Christina – and Stewart. Let me call them for you."

Mayella gave a derisive snort. "I know why you want to call her, George. I know you and your Latin ways."

Jorgé smiled and shook his head. "You old bigot."

"Don't pull out your sweet talk now. I can't change the way I am."

"You can't or you won't?"

He pushed his chair back to leave, but with more strength than he expected from her, Mayella's hand shot out to clutch his arm.

"No. Don't go, George." Her eyes were closed.

Jorgé pulled up to the bed again and patted the back of her hand. "I won't leave you, Mayella."

She lay there with her eyes closed for a long while until Jorgé thought perhaps she slept. He was startled when she spoke again.

"And just why is that, George?"

"Why is what?"

"Why didn't you ever leave me? Expecting to inherit a share of my estate, no doubt."

TWO MOONS OVER CEDAR HILL

He pressed his lips together into a firm line again.

"No doubt," was all he said.

"You've been waiting for her to come back."

"You've made it clear she's never coming back."

"I saw to it she wouldn't."

"You sent them away, your children - family – the only thing you have that I ever coveted. Why? By what means? Tell me that at least."

Mayella opened her eyes. "Christina - I told her you were after this farm." She looked up at Jorgé and clucked her tongue. "Imagine that – an old man like you – nearly old enough to be her daddy." Her eyes darted around, taking in every memorized line of his face. "I told her you meant to have this farm one way or another – even it if meant marrying her to get it - another damn foreigner coming along, trying to snatch up a piece of America."

Jorgé held Mayella's hand in both his, leaning his elbows on the side of her bed, he bent down to kiss the back of her withered hands, despite her, to spite her, in spite of her bigotry. A muscle twitched in her jaw, but she gave no other outward sign of agitation or revulsion over the intimacy.

She continued. "I told her, if she didn't leave, stop foolin' around with you, I'd disinherit her and Stewart."

"Chita has no expectation of a birthright." He kept his elbows on her bed, hovering over her.

"But she would do it for her brother. She'd do just about anything for that boy – even give up… her home."

"But at what cost to you, Mayella?" He sat up, still holding her hand. "You've given up your family – when you need them most."

Mayella closed her eyes again and nodded. "Two in the bush in exchange for one bird in hand." She licked her lips and Jorgé reached for the glass and straw on the bedside table. He touched it to her lips and she drank, keeping her eyes shut.

"I saw to it, alright. You were too old for her… and a damn Mexican to boot. You know how I feel about intermingling the races, weakening the blood."

"I thought that was the result of inbreeding."

Mayella smiled. "Probably how I come by the name – Breeden."

Jorgé laughed and that gave Mayella the strength to open her eyes. He smiled, but his real thoughts were hidden by cherubic amiability. His round face, though nearing forty, would have seemed quite boyish if not for the little gray that touched the sides of his hair now. He was beyond any vanity that might make him self-conscious of the lines at the corners of his smiling eyes. He loved

TWO MOONS OVER CEDAR HILL

being outdoors the best and the elements blessed his dark skin with their kisses.

Inside, he was as steady as a rock, with a purpose and drive that was more tightly tied to the farm called Cedar Hill than if that estate had been his birth right.

Living so many years with Mayella had forced him to look for and find something good about the older woman's prejudice. The good thing about Mayella was that she could be trusted to say precisely what she felt, no matter how flawed. And she was the only person too perceptive to be fooled by his pretense of perpetual good humor.

Her smile faded. She kept her eyes closed and then slept.

When he was sure she was sleeping, when short puffs of air parted her spit-stuck lips, Jorgé gently tucked her hand back under the covers, then rose silently from the straight backed chair and picked up the tray from the floor at the end of the bed. He patted the side of his leg to call the dog out of the room, but stopped at the upstairs bedroom window. This room and his room across the hallway had the only two windows that looked out on the orchard. He looked out on those trees every morning when he woke and every night before he turned in. It sat on a low rise, the first wave between the bay and the Blue Ridge Mountains to the west.

He turned and was almost out the door when Mayella spoke again.

"How are our babies?"

He understood Mayella's reference to the apple orchard. Those trees were the only "children" she had left and they were the only children he would probably ever sire. It represented the culmination of a childhood dream – to be the one who grew the apples rather than the one who picked them.

"Last of the pickers left this morning. Most of the late harvest apples are in. We had a good haul this year. Best yet, in fact."

She nodded. He thought she drifted off again. He turned and once more, she spoke. "Christina's coming home tomorrow. I've fixed things with her as best I can. It's in your hands now."

Jorgé turned sharply at the door to look at Mayella, but her eyes were still closed and her breathing regular. In so many words, she had granted him his only wish of the past ten years – to see Christina… and make up for letting her down ten years ago.

TWO MOONS OVER CEDAR HILL

Chapter 8

River's Edge, 1864

Lyonses, Jack's father's side of the family, did not fight in the war. They did their part by sending their slaves to participate. They paid a salary to the poor white subsistence farmers and those who worked in the brick field to take an active role. Lyonses chose to see it as their role to ensure that the machinations of everyday living and money making continued while the Thompsons, on the neighboring estate, held office to ensure states' rights and took up arms when there was no choice. The Lyons family took advantage.

Jack Lyons blotted the wet ink from the letter and hesitated before folding the paper around it like an envelope. On the outside, he wrote, "Grays Thom'son".

He nursed his bruised and bandaged knuckles. A fire burned in the grate and he stood staring at the flames a long while, rotating the letter between his thumb and forefinger. This was the sort of skill a girls' school was supposed to teach Grace – paper folding, writing, maybe reading, maybe not. It was not supposed to fill her head with ideas about the war and politics. The school was to be blamed.

When the letter slipped by accident from his careless, bandaged fingers and fluttered to the floor, he scrambled to catch it before it should disappear, but it drifted away from the fire rather than into it.

Jack Lyons was a gentleman and as such, he had to accept his own responsibility in the death of Salter Lyons. Of course there would be no inquiry. No one to answer to. Salter was property in his eyes, no matter what Mr. Lincoln's proclamation said to the contrary, but....

He put the envelope on the mantle over the fire, turned and picked up a saddlebag and left the house by the front door, closing it quietly behind him. It was late morning and the sun was rising toward mid-sky. The table would be laid by two o'clock, but by the time ham was on, he would be four hours down the road. The house would continue to function. The lives of slaves were simple. Only Salter chose to complicate his life.

When it was discovered that the master was gone, Ol'Cedric, the one he saw last at night and first in the morning, might wonder. He would go about his usual routine of closing up the house at night and laying the morning fires. He would find the letter and ensure its delivery to Grace. Then they would all learn of his fate.

Grace would weep and everyone would think it was for him. Some would shun her for her part in his leaving. He regretted that, but she had made her own bed to lie in. He tried to convince himself that he was without fault. Salter was careless. He had gone against nature in attaching himself to Grace.

Jack threw a saddle on the only horse left in the stable. One of the brickyard laborers looked up from under the mud filled canvas sack he carried on his shoulder. His face was a slightly darker shade of brick. He did not dare ask what business the master was about. Instead, he silently doffed his hat, then turned his attention back to the task of mud hauling as Jack's horse slopped past.

For three days, he rode the muddy tracks of Three Chopt Road to Richmond, following in the footsteps of other notable statesmen who had fought and led their country to battle and themselves to greatness. Jack Lyons, in attempting to cross the James River, would die a peaceful death, only to be reborn in another time, given another chance to make amends.

His estate, River's Edge, would be passed on to a first cousin who would see it to its stagnant survival under the name of Breeden.

Chapter 9

Cedar Hill, present day

*"Oh freedom, oh freedom, oh freedom over me.
And before I'll be a slave, I'll be buried in my grave,
And go home to my Lord and be free."*
— Anon.

Mayella Breeden was not a woman given to tears, but her regrets were enough to make her eyes spicy.

She had lain awake listening to the creaking attic floorboards overhead until they stopped two hours ago. Now the house was quiet, the ghosts at rest.

Across the hall from her room, Jorgé slept with his door closed. Treeny, in the room next to Mayella's, kept her door open at night, but the woman slept like the dead, waking only when her own sleep apnea cut off her own breathing long enough to wake her.

Mayella felt better than she had in months – the morphine drip providing immediate relief, so it was a wrench to unplug the white plastic coupling from the spigot in her left arm. The temporary relief gave her the strength she would need to continue. Gingerly, Mayella rose from the side of the bed, taking one of the full amber pill bottles with her. She expected to stagger as she did when she went, with assistance, to the toilet. She felt unexpectedly strong as she moved across her room and out into the hallway.

Mayella put her wrinkled hand to Jorgé's door. She had been the cause of years of hurt. She had no desire for and lacked the courage to stick around to witness the resolution of her offenses, but she could take some small comfort in knowing that her actions now could ensure that resolution happened when she was gone. She let her hand lie on his door for a moment before she moved off down the hall.

The stairs were trickier to maneuver. A dull pain throbbed through her body and her bones ground with each step as if the cancer had eaten away her cartilage. She held tight to the banister. She lured herself with the promise of resting at the chair in the downstairs hall, but she lied to herself, using the chair as a carrot on a stick. Instead, she treated herself to one of the pills in the bottle clenched in her hand. Again, she promised herself she would rest once outside on the porch. She passed the chair and opened the front door, knowing full well that if she stopped now, she wouldn't be able to get up again. They would find her body in the morning, slumped in an undignified heap in the floor. But everything had a reason and her own death would have meaning and importance if she had anything to do with it. Where her body was found meant everything.

Everyone slept as Mayella crept from the house. Still in her long night gown and bare feet, she did not even bother to close the front door behind her, so Beebo, the ancient golden retriever, gone gray about the muzzle, followed her outside.

The moon was only about half full, but had it been pitch black, Mayella might have found her way across the farm. The cold burning the soles of her feet took her mind off of the pain that was creeping back into the rest of her body. She moved down the moss covered brick walkway toward the circular drive, also moss covered, then followed its grassy center.

The black, four board fence that bracketed both sides of the driveway was bisected by a gate and this was where Mayella stopped long enough to pull off the chain. The gate swung open without resistance and she knew it must be fate allowing her to reach her destination.

Beebo brushed her thigh and she fell. The dog whined and Mayella pulled herself up to her knees. The amber pill bottle was lost in the grass and frantically, she searched on her hands and knees, thinking herself too cocky for her own good. The ground was cold. It was too late to try to make it back to the comfort of her death bed now anyway. The feeling in her hands passed from cold to hot, then to numb. The pill bottle pressed into her shin and she groped it with relief. The exertion left her depleted and she popped another pill, then crawled until walking was the more appealing of the two. She had to be upright to see over the soy bean stubble to the iron fence that surrounded the family cemetery.

    She could not tell if she had lost her vision or if it was just dark. Mayella cursed and willed herself to keep going, stumbling over the rough rows and bumping into the dog, then holding onto Beebo's collar for support. She had to get inside the fence – to the exact spot or she would surely go to hell.

    She had made matters worse between Christina and herself by attaching strings to her return. Mayella longed to be back in her bed where she might die in relative comfort, a comatose stupor, but then she reasoned, what was pain and discomfort in the here and now compared to eternal damnation? She trudged on, hands outstretched until she rammed her thigh into the iron fence. She did not need to find the cemetery gate. She fell, head over ass, into the plot. It took her a moment to recall herself. Blood dripped from her hand where the catheter, her spigot to anesthesia, had torn out, but this time she held tight to the pill bottle. The dog whimpered outside the fence. Mayella ignored him. She waved her arm in the air, thought she caught a glimpse of something dark in front of her, and dragged her body toward the grave stone.

Sofie Couch

She could not see well enough to read the name, knew it was not the resting place she sought, but she ran her hand over the stone to try and get her bearings. It was clean and smooth. She felt the letters etched into it, found the deepest imprints and ran her fingers around their edges, reading to herself.

"S-T-E-…. Stewart Breeden, Senior." *Unfaithful, son-of-a-bitch gambler.* Her late husband. She pulled herself up on his tombstone, receiving more assistance from him in this way than he had ever given *alive*. She could see the shadowy outline of the next two stones. She stumbled there. The second one was relatively smooth – too new still, and she knew it to be the grave of her first child – born as still as stone. He would have been in his late twenties if he had lived. She moved on to the third. This one was older, moss and lichen covered and she only ran her hand over the top of the stone. She knew the letters to be indiscernible in the pock marked stone. She moved to the next, then the next row. There, her foot hit a groundhog hole and she fell face first, her chest directly over the heart she sought. She knew even before reaching to the stone, but her hand went there anyway.

And by the grace of fate, her vision returned or the moon cast its glow directly on the stone and she knew she was lying on the grave of Grace Thompson, 1848-1865. The symbol of a star and double moons, the origin and meaning of which had

TWO MOONS OVER CEDAR HILL

been lost, worn with rain and time, but it was still visible there above the name.

Mayella found her smile. She was the only one who had figured it out in all these years. No one else had put the pieces together as she had and it was one of the dogs, Beebo's predecessor, who had given her the clue she had needed. It was with a happy heart that she opened the pill bottle, emptied its contents one-by-one into her mouth, then lay her head down on her arms and closed her eyes.

Outside the fence, Beebo whimpered.

Chapter 10

Cedar Hill, 1855

He came and went as obligations demanded. Grace loved her father with the adoration of a disciple. He took her with him about the farm, her tiny hand in his. He always told the same stories and as they rounded a turn in the wagon road she knew what he would say when they passed a particularly rutted spot.

"No other animal on the earth has wrought such devastation. Maybe not since the dinosauria."

He had told her about those long dead animals a hundred times before, but she still asked, hoping for more detail. She did not believe in fairy tales, never had, but because her father said these mythical creatures existed, she believed him.

"How big were they?"

Her father smiled, but kept looking straight ahead. He knew she knew the answer to her own question. She had always been an inquisitive child.

"One foot print from dinosauria might have been as big as that mud hole in the road there. If his foot came down on us right now, we would not even have time for prayer." He smacked his hands together like the foot coming down on them. "We'd be turned back to dust and made a part of this land along with the giant lizards."

TWO MOONS OVER CEDAR HILL

"Ah, but you said Thompsons have been here since the beginning of time."

"Well, I don't suppose it has been quite that long. This soil probably hasn't even been here that long." And he looked over his shoulder at the hill behind them. "It does seem though, that time lasts longer here than any other place. I think it's because this very hill – the first substantial rise in the landscape between here and the ocean that juts up and tries to keep the sun from setting. This one spot is blessed with just a few more minutes of day light than any other place on earth."

Grace liked that new addition to the story and stored it for recall later.

Twenty years ago

Mayella held Christina's small, child hand in hers and they walked about the farm, the matriarch and the heiress presumptive. The dozen or so dogs that followed on Mayella's heels admitted and protected Christina as one of the inner circle and she had no fear of them. Christina had not yet felt her importance to her mother and her mother's partiality to her, but she had noticed that her twin brother, Stewart, never accompanied them on these morning walks and it had nothing to do with his visual impairment. He could keep up with the best of them and he knew the farm better than almost anyone – almost as well as Jorgé. This morning they were up so early the sun had only begun to seep over the low horizon to the east.

Mayella glanced behind them. "You see that hill back there?"

Christina looked behind them to the distinctive rise in the land. There was one ancient cedar tree that stood taller than any of the others and she promised herself to walk there some day when she was grown-up.

"They reach up and hold the sunlight here on Cedar Hill longer than any other place on earth. That's why it's so special."

She accepted her mother's words as fact. It was the first time she felt the connection she and her mother had to this bit of land.

Tidewater, present day

The sound of the death rattle woke Christina with a start. The coffee maker in the kitchen sputtered and coughed up its last drops. She looked to the alarm clock that winked a mocking, red, digital "2:32 - 2:32 – 2:32 – click - 2:33…."

Outside, there was a hint of pink in the east which meant the power must have gone out two and a half hours ago. It was about time to wake up anyway. Christina rolled out of bed, going knees first onto a box lot of stuff from an auction and she swore when something cracked.

TWO MOONS OVER CEDAR HILL

Every square inch in the apartment had become staging area for the boxes of bric-a-brac – mementos that measured somebody else's family and life - that she would price and put in Richard's shop downstairs. She surrounded herself with history, the guardian of heirlooms displaced from their families, and she treasured each trinket that came into her care as though it was her own family memento and mourned its loss when it was sold.

She opened the box and pulled out the pocket watch with the smashed face, its hands bent and immovable now. It was like the one her father had worn and with the ruination of the watch, Christina mourned her own lost history. Cradling the watch, she lowered it into a cedar jewelry box and nestled its remains on a cotton embroidered handkerchief before maneuvering around several floor lamps that were waiting for re-wiring. She padded out of the room.

In the kitchen, the coffee was already made and the skunk coffee smell wound itself around her like a comfortable quilt.

"You're up early."

"Couldn't sleep." Stewart, spoke through a mouth full of toothpaste. He brushed at the kitchen sink, left the water running, poured coffee into his cup, then spun around to scramble eggs before they stuck to the pan, all the while holding his toothbrush clenched in his teeth… and all blind.

Sofie Couch

Christina switched off the tap.

"You came in late. Not that I'm keeping tabs on you or anything, but I wanted to talk to you."

"Late night at work. Custody case. Kid's caught in the middle. Same ol', same ol'."

She picked up the coffee cup Stewart had left on the counter, took a sip, winced, and then returned it. "Ugh. You bought that crap coffee with the picture of the sea captain on the front, didn't you?"

"Um-hum," her brother confirmed before spitting toothpaste into the sink. The only time his blindness was a handicap was when Christina left dishes in the sink. "You know how I'm a sucker for those pretty labels," he mocked.

"You know, just because it tastes like sea water, doesn't make you an old salt."

Stewart pounded a fist to his chest, then groped for the spoon holder. He dropped in his toothbrush. "Grows hair on your chest."

She poked two fingers between the buttons of his denim shirt and closed one eye. "Better keep drinking." She took his toothbrush from the spoon holder, hosed his white foamy spit from the sink, and then turned to leave for the bathroom.

"Wait a minute," he called after her. "What'd you wanna talk about?"

TWO MOONS OVER CEDAR HILL

"Mama called yesterday. She wants us to come home." She dropped the bomb with nonchalance.

Stewart stiffened. "Get outta town."

"That's my plan." Christina took a deep breath. "She's sick. Afraid she's going to die. Wants to make amends." She finally looked up at him.

"Woah."

"Woah."

He tipped his head, turning an ear toward her. "And is everything as we left it?"

"I suppose so. She didn't give a change of address."

"I mean, is every*one*... where we left them."

"She did mention Jorgé, so, yes. He's still there... with her." Stewart nodded, but wore a doubtful expression. He mindlessly chopped and mixed eggs in a pan with a spatula. He would know when they were done based on the feel and the sound.

"Did she mention...." But he trailed off without finishing, then he swore. "She's burned a lot of bridges."

Christina nodded, but it was time. Stewart buried his anger in his work and that wasn't healthy. She buried her hurt under a mountain of antique crap that was slowly hemming her in. Also, a nagging thought kept recurring. Just a few nights ago she had attended an auction - an estate consisting of the worldly possessions of six siblings, none of whom had ever married, none of whom had relatives to whom they might leave the crap that represented the time they had spent here on earth. She wondered if she and Stewart were similarly destined. Stewart had not yet shaved and his chin bore the stubble of a grown man. Her "baby" brother, her family, and they were both showing every sign of being the end of their line. It was time they both started living again.

"When do you leave?"

"I leave this morning."

He smiled without humor. "What? She didn't want to reconcile with her estranged son?"

"She asked for you."

Stewart spooned a large dollop of mayonnaise, then with both hands, to determine placement, he blobbed it on a plate. Christina watched with revulsion as he dumped scrambled eggs from the fry pan into the center of the mayonnaise, on purpose.

Around just her, he didn't bother to wear his opaque sunglasses, and his eyes rolled erratically. "Must be serious. You don't need to protect me from her, you know."

"I'm not protecting you, Stewart," but she was a terrible liar and Stewart grinned.

TWO MOONS OVER CEDAR HILL

He straddled a chair and plopped down in front of his plate. Christina put her hand over her nose and mouth.

"What sort of conditions did the ol' battle ax attach to our coming home?"

"What makes you think there were conditions?"

"There were, weren't there?" He took a healthy bite.

"She's a sick woman, Stewart."

"What conditions?" He spoke through his food.

"She might have mentioned our inheritance." Stewart snorted.

"Truly, I think she was just desperate to get us to come home. Which worries me. Maybe she is very ill or maybe she wants to make up for... everything."

Stewart only shook his head. "Damage is done. Mama has an ulterior motive. You can bank on that." He took another bite, then spoke around the eggs. "So, you ever gonna tell me what you two really argued about?"

"I told you, Stewart. She wanted me to take over managing the farm. I refused to displace Jorgé and I left so she would have to keep him on."

Stewart shook his head. "I wasn't talkin' about you and Mama. Any fool would have known that for the hollow threat it was. I meant you and Jorgé. What did *you* two argue about?"

Sofie Couch

He read her like a book, so she turned her back on him, speaking over her shoulder and ignoring his question. "I'm going back… briefly. I can call from there to let you know how she is. I'll try to get back here by Wednesday. Will you be okay?"

"What about the shop? Richard gonna let you leave the bell jar?"

"Stewart… please."

Holding his plate up at chin level, he shoveled the rest of his mayonnaise eggs into his mouth, and swallowed before continuing. "I just don't trust that guy."

"Why?"

Stewart stood, twirled toward the sink, knowing this kitchen as well as their childhood home. He swished his plate with a soapy sponge, rinsed, and then placed it in the drainer. He turned again and on his way out, patted the top of Christina's head as he passed her in the doorway. "He has some ulterior motive. Beware a man who wants you for more than your good looks." And before she could sputter a protest, he darted ahead to the bathroom and locked the door behind him.

There was a bitter taste in Christina's mouth. Stewart had an uncanny sense when it came to people. She felt things taking an uncomfortable turn and it had nothing to do with the smell of

TWO MOONS OVER CEDAR HILL

mayonnaise eggs and skunk-coffee at five in the morning.

Chapter 11

Cedar Hill, thirty years ago

Stew Breeden, Senior, ran a hand over the horse's flank like a man running his hand over the thigh of a woman. The teenaged Mexican kid watched alternately the horse and the man who had made the poor investment. The horse twitched and jostled around under restraint.

The kid tightened his grip on the horse's halter and murmured in the tones he thought a nervous woman would want to hear, although at only barely thirteen years old, he was going on instinct rather than experience.

"He'll take the crown."

The kid nodded.

"You're saying 'yes,' but your face says no."

"She has the structure..." The kid's accent was still thick having lived here just five years since being orphaned with no choice in the trade he was being taught. "But I don't think the temperament."

"Oh, she's got spirit, alright." And Stew thumped the horse on its rump and nearly sent it over the edge. The kid had to plant the heels of his boots into the soft dirt under foot. He had no fear of the animal. The smile Stew Breeden had worn since buying the horse began to melt as his manic high began to give way to the realities of the flaw in his choice.

TWO MOONS OVER CEDAR HILL

"She has not the temperament for racing. Maybe… in a generation or two…."

But Stew Breeden wasn't listening any more. He turned his back on horse and boy and strode out of the barn. Over his shoulder he called, "Then next time, damn it, you come along and pick out the horse before I set down the cash."

The kid had advised against the purchase and Stew had ignored him. What did a thirteen year old kid know about picking a winner anyway?

"Maybe you'll put more effort into training the horse if you know I spent your allowance on her."

They both knew there was no more money and the one thing Stew Breeden was sensible of was that horses were expensive. The kid settled his hand on the horse's neck and could feel its heart racing. Like the purchaser, the horse was flighty.

Stew Breeden stopped at the front steps of the home that had been passed down through generations of Breedens and he swore. He looked up at the façade. The kid joined him in his attention to the house. One man cursed the poor management by previous generations that had left him in this embarrassing state, acquitting himself of responsibility. The other man, mature beyond his thirteen years, looked at the house and saw his connection to it as fate. Stew Breeden could sell off pieces of the farm, but even he had to recognize that as a limited resource and when it was gone….

…The kid would have no home… no connection to any place on this planet.

Preservation of the farm was the single goal they both worked toward. The hill to the north-west fell away in a topographical wave, dissolving into the flat land that ran into the wide York River. The Breeden ancestral home sat atop Cedar Hill.

Both estates boasted families that had survived the Civil War and Reconstruction. Both were the size of small kingdoms. Both were old Virginia money. Stew thought of his neighbor, Mayella Thompson, who was a distant cousin. A third cousin perhaps? Not the kindest face to look upon. However, she did have the only asset any woman needed. Money.

Stew Breeden did not give the horse another thought. Instead, he strode inside his house, the king of his realm, showered, changed, and then made his way on foot down the old wagon road that used to connect the two estates with civilization. It was time he began showing his respects to his spinster third cousin.

Jorgé, just a boy, watched the man leave without a word. He comforted the horse, walked it to the pasture, then stood back and dreamt of the profitable use *he* would make of the fallow land stretched out before him.

TWO MOONS OVER CEDAR HILL

Chapter 12

Cedar Hill, present day

Jorgé bolted up in bed, then paused to listen. The rooster crowed. Foxes? No. Had something fallen with a crash in the house? No. He listened. The house was silent – in fact, too quiet.

He lay back on his pillow, tossed once, then gave up his fight to sleep. He rubbed his hand over his face, pushing one eyebrow backwards. When he had lain his head down on his pillow the night before he had had difficulty falling asleep for thinking of all that needed to be done to prepare for Christina's homecoming. It was time to get up anyway. At least, his internal clock told him it would be time in another half-hour or so.

There was no movement out in the hall, so it was unlikely that Treeny was up which meant Mayella probably had slept well too. That, at least, was a comfort. She should have accepted the morphine drip a week ago.

Jorgé threw his naked feet over the side of the bed. His actions, a routine. He had no need to switch on a light. Silently, he moved through the doorway, into the hall, downstairs and it was there, in the front hall that he first felt the disturbance to his routine.

Cold air crept up from the floor. He fumbled for the light switch. The front door stood wide-open. He walked to the open door, looked outside, and then closed it, a furrow at his brow. He pulled down the rolled up sleeves on his plaid flannel shirt, then stepped back into his deep-grooved rut as he moved toward the stairs that led down to the kitchen in the English basement.

Another break with routine – the dog hadn't followed him downstairs. "Beebo?"

There was no answering clickity click of claws as the arthritic dog scrambled and clawed his way into an upright position, as he usually did. Jorgé flipped on the second light. The stairs down to the kitchen were cold and still. No Beebo.

The dog had begun to show signs of dementia and Jorgé wondered by how much, if any time, the dog would outlast Mayella.

Then he noticed, the grandfather clock that stood in the front hall was silent, it's pendulum still for the first time in, probably, years. He turned back around to re-trace his steps, a premonition making the hair on his arms stand on end, so by the time he returned to Mayella's open door, he dreaded what he would find there.

The room was dark. Jorgé walked to the bed and reached out a hand. Before touching anything, he prepared himself to come into contact with her stiff, lifeless body. His hand touched chenille. It was flat... and cold. He ran his hand over the bed. It was empty.

TWO MOONS OVER CEDAR HILL

He fumbled for the bedside light, knocking over the pill bottles as he did so, one of them spiraling off the table, caught by the drawer that was open a crack. His eyes frantically ran over the rumpled bed clothes, then to the tube from the Fentanyl drip that dangled from the rack, a puddle on the wooden floor below the open stopcock. Jorgé looked to the adjoining bathroom. Its door stood open too and it was dark inside. He rushed to the doorway, flipped on the light and looked inside. It bore the tidy paraphernalia of the sick, but no sign of Mayella.

With overlarge strides, Jorgé moved around her bed, out the door and to the room next door to Mayella's where he knocked sharply on the door facing. Treeny left her door open so she could hear Mayella if she called, although he suspected her hearing was no better than the old dog's. The housekeeper sat up in bed, suddenly awake.

"It's Mayella. She's not in her room."

The woman rubbed her sleepy eyes awake, then she grabbed the pink cardigan beside her bed.

Jorgé left her thin lipped in the doorway and ran down the hall, opening and slamming doors in his frantic search. Mayella was barely strong enough to move from her bed to the toilet. It was unimaginable that she might have gone far, but when the upstairs revealed no sign of her, he yelled to the now awake Treeny. "You look downstairs." He remembered the open front door and knew in his heart they would not find Mayella inside the house.

The front porch stood a full story above ground level and usually provided him a proud view of the farm he had had a hand in creating. Today, a dark shape moving in the front field caught his eye and Jorgé ran down the steps, mindless of anything other than the dog that pranced and barked from outside the wrought iron square of fence that stood on a low swell of the soybean field. Jorgé sprinted along the driveway toward the main road. There, half way along, he saw the fence gate standing open where they let the tractor in for thrashing. His heart pounded in his chest.

"What the devil were you thinking?" He spoke aloud, but his words were lifted and dissipated until they were lost on the frosty morning air.

Arthritic Beebo whimpered, then barked again.

"*Madre de dios.*"

Faster than his body was used to traveling, Jorgé ran the distance to the old dog and saw, before even reaching the spot, Mayella's body inside the cemetery fence. Jorgé planted one hand between the spiked pickets and launched over the intricate, rusty, wrought iron surround. But inside, and with immediate reverence, he stopped.

Like a lost child found sleeping in a thicket, Mayella's body lay in the tall bramble. She was on her stomach, her head tipped to the side and resting in the crook of her arm. Her legs were gently bent as though she had finally found a comfortable position.

Slowly, Jorgé approached, then knelt beside the body. Mayella was dead, an empty amber pill bottle to the side of her face, tipped at an angle toward her mouth that implied the details of her *finale*.

With a loving hand, he reached out to touch her gray hair. It was wet with dew that had taken from it the crazed look of a person tortured with pain. Instead, it fell about her face in loose, damp curls, a blush of frost on her eye lashes. With a twist of his stomach, he saw the resemblance between Mayella and her daughter – a face he had not seen in a little over half a decade. The resemblance was so close, it froze his heart until he could no longer look at Mayella. He turned his eyes to the gravestone over her head… the gravestone lichen covered, worn by time and elements… the gravestone….

And as if a cold hand had reached up from the ground to grip his heart, Jorgé dropped to his knees, catching himself on the stone. His face was inches from the ancient engraving and it mocked him. The star and double moon symbol, so familiar to his own heart, was there in front of him. The name under it, "Grace Thompson," – G.T. - confused, then mocked him and everything he had held dear.

Sofie Couch

Outside the fence, Beebo whimpered. Inside the fence, Jorgé wept, his hands on the stone and his tears falling on the face of the women who, as her last act on earth, ensured he knew the truth of the only thing he had left to cling to – his history was a fiction.

TWO MOONS OVER CEDAR HILL

Chapter 13

Cedar Hill, 1863

A man can take pride in seeing to the welfare of his family. Salter had watched his siblings as they were, one by one, buried, sold or traded to other white land owners. A man can take pride in his choice of a wife. Salter would be denied his choice of his life mate. A man can take pride in his home. Salter's house was only as warm as the ground below him. It leaned against a stone chimney and the chimney leaned against the house. It was one of the better built out lying dependencies and he pointed the cracks between the logs himself, so it was nearly air tight. It used to be a smoke house and it still choked its inhabitants with the smell of ham without affording the consolation of taste.

Salter held the exalted position of "mason" which meant he was used to hard labor. He was to blame if the bricks were weak, an animal died, or one of the brick yard laborers fell sick. No one lost much sleep if a slave died and no one took time to bury them until the workday was done.

And yet, with so few prospects, Salter held his head high when no one was looking. Until one day when Grace Thompson looked.

Grace was, once again, in a place she wasn't supposed to be. Lying on her stomach on a wool blanket under a mountain laurel, her diary open in front of her as she jotted notes alongside lead pencil sketches of a brazen family of white tail rabbits. It was late August and what little sunlight managed to filter down through the trees warmed her back through dress and josie.

In this inconspicuous place she went unnoticed by Salter who walked right up to the very warren she was watching, crouched beside it and waited. He blocked her view of the hole, but she put her pen and paper aside and instead, watched him from behind as though he was another animal specimen to be sketched in her book. Certainly, she had seen Negroes up close before, but never one of the brickyard laborers. She thought this man was quite possibly the largest man she had ever seen before, with muscles down to his fingers. No one had ever warned her to fear the Negro men on the farm. And Grace was not given to fear of animals. She did not place him within the same species as herself and he was as foreign a curiosity as some western animal in her Daddy's book by Mr. Audubon.

And how curious that this black man would think himself capable of catching a rabbit without the aid of a gun or snare as though he simply expected the rabbit to pop his head out with the scent of a predator outside his hole.

Grace wondered if maybe the men of his species had no scent. She was a firm believer in Mr.

TWO MOONS OVER CEDAR HILL

Darwin's theories and thought that might be an advantageous thing for a race of hunters. While ruminating on that thought, the man squatting beside the hole suddenly lunged into action. His hand dove down. There was a brief, futile scuffle of rabbit feet against hard packed dirt, then a sharp crunch as the man snapped the rabbit's neck.

He rose, turned to leave, and then stopped, with the rabbit hanging limp at the side of his leg. Grace slowly looked up, her eyes traveling up the side of the man's ticking pants, past his linen shirt and finally, to his face. He was looking back at her, but with his back to daylight and her in the shadows and used to shaded light, his face looked like a different sort of rabbit hole in the sky.

"What're you doing down there?"

Grace scrambled to her feet, brushing off the front of her dress. "Watching rabbits."

He looked both ways as though expecting someone else to pop out from under the laurel bushes.

"You best get back to the house, Miss Grace."

"How'd you know my name?"

He looked worried as he checked both ways again.

"You go on back now, Miss Grace. You shouldn't be out here on you own."

"What's your name?"

"Salter. Salter…" he hesitated, "…Lyons."

Grace stood a little taller and stepped out from behind the laurel with her hand extended.

"Pleased to meet you, Mr. Lyons. You from over the brick yard? At the Lyons's place?"

He looked at her hand, but did not take it.

"You oughta be getting on back to the house now."

"Why didn't that rabbit smell you?" She nodded toward the limp animal still held in his hand by the scruff and taking a step closer, she inhaled deeply.

Salter averted his gaze from no one, so he held her direct stare. "Why di'n' she smell *you*?"

"I wasn't as close."

"They can smell you though." He took one step closer, still a yard separating them, and he inhaled deeply. "You wearin' basil."

"I most certainly am not."

But in contradiction, Salter nodded. "You wearin' basil water. I can smell it."

"My daddy got this perfume for me from a gypsy woman over in Richmond."

Salter nodded. "It's made of basil stirred up in water. Maybe some mint in it too. Rabbit come out his hole thinking he smells dinner."

Grace watched him with suspicion. "What about you? Are you wearing basil water?"

Salter shook his head. "I rubbed down in violet water."

TWO MOONS OVER CEDAR HILL

Before he knew what she was doing, she stepped right up to him, lifted his forearm to her nose and took a good long sniff. He stiffened. She looked up at him, still holding his forearm. She was smiling.

"Well, I'll be. You sure did. Violet water. Just as pretty as a woman," but beneath the soft scent of violet water, she smelled something musky that emanated from him – from his arm – and she liked the smell that reminded her of her daddy and she felt comforted by it. "But something else too. Something…."

Salter took a step away from her. "Listen, you'd best to get back home, Miss Grace. Ain't safe for you to be out here on your own."

She laughed and Salter thought he had never heard a sweeter, more natural sound. It rivaled the sound of birds first thing in the morning.

"Are you afraid in the woods?" she asked him.

"No."

"Me neither. There's nothing out here to hurt a person who's minding their own business."

He could not argue that point with her. This land was his home. He was born here and he would die here – but not as a result of anything that was a part of the weave of the land. He saw a common bond with the girl in front of him and in an instant, against all reason, against years of oppression and better sense, he fell in love with her and he knew who he would choose for his wife if he were free to do so.

But instead, he said, "Go on back to the house, Miss Grace."

TWO MOONS OVER CEDAR HILL

Chapter 14

Tidewater, present day

Stewart intentionally waited until he heard the cowbell clunk on the downstairs shop door. Christina would be on her way home – back to their childhood home. He picked up the phone.

"Hey. It's Stewart. I won't be able to make it in today."

There was a long pause and concern on the other end.

"No. I'm fine. I just need to buzz home for a long weekend. Can you cover my caseload today? No. I'm fine. Really. Thanks. And you'll take my caseload of kids for the day? Thanks."

Stewart felt for the base, then returned the receiver and went about the business of draping a necktie around his neck. He soundlessly navigated the steps to the antique shop below and straight into the disapproving notice of the parasitic idiot who took advantage of Christina's insecurities for slave labor in his shop.

Stewart made a show of smelling the air. "Morning, Richard."

Richard gave Stewart the briefest of nods. Ten years and he still didn't get that blind people cannot see a nod. Richard sipped at a cup of coffee, hot from the sound of it. He was sitting at the front counter and distracted himself with a perusal of the newspaper. Stewart could tell by the sound.

Richard smelled like fake leather and musky cologne - another fixture in the shop, an *objet d'art* that needed deodorizer to conceal its stink.

Stewart moved toward the front desk, smelling the coffee and guessing correctly that there was another cup there for Christina. "Aw. Did you bring that for me?" Stewart feigned reaching for one of the cups.

Richard reached for it, as if to snatch it away, then recalled that Stewart couldn't see and was only messing with him. Richard glared – to no effect.

Stewart let his hand fall and shifted the saddle bag he wore slung over his shoulder, eager to be gone, but hesitant to miss an opportunity to screw with Richard. "You know, Christina has a favorite brand of coffee she drinks... almost exclusively?"

Richard lowered his newspaper, but gave no verbal response.

"Yeah. That one with the picture of a sea captain on the front." Stewart shrugged. "If you wanna score with her." It would not occur to Richard that Stewart had never actually seen the sea captain on the label before.

"Stewart, you 'score'. I woo."

Stewart muttered under his breath, "You slither, Dick."

"What's that?"

TWO MOONS OVER CEDAR HILL

"I said... mustn't... dither... around here, Rick. If Christina calls from the road, you'll cover for me, won't you?" Stewart expertly spun his necktie into a tight Windsor knot — one of the completely useless skills his father had taught him. As a child he had clung to any bone his father threw his way, even a useless lesson in spinning a tight noose.

Richard watched the maneuver with so much surprise, he put down his newspaper, no longer interested in the obituaries and in finding out who might have died leaving behind a fortune in antiques and cheap property.

"Well, I don't think I've ever been more impressed in your presence, Stewart. That was inspiring."

"Hmm?"

"Nice Windsor." Richard increased his volume whenever he remembered that Stewart was blind.

"Oh, I'm full of surprises." Knowing the clear path to the shop's entrance, he started toward the door, turning his back on Richard.

"Hold up there a minute, Stew, will you?"

Stew? Stewart turned, suspicion making his spine go straight. He let the saddle bag slip from his shoulder to the floor.

"Speaking of surprises, I suppose Christina told you she's going home this weekend?"

"Yep."

"She's never mentioned your mother before now."

"We did have one."

"I guess I do have to credit you with that."

"Yeah, well, she doesn't like to talk about our past. I don't talk about *her*... with strangers."

Richard folded the newspaper with anal retentive precision, finally giving Stewart more attention than he had shown for him in the nine years since they'd first met. "I'd hardly call myself a stranger. I've known the two of you for... years now."

"Yeah, ever since you hired her in exchange for room above and slave wages below." Stewart waved a hand around the chocked full antique store.

Richard shrugged. "Just a matter of being in the right place at the right time." He tapped the newspaper against his crossed leg.

"Convenient, that." Stewart turned again to head out.

"I know you don't like me."

Stewart shrugged. "I don't trust you more." Stewart hated being transparent to Richard. He hated that his sister saw anything to admire in Richard and he spent his effort waffling over whether or not he really disliked Richard or whether he was just jealous. Jealousy over another man's interest in his sister stuck in his craw. He wanted a valid reason to mistrust Richard, but the solid evidence always lurked just out of reach.

"It's just that," Richard paused for dramatic effect, "…I can't imagine Christina having a falling out… with anyone… but especially not her mother."

"And that's just the thing, Richard. You don't know Christina. The Christina you see here," he waved a hand around the shop, nearly smashing into a lamp with hanging crystals, "isn't the same sister I had ten years ago. When we left home, she changed – left a part of herself behind."

Richard wore a skeptical twist on his mouth. "What could they have argued over?"

"That's a question you'll have to put to Christina."

"She has never hinted at the reason for her falling out with your mother?"

"I didn't say that, Richard. I just never believed her version of things."

The resentment that Mayella bore Stewart was never a secret. He knew it had less to do with the person he was than the person his father had been and his resemblance to his namesake. Stewart's memory of his father still bore a touch of childish glow – but only a touch. Stewart had plenty reason to resent his mother. He wouldn't share the half of it with Richard.

"What of this farm manager?"

Stewart shook his head. "Jorgé? Is that what she called him? The 'farm manager'?"

"She was in love with him?"

Was that a flicker of jealousy? "I guess that much is obvious."

"And I take it, your mother fired him anyway."

Stewart blew off the suggestion with a wave of his hand, taking on a Jorgé mannerism at the mere mention of the man who had been more father to him than his real father. Stewart ignored the sense of loss for having been away so long.

"The farm could never survive without him. He's still there. My mother manipulates people by threatening to revoke that thing she possesses that they want. She's no fool. She knows without Jorgé the farm would go to ruin. Use of money and social influence is more her style."

"Do you think your mother offered her money to return? That that was Christina's motivation for leaving?"

"No. Money's not what she cares about."

Nor did Stewart. His mother had gleefully taken from Stewart something that could never be replaced, a secret he still kept close to his heart. So what, he wondered, had their mother done to Christina, that she would leave her home in favor of this life of exile, peddling the historical vignettes of other people's lives?

TWO MOONS OVER CEDAR HILL

"History. Christina cares about family history."

"Given a choice, she'd be home… and I intend to find out why she isn't – why she chose to leave home – her roots – to run away from home with me. I'm gonna find out why - something I should have done years ago."

And with that, Stewart strode out of the shop, leaving the cow bell clunking behind him.

Out on the street, he popped the red-tipped, white cane out of his back pocket, unfolded it, and adjusted the saddle bag over his opposite shoulder.

As he walked away from the shop, he knew this might be the last time he "saw" this place. In ten years, he had found peace with his mother's actions, if not exactly *peace*, with her, but there was Christina to consider. She left, supposedly, for him. He meant for her to be reinstated at her home.

Twenty-five steps, and he turned around the corner. Christina's admiration of Richard was another thorn in his side. He hated that she found anything to admire in Richard. She admired him for his renaissance qualities. He did seem to know more stuff about stuff than almost anyone he had ever met, maybe with the exception of an aunt with eidetic memory, but Stewart had always felt as though Richard had somehow wheedled his way into Christina's notice, being all too conveniently positioned in their late father's ocean front commercial property. He brought out an irrationally protective response in him.

    Stewart paused after ten more paces, and tapped his cane until it clanked against a sign post. Extending a hand, he reached for the sign, recognized the shape as the bus stop and within a minute, the bus pulled up. Stewart flashed a pass at the driver as he mounted the steps. There was a reason Christina allowed herself to be exiled from her home and he was determined to learn the truth of it – and the truth was usually pretty close to the physical source.

TWO MOONS OVER CEDAR HILL

Chapter 15

Cedar Hill, about twenty years ago

"I think I've figured out where it is."

Stew Breeden's ex-wife looked up. "Oh really?"

The one thing Stew Senior had never figured out was how to dance around Mayella, who held the strings to nearly everything.

"What is the one place they might have buried a treasure – where the Yankees wouldn't find it – or think to look?"

Mayella put down the book she had been reading while the twins slept. "I have no idea, Stewart."

"A grave! If there was a fresh grave, no one would think to dig it up to search for something that had been buried. I was just out in the field – at the family plot – and there's a grave that would have been dug about the time the family treasure disappeared – 1864. It's hard to read the stone any more, but it makes sense. If the family was afraid their only source of wealth would be looted, then they would try to hide it before the northern army marched through. What better place to hide it?"

Mayella reached up to toy with a clay pendant that hung around her neck. She turned her attention back to the book she had been reading before

Stewart came in with his latest "get-rich-quick" scheme.

"Then how come they to lose track of it? You'd think someone woulda gone back to unbury it when the war was over and times were hard."

"I don't know what your crazy ancestors coulda been thinking? But I think it's worth a little pokin' around, don't you?"

Mayella took her hand away from her necklace. "And who do you think is gonna do all of this pokin' around? Presumably, you're not proposing digging up the family plot on your own?"

"I could. But it'd go faster with Jorgé putting his shoulder to the task."

Mayella snorted. She knew that was Stew-speak for Jorgé doing all the digging while he supervised.

"I will not condone you desecrating the graves of our ancestors."

"For a fortune in buried silver and gold coin?"

"For any reason, but not just because you got some notion in your head that that must be where it was buried… if it was ever buried. More likely than not, it was a fiction invented by dog-tired parents to tell their children at night – a pirate treasure story."

Stewart Senior turned and stormed out, slamming the door on his way and waking both babies.

TWO MOONS OVER CEDAR HILL

"I hope to hell I find it, Mayella!" He yelled from the front porch. "I'm gonna demand 50% on top of my 10% finder's fee!"

The teenaged Jorgé installed the timbers for a cold frame. Mayella had agreed to allow him to dabble in organic produce if he could do it without expense to her. Today, Stew Breeden, Senior stormed past him without speaking. He had just had another "interview" with his estranged wife and those discussions usually revolved around finances and never ended well for Stew Senior. Neither was he speaking to Jorgé, because he was still miffed about losing his services in the separation settlement with his wife. He kept life rights in his old home and the freedom to live his life as he wanted, under the restraint of an allowance. Mayella kept the children, infant twins, and the services of sixteen year old Jorgé.

Jorgé looked up in case Stew Senior decided to grace him with his notice. He did not. Jorgé was curious to know how the training was going with Stew's latest equine acquisition.

A wheelbarrow stood nearby and it was filled with the black, organic soil Jorgé had been curing all winter. Now it was early spring and time for the seeds to go in. The ground was beginning to warm and in the frames once he attached the old salvaged windows, he would plant seeds without fear of late frost.

Mayella meandered out to the south side of the barn to inspect his work. She held two babies – one on each hip – and a half dozen dogs followed in her wake, trying to trip her and vie for her attention. She never had a harsh word for her dogs.

"One thing I'll say for you. You're persistent as hell."

"Wasted effort if I did not believe it would succeed." Jorgé did not look up at her, but pushed the nose of one of the dogs away from his crotch and kept working, moving the soil with a spade and working it in with the top soil he had just amended.

"You and Stew Breeden have too much in common."

He paused mid-shovel, looked in the direction Stew Senior had left, then kept working. "Mr. Breeden is a driven man."

Mayella only snorted. She stood behind him, supervising the production. If the organic produce turned out a yield, she would nod with approval. If it turned a profit, she would take credit for the idea. Jorgé didn't care. He was only trying to strike a balance.

"I've got something for you."

He took another shovelful from the wheelbarrow, mixed it in, and then stopped to give her his attention, expecting little.

TWO MOONS OVER CEDAR HILL

She handed over her male child, Stew Junior, and Jorgé took the infant into his arms while Mayella reached to her pocket. "I ran across this the other day." She fumbled in her jacket pocket and pulled out a necklace. The medallion was made of some sort of baked, red clay and it spun on a leather thong. "Thought you might like to have it back."

He shifted the baby to his hip, took the necklace into the palm of his dirty hand, turned it over and took note of the initials etched into the back, "G.T. + S.L."

"Looks old." He inspected it from all sides. "I didn't lose it." He tried to hand it back to her, but she was already reaching for the infant son.

"It's yours, alright. At least, it should be. Your Mama gave it to me long time ago, when she kept house here and," she nodded in the direction Stew Senior had headed, "over the way. I gave her some sort of little bauble. Your mama was always a proper woman. Probably felt she had to give me something in return. Gave me that little chunk of clay to hang on to. Said it'd been in your family a long time. I thought you might like to have it back."

This time, with reverence and a palpitating heart, Jorgé turned the stone over and inspected both sides, then rubbed his thumb over the clay. The "G.T." he did not recognize, but the "S.L." he took to be the initials of some long dead relative – another "Lopez". The week before he had learned a new word to add to his vocabulary: enculturated, and it had depressed him for a full seven days. Now, his spirit felt lighter.

"Mayella. I...." But she had already turned and was headed off in the opposite direction, back toward the house with her young children, followed by her pack of faithful canine courtesans.

Present day

Mayella was dead.

"Look – at - it. Look at it!" The ghost of Mayella shouted into Jorgé's ear.

Jorgé put his fingers to the inexpertly carved tombstone and caressed the lichen with reverence and anguish. As he traced the letters carved there, "G.T. + S.L.", he wept.

"You understand now, don't you?" the ghost of Mayella asked.

"I don't understand you, Mayella," Jorgé said aloud through his tears not expecting an answer.

"You will understand."

"You hate-filled woman." And like Beebo, the last surviving dog on the farm had done the night before, Jorgé turned his head to the sky and cried. "You torture me from the grave!"

Mayella's spirit felt sadness. "I love you from the grave." Her soul was wrought with regret and she cried. "I've only ever loved you."

TWO MOONS OVER CEDAR HILL

She watched from some position suspended just over his head, so close she might reach down and caress his black, shiny hair that was beginning to show flecks of gray if she had had a hand with which to do it. Instead, she could only watch, an unwilling spectator, a specter, as Jorgé struggled to recover from the blow. He looked at the stone beside Grace Thompson's. It read, "Jamie Thompson." A relative, but that stone was simple, with no adornment like the symbol on Grace's headstone.

Jorgé wiped his nose on the back of his shirt sleeve, then bent and scooped up Mayella's body from the ground. He carried her in his strong, sinewy arms as if she were some sort of stiff child, her body retaining the bends it had assumed on the ground, her arm still folded with her head in its crook.

Looking down on her face, Jorgé wept some more. She understood then that he wept, not for her, but for the resemblance he saw in her face to Christina. The instantaneous level of her understanding was surprising.

She also knew that most people in her situation would have gone on to another place and while she wanted to, she could not. All her efforts would be for naught if she did not stick around to help. The living - and the dead - still needed her assistance.

Beebo hobbled beside Jorgé, but looked up, not at him or the body he carried, but to the spot over Jorgé's shoulder, to Mayella's spirit. The dog walked with its tail tucked between its legs, going ahead of Jorgé, then glancing back, running ahead, then glancing back.

At the house, Beebo ran up the stairs, his overly long claws clicking on the hardwood floors that had seen better days. The dog went to his basket beside Mayella's bed, could not find a comfortable spot and finally crawled under the bed where he would stay for the next two days.

Jorgé came lumbering up the stairs under the strain of Mayella's body in his arms – nothing compared to the burden of the truth that was written in stone.

Treeny threw her back to the wall, going white about the lips. "No. Not yet," she whispered.

Jorgé entered the room and laid Mayella's body on the covers in the same position he had found her in the cemetery.

Treeny cried in the doorway. "She shouldn't have gone this quickly."

Jorgé wiped his eyes and nose on the back of his shirt sleeve before taking a deep breath.

"I have little experience of this. I think we should call the home health agency to ask their advice."

TWO MOONS OVER CEDAR HILL

He moved to leave the room and Treeny hung back. Jorgé took one long last look at Mayella, then looked up and for an instant, her spirit thought perhaps he was looking directly at her.

"You have taken from me the only thing I had left in this world," he said, presumably to no one.

Mayella's spirit whispered. "I have given you everything you've ever wanted from this world."

Chapter 16

Present day

Christina climbed out of the rust red pick-up truck, pressed her hands into the small of her back and stretched backwards. When she leaned forward, bending over to touch her toes, the necklace around her neck fell out of her blouse, a rude reminder that some things that had been buried for a long time were about to be unearthed.

She shoved the necklace back in her top. Other travelers stopped – the women heading toward the rest area ladies' room - the men heading mostly toward the coffee vending machines.

She followed the flock, locked the door on a stall and, in lieu of engaging a pair of shoes in conversation, found a different sort of comfort, then pulled out the necklace again. Holding it in her palm, she turned it over, looking first at the design on the front and secondly at the initials pressed into the back.

Terracotta, brown with oil transferred from loving hands. She massaged the front. It had been a gift from Jorgé at her *quincinera*.

Cedar Hill, 21years ago

A fifteen year old Christina accepted the beautifully wrapped gift from her father – the last of

TWO MOONS OVER CEDAR HILL

a small avalanche of birthday gifts for the twins on their fifteenth birthday. There had been ever practical sweaters from their mother, artwork from Annabelle, her best friend, music from Stewart Little, pirated and recorded on MP3, and a refurbished horse saddle from Jorgé for Stewart Little and a re-built mini-bike for her that their father claimed credit for giving. They both knew who did the work on it.

Her father grinned at her from the head of the table looking almost as if he sat there every night. Christina hated these mandatory "family" functions where her parents feigned tolerance for one another.

Christina removed the bow from the box and slowly peeled away the gift wrap. She wanted desperately for there to be something appropriate in the box, not for her own sake, but for her father's sake. She wanted her father to meet her mother's high expectations. She lifted the lid and caught her breath. A diamond tennis bracelet winked at her from the velvet lined interior.

"Daddy. It's beautiful." She held it up by the clasp and let it sparkle under the light of the chandelier. "Look, Mama. Isn't it beautiful?"

Mayella took the bracelet for closer inspection. Stew Senior swelled and smiled down the table at the familial collection. Jorgé and Christina's friend, Annabelle, the only two invited guests, sat opposite Christina and Stewart.

While Stew Senior expounded on the quality of the diamonds, and as Mayella inspected them for authenticity, Christina spied the corner of a card that peeked from under the cotton lining of the box and pulled out the note. She read to herself: "To Trinity, With all my love, Stewart."

Christina felt her stomach turn. She hastily slipped the card under her napkin, found her smile and painted it back on in time to take the bracelet as her mother returned it to her.

"It's an extravagant gift for a child."

"Thank you, Daddy. It's beautiful," Christina painted over her mother's comment. She laid the bracelet back in the box on the cotton and covered it with the lid. When she looked up again, Jorgé's attention was not on her or the gift box, but on her napkin where she had hidden the note. Christina put her hand over the napkin, crumpled it and pretended to wipe her mouth. Jorgé's eyes followed the napkin to her lips, then to Christina's eyes. She smiled with a quiver at the corner of her mouth. He wasn't so easily fooled.

Christina stood and gathered her plate, then Stewart's.

"You don't do dishes on your birthday," her father scolded, but made no effort to intercede.

"It's my night to wash."

Jorgé rose from his chair and took his and Annabelle's plates to the dumbwaiter. Only Christina noticed when he slipped out of the dining room and she was relieved he did not press her for the contents of the note.

She had loaded all the dishes and was in the basement kitchen retrieving the bus bin from the dumbwaiter when Jorgé returned, coming in from the outside.

"I have one more gift for you."

Christina couldn't meet his eyes, so she stared down at the ill-wrapped box in his hands.

"Sorry. My fingers are better suited to harvesting apples than tying pretty bows." He thrust the hastily wrapped box toward her.

Slowly, dreading what she would find in the box, she undid the jute bow and brown paper wrapping that, she was certain, he had only just hastily wound around the gift.

"But you've already given me a gift, Jorgé."

He shrugged. "Where I come from a girl becomes a woman on her fifteenth birthday. A mini bike," he shrugged, "that is your little girl gift, Chita, but I know you are old enough now to appreciate and care for a thing of great value." He winced. "Well, great sentimental value, at any rate."

She knew he had nothing of monetary value to give her, both of them being financially dependent upon Christina's mother. He was fifteen years her senior and had fallen in the middle of the Breeden generations – not a member of the family, but kept close enough to prevent any complaint over low wages.

She pulled off the brown wrapping paper, but that was easily enough done. There was no tape holding it closed, just the string. Inside was an old cigar box and Christina laughed.

"Gee. Thanks, Jorgé. Cubans. Good thing too, 'cause I was all out."

He chuckled. "Don't smoke'em all at once." He tapped the box. "Look inside."

She was smiling as she opened the box, but her smile faded when she saw what lay inside.

"It's not as beautiful as your bracelet, but to me it's priceless – a family heirloom – the only thing I have from my Mamá."

"Jorgé. I can't… I can't take this from you. It belongs in your family." She knew the medallion to be the one he always wore. She grew up alongside Jorgé, separated only by fifteen years and she couldn't remember ever seeing him when he wasn't wearing it.

"No. Look at this." He pulled down the collar of his tee-shirt to expose a well-oiled leather band that he wore around his own neck.

"This," he said, "is the original cord and I will keep it. It has the sweat of my ancestors on it." He pulled it from the neck of his shirt and gave it a kiss.

"It looks very old," she said, looking from the leather band, then down into the cigar box, almost afraid to touch the old pendant.

"So old, its history is lost." He took the medallion from the box and flipped it over, exposing the twin moons and star symbol. "I know little of my ancestors. I can remember my Mama and Papa only vaguely."

Christina touched the medallion with reverence and turned it again. On the rear of the medallion, the initials, "G.T + S.L." were scratched, but almost worn smooth.

"Thank you, Jorgé. I love it," and as he had done, she lifted the medallion to her lips and gave it a kiss.

"I knew it would find a worthy guardian in you, Chita."

The then fifteen year old Christina "Chita" Breeden, as he had dubbed her, put her arms around his neck and kissed his scratchy cheek.

"I'll keep it safe. I promise."

"I know you will."

Present day

And she had.

Sitting in the stall, Christina ran her fingers over the gold chain. It was a later addition that Jorgé had given her shortly after. It was fourteen karat and didn't really match the red clay-fired medallion, but it must have cost Jorgé the better part of a paycheck.

She lowered the necklace down her blouse again, shuffled her clothing back into position and rushed out of the stall to the sink before the automatic toilet finished flushing.

Outside her truck once more, she dreaded the four more hours of interstate driving ahead of her. The last leg of the journey to the gallows takes the longest, but for her mother's sake she had to keep going. She realized, as she merged into traffic, it wasn't Mayella with whom she was dreading a reunion. It was seeing Jorgé again that she dreaded.

The sadistic side of her rehearsed the words she would say to him when she returned his necklace.

TWO MOONS OVER CEDAR HILL

Chapter 17

Cedar Hill, 1863

Salter Lyons watched Grace from afar and found more reason to notice than to ignore. At night, he argued with himself over the fool heartiness of noticing her at all… of loving her, if he was completely honest with himself.

His lot in life was the exact opposite of hers. He had every right to resent the girl. He had practically watched her grow up at the same time he watched his own family separated. She had barely noticed him at all. He overheard and listened. She expressed her thoughts and feelings more than any person he had ever met. Her family was in the thick of the war, torn between sides, while he felt like an outside observer. He was a free man according to Mr. Lincoln's proclamation, as if that had ever needed proclaiming. Her family had much to lose and he had everything to gain. She was as fair skinned as the inside of a new potato while he could not boast a hint of red-bone in his hide. He was as black as the sun could cook a man without killing him.

No matter how much the war changed things, he and Grace Thompson had no chance of a future together. Still he felt safe in admiring her from afar. What harm could there ever be in looking? But eventually, it would not be from afar.

Sofie Couch

River's Edge abutted Cedar Hill and it was his home. His Mother's stories were about the earth and man's connection to it. According to her, no one owned the land and Salter respected his mother who continued to live through her stories.

With that as his theology, Salter was able to cast aside resentment for his oppressors. He was a free man in his heart. He made a decent living through his craft, which circumstances forced him to share with the white landowner. He convinced himself it was part of a pay-off for his education in the field of masonry, his indenture. He was but one animal. His impact would be measured, then erased with years in direct proportion to the harm he had caused the earth. He would find immortality through his deeds that were of benefit to the earth.

Salter slapped mortar on a brick, then laid it with a precise eye. He tapped the red brick into place and over the top of the brick, he saw, coming out the back door of the Thompson house, Grace Thompson. With footsteps that looked as though she stepped over clouds, she approached the work site. Salter remembered her taking his arm and sniffing it the first time they met.

"You'd best not come too close, Miss Grace. Is awful muddy around here." He reached to the buttons on his shirt and closed them.

"I've been watching this whole past hour." She spoke softly and pointed back toward the house and to a window on the upper floor. "You make it look easy."

"It is." He swelled.

He went about his work and eventually she moved away.

It wasn't conceit, but a fact that Salter had become the most experienced mason at River's Edge. He did not doubt there were others in the county who were better, had better tools, but he had more practice than most since his labor came cheap, almost for the asking. He was not blind to the inequity in this, but believed the likelihood of a better situation further north was slim. At least here, he was home and home was the occasional glimpse of Grace.

The next day, he worked on the same folly, but this time, with his back to the main house. He could almost feel Grace watching him from her upstairs window, but he waited through most of the morning before chancing a look. She was not there.

Jack Lyons rode up and sat astride his horse inspecting Salter's work. Salter thought nothing of it until the boy rode away without comment and tied up at the Thompson house. Annoyance turned to jealousy as he watched him go into Grace's house for mid-day dinner.

Salter ate a cucumber and drank three jars of water knowing that heavy food in this heat was death. Jack would not last a day in this heat.

At the end of the week, Jack showed up again, this time on foot, and disappeared inside the house again.

Footfalls coming from behind him made Salter look up. He expected Jack, but met the steady gaze and sweet smile of Grace.

"How do you do that? Work all morning and into the afternoon without stopping for a break?"

Salter mixed mortar with a hoe in a large wooden trough. He glanced at her, pretending to hardly notice her, then kept mixing.

"'Round two, three o'clock is the hottest part of the day. I work early and keep working 'til then. Then I quit. Gonna rain soon anyway."

"Here. Brought you something from the house."

She held out a square something wrapped in a piece of muslin. Hesitantly, Salter took it from her, careful not to touch her hands… pretending it was because his own hands were dirty. Under the muslin was a large chunk of cake and he breathed in the sweet, warm smell of it.

"That looks real good, Miss Grace." He looked to the house when the door opened again. This time, Jack Lyons came out and cut a direct path toward them. Salter felt a drop of rain hit his cheek. A little shower would make the humidity all the worse the next day.

TWO MOONS OVER CEDAR HILL

Salter covered the cake and put it behind the brick wall he was working on.

"Aren't you gonna eat it?"

"Thank you, Grace. I'm about to quit for the day. I'll have it when I get home. I'm sure if you made it I can't help but like it."

He saw a scowl come to her forehead and he wished he could take back his words. It wouldn't kill him to take a small bite and make over it.

"I didn't make it. I don't know how to cook."

"You... don't know how to cook?" He smiled, thinking she was joking, but she didn't smile. He sobered. "I'm sorry. I thought you went to some fancy girls' school up in Charlottesville."

"They don't teach cooking."

"Folly's looking good, ain't it, Grace?"

Jack surprised him with the speed he had covered the distance from the house. They sprang apart.

Another drop of rain hit the back of his hand.

"Well, the masonry is exceptional, if that's what you mean." Grace tipped her head and ran her finger along a brick on which Salter had made some precise mathematical calculations in lead pencil. "Can't tell much about what it's going to look like in the end. Seems like a pretty big extravagance if you ask me."

Salter kept his smile to the inside. Talking Mrs. Thompson into a brick Grecian temple had been Jack's idea. Salter was constructing it from an old picture drawn in a book from Mr. Thompson's library.

"It'll make a fine site for a party. Maybe a wedding party – someday soon," Jack hinted.

Salter cut his eyes from his work to Grace. He saw the way her back went straight. "I don't know anyone who is thinking to be married anytime soon."

Jack grinned like a 'possum that's just cleaned up the scraps after All Day Doin's and Dunner on the Lawn. "No sense waiting until the last minute. And Salter here's about the best brick mason around these parts. This 'ere structure'll be here for five hundred years and folks'll wonder about the couple that stood under the bower."

It did not feel like a compliment. Jack was showing off his property to Grace and for the first time since he had known the boy, Salter resented him. The rain began to pick up as dark clouds rolled in and saddled up to the hill.

"Well, I'd best get on back to the house before I drown." She put a hand to her brow and looked up at the sky, then back to Salter who was stooping to pick up a large sheet of canvas oil cloth. "Looks like it's comin' on two o'clock, Mr. Lyons, but I believe the rain will stop you before the heat does."

Salter straightened, uncertain at first to whom she was speaking. He rarely heard the title, "Mr.

Lyons," and for an instant, he felt regret that he did not have a name of his own to transfer to a wife. An enslaved man had no last name of his own to pass on to wife or child.

"Yes ma'am. I believe it is." He flipped the oil cloth in the air and let it settle down over the top of the brick work that was still wet. The rain on the oil soaked cloth sent a different smell into the air. He hid his notice of Grace behind his work.

Grace made no effort to make herself scarce.

Now the rain speckled the pile of sand by the mortar box.

"I should walk you back home, Grace." Jack held out his hand.

Grace turned pointedly away from him.

"Caught any rabbits lately?"

Salter smiled while he leisurely gathered his tools and cleaned them in the bucket of water. "Caught a ground hog the other night."

"Ground hog? You eat it?"

"I sure didn't let it go to waste," but he smiled so she wasn't sure if he was teasing or not. "Don't eat no 'possum though. They tastes worse than a turkey buzzard."

She laughed and it trickled up his spine. He could see Jack's indecision. The rain was getting harder, but he had a duty to see Grace safely home.

"Listen. I'd best get back to work. Get this loaded." He nodded toward the large canvas bag in which he carried his tools.

Jack took a few steps toward the Thompson house. When Salter looked up, he could see Mrs. Thompson watching them from a window.

Grace whispered. "I think you've been avoiding me."

Salter shifted nervously and scrapped at a bit of dried mortar on his trowel. "Ain't nothing to avoid. Why would I avoid you? Or not avoid you?" He spoke between clenched teeth in a tone soft enough Jack couldn't hear.

She shrugged. "Don't know. I thought, maybe you've seen Jack Lyons calling a lot and that made you stand-offish."

"It's time he settle down."

She shrugged again. "Maybe. Just not with me."

He looked up and she held his gaze for a long while.

And as if he could smell the invasion of his territory, Jack Lyons closed the gap between them, taking Grace by the elbow.

Grace looked at his hand and he released her.

Salter looked to the young man who had an inequitable share – of everything.

"He's a good man. You could do worse." He spoke so Jack could hear him.

TWO MOONS OVER CEDAR HILL

Jack looked like a man who had just had his fill and was looking forward to dessert. "Your mama is calling you in from the window, Grace."

Without a parting word, Grace turned and headed away from the house, toward the base of Cedar Hill's namesake. Jack ran to catch up with her.

"I'll be leaving for school next week."

"I was talking about that with your mama. And we think you may not need to go back to school this year."

Salter cringed. The rain had picked up to a steady rhythm, but Salter could hear them clearly. Grace stopped walking and turned on Jack. "What right have you to discuss whether or not I need to go back?"

Jack looked taken aback. "It was a thought. Just something we were discussing."

"My father will be most distressed to learn that you and mother have decided on the perpetuation of my ignorance. I think he will side with me on this." She picked up her skirt and slip. "If you don't mind, Mr. Lyons, I am going on a scientific excursion. Your presence would interfere with the results."

He stopped and looked at her dumbstruck. She was several steps away before he spoke.

"I just thought we might talk about the future of our two families."

She turned. "I'm sure I would be poor counsel. I know little about brick making."

"Salter's getting married," he blurted out.

Salter, who had been rather enjoying eavesdropping on the exchange stiffened.

Grace raised her chin, pretending a lack of interest.

"I'm going to pick her up in Richmond in a couple of weeks." He shoved his hands into his coat pockets and nonchalantly moved toward her.

"I think you'll find that to be a fool hearty investment. The war'll be over soon and your labor will be demanding the wages they deserve."

"You think we won't win the war?"

Grace shook her head.

"I think highly of Salter." Jack walked toward her, pretending he wasn't getting soaked and it didn't bother him. "He's a good worker. Devoted to his family. You get that sort of devotion from them when you treat them fairly."

Grace walked away with her fists clenched. Salter bent back to his work and seethed with anger at the boy. The rain fell, weakening the brickwork he had spent the morning laying.

TWO MOONS OVER CEDAR HILL

Chapter 18

Cedar Hill, Present day

Mayella's body was loaded into a dark van. Overhead, the clouds darkened and threatened rain and Jorgé watched the sky, then the retreating van. Jorgé watched until it was out of sight, then he made a dreaded repeat journey back out to the family cemetery in the center of the soybean field.

The beans had been thrashed, leaving only twelve inch dried remains. The field would host a season of rye grass and clover next summer, then lie fallow for a year of cattle grazing and rest.

His breath came out in frosty puffs. It had not felt this cold when he was here a few short hours ago. The sun was up full in the sky now and this time, instead of launching himself over the wrought iron fence, he found the gate, forced its rusty hinges to move and took leaden steps to the spot where he had found her.

It did not look like the same spot, yet the markings on the tomb stone were undeniable. "Grace Thompson" – he knew her as "G.T." He wondered who "S.L." was. Certainly not of his family as he had long believed. The star and double moon symbol he knew even better than the initials.

Mayella had given him the necklace, saying it had been a gift from his mother before she died. His mother died cleaning the homes of wealthy white

Americans shortly before his father died of grief and a horse kick to his head and a boy had become an orphan and adrift from the migrant community that was his only family. The necklace had been his only link to his history.

For the Lyonses, it was easy to convince themselves it was their civic duty to employ undocumented laborers, who came cheap. It was not exploitation, rather, part of the trickle-down theory of wealth they bought into on election day, but when those same migrant workers died, leaving behind an adolescent boy – too young to set out on his own, and too illegal to officially adopt, their blend of politics abandoned them.

There being no known next-of-kin, Jorgé had been kept on as something less than family and something more than a pet. He fell in the gap between generations of Breedens, acting as something like a favored uncle to Stewart and something else to Christina. Only one person recognized Jorgé's desire for family and history. Mayella. She made an avocation of finding a person's weakness.

Jorgé had worn the necklace around his neck until he had found a worthy caretaker. He still wore the leather band.

He kneeled back down beside the tombstone to more closely inspect the etched marble, running his hand over its time pocked surface. The design

TWO MOONS OVER CEDAR HILL

was unmistakable – two moons and a star. It still had no more meaning to him, but now it held far less value.

It might be a family crest, but for certain, it was not *his* family's. Worse though by far than losing this thing that had once meant so much to him, was learning that he had given to Chita a thing of undefined virtue – no better than the bracelet her father had given her second-hand so many years ago. In giving it to Chita he never thought of it as leaving him, but now it was a taint that he had passed on to one of the only people he could call family.

Jorgé rose suddenly from the ground. Mayella was no fool. She had been about something. What had she told him? That she would make things right by him? He shook his head, unable to recall her exact words, but looking at the stone again, he knew there was method to Mayella's madness.

With Mayella she always looked for an ulterior motive, but only because she always had an ulterior motive for her actions. His gaze traveled to the house, imagining Mayella, racked with pain, coming out into the night. He closed his eyes. She had been in her nightgown, no shoes. The iron gate was closed. How did she get into the cemetery? Climbed? He looked across the field. The dew had mostly burned from it, but he could still make out the crushed and zig-zagged path that Mayella had taken. He stepped back to the edge of the fence and looked at the bramble that covered most of the graves. There was a very distinct path beaten across the hitch-hikers. Her feet were bare, so she must have crawled.

Jorgé could imagine Mayella stopping at the different stones, straining to read them or perhaps feeling them. She had moved down a row of six gravestones, then the next row, only to stop at the one grave that would have offered the least comfort – the one with a giant groundhog hole in its center. She stopped at this stone for a purpose.

Hastily again, Jorgé launched himself over the fence. He ran the distance across the field to the gravel drive, then ran to the house and up the stairs to Mayella's room.

Treeny rose suddenly from the side of Mayella's bed. Jorgé stopped in the doorway.

"I didn't hear you come in." She wrung her hands.

"Treeny." Jorgé stopped as though he had hit a brick wall.

The woman looked up from clenched hands. Jorgé thought perhaps she had been praying before his jarring entrance. He forced himself to slow down and consider one of the many people who would be affected by Mayella's death. He walked to the ladder back chair and pulled it up to the bedside as he had done so often over the past few weeks when Mayella had lain there. He reached out and

TWO MOONS OVER CEDAR HILL

Treeny shoved her tissue up the sleeve of her cardigan before putting her hands into his.

"It's been a full morning. I haven't had time to consider.... Are you okay?" he asked of her.

Treeny lifted her eyes from the vision of her hands in his. Her eyes spontaneously filled with tears. "It never gets any easier, you know?" She sniffed. "I mean, I've lost family before. I knew Mayella was on her way out, but somehow, every time, I block out the fact that we're all on our way out – our bodies in a downward spiral."

Under the bed, Beebo thumped his tail on the floor. Jorgé ignored the sound of the dog.

He looked around the room that had lost much of its reverence under the disinfectant smell and the medical equipment. "Mayella was lucky to have had you near her at the end."

Treeny removed her hands from Jorgé's soft clasp, pulled out the tissue again and wiped her eyes. "Do you think they'll want to keep me on?" Her eyes were dry as quickly as they had become moist.

Jorgé patted the back of her hand. "There's no need to think about that just now."

"I've gotta think about it now. Mayella's gone and I've got to take care of myself. I guess that's not something I've ever been very good at." Her gravely smoker's voice was testament to her poor care of herself. "It's just easier to take care of other people."

"Do you have family?"

Treeny shook her head. "No. Well, I've got a son. We don't talk much anymore."

A sigh slipped out. Jorgé watched in wonder as the people around him allowed their families to slip away from them as if they meant no more to them than casual acquaintances.

"No one will ask you to leave here." He sat up straight in the chair, bracing himself for the eventual reunion. "Mayella's children will be arriving… probably in the next day or two. They're good kids. They won't be throwing anyone out if that's what you're worried about."

Treeny made no sign that she was going to vacate Mayella's room any time soon, so Jorgé gave her an excuse to move. "Perhaps we would both feel better if we were busy. I know it will be an unpleasant surprise for her children to return to this." He pointed toward the I.V. "We could begin by clearing her room of its medical taint."

Treeny brightened. "Maybe I could help by freshening up the room too."

"There. That's the idea."

Treeny stood and began removing the medicine bottles and water glass from Mayella's nightstand, then she turned and pulled the rumpled sheets and chenille spread from the bed, throwing them over her free arm.

TWO MOONS OVER CEDAR HILL

"I'll just pop down the hall for fresh sheets – maybe pull a box or two from the attic to stow some of this stuff."

"Mayella was lucky to have found you when she needed you most."

Treeny moved out of the room with an armload of stale linen, leaving Jorgé to look freely around the vacant room. He pushed his chair back from the bed, lining it up with the wall again and for the second time, he noticed the large puddle of clear fluid that was soaking into the wood floor. He looked up at the ceiling, then back down at the I.V. dispenser. It was still plugged into the wall, the plastic tube that had fed the medicine into the back of Mayella's hand dangled from the pump. She had had to turn it off and unplug herself from the morphine drip that she had only just submitted to. Jorgé looked over his shoulder to ensure that Treeny had gone down the hall with the linens, then he moved to the bedside table. He hesitated, but the top drawer was already open a crack and an amber pill bottle there where he had knocked it earlier in his search for Mayella. It was there, under the bottle, that he found precisely the thing he knew he would – a letter – addressed to himself in Mayella's spidery handwriting. Taking up the seat on the edge of the unmade bed, the same seat Treeny had only just vacated, he very slowly opened the letter and began to read.

Sofie Couch

It was not like Mayella to leave an incomplete trail. There was something here and he had to find it before Chita or her brother returned.

Treeny sat down on a crate, pulled the tissue out of her sleeve and unfolded it. From inside she took a thin gold wedding band, one side of which had been worn so thin, it was almost broken.

With a shaking hand, Treeny slipped the band onto her left-hand, ring finger, wiped her nose on the handkerchief, and then turned back to the job at hand, packing away Mayella's things.

Behind her left shoulder, the ephemeral image of a man, dead 150 years, watched her from his perch atop an invisible trunk.

TWO MOONS OVER CEDAR HILL

Chapter 19

Present day

"*Dear George,*
   By now, I will have left this earth and with some regret, I can't say that I'll be sorely missed by many. I hope you find yourself free to miss me just a little.
   You know my disposition where my children are concerned. I told you I had fixed things with Christina and Stewart. Well, the truth of the matter is that I need your help... and asking for help isn't my way, thus the chain of events that have led you to find this letter.
   In the second drawer of the night table you will find a folder. In it, I have left two separate documents. Read them both. It's for you to decide which of the two to put forward as my last Will and testament. It's legal. You will remember my lawyer visiting on a regular basis some weeks ago. He can bear witness to my sanity at the time of writing. Either way, I will be pleased with the outcome.
   I know you must think I am a heartless old woman, but it's because of my weak heart that things have come to the head they have. I am who I am and I will not soon change. If my previous actions have been harsh I will not apologize. Just know that I acted as my conscience directed.
   You have been a faithful servant and dear friend. I am saddened that I am unable to claim you as anything more.

   Yours In Parting,

Sofie Couch

Mayella Thompson Breeden"

The spidery penmanship was unmistakably Mayella's and in the frantic confusion of the morning, it had gone unnoticed. It lay folded in the top most of the three drawers in her bedside table. As if it contained something venomous, Jorgé opened the second drawer with caution. It was empty save for a thin manila envelope.

Sitting on the edge of Mayella's bed, he leaned over and peered deeper into the drawer before removing the two thin sheaths of paper, both stapled at the top left corner, and both bearing the title, *"Last Will and Testament"*.

Overhead there was a small crash on the attic floor. Treeny called down in muffled tones. "I'm okay. Just knocked over a stack of crap."

Jorgé looked back to the Wills, one in each hand, and dropped his chin to his chest. Mayella drew on his reserves. Not knowing what he might find, Jorgé finally pulled the serviceable black framed glasses from the breast pocket of his plaid flannel shirt and read, a scowl digging deeper into his forehead as he read.

"Caramba."

He shook his head and pressed his fingers hard into his temples. She left him… everything.

TWO MOONS OVER CEDAR HILL

He tried to imagine Christina's reaction to reading this. Mayella had made certain that Christina's opinion of him was tarnished at best. If she read this, she would think he had something to do with the bequest. Even after death, Mayella tied strings to everything.

He put the second Will on top of the first and began to read, skipping over much of the jargon he had waded through in the first Will. But half way through the first page of the second Will, Jorgé stopped, pulled off his glasses to blink hard before reinstalling them lower on his nose as if this might make the meaning more clear.

His arms went limp and he dropped his chin to his chest again, this time in defeat. Not a man given to profanity, as the meaning sunk in Jorgé whispered his heart-felt assessment.

"*Mierda.*"

Mayella wanted nothing short of his soul.

Jorgé forced himself to wade through the shorter document to its end. This was more straight forward. It would be uncontestable if he chose to present it as her latest Will.

Without hesitation, he folded the first Will – the one leaving everything to him and shoved it, along with Mayella's letter, into his breast pocket. The second Will, he flattened and held it to his chest.

Sofie Couch

At the door, he took one more look around the room, then closed that door too.

He crossed the hall to his own room, then beside the bed, he went down on his hands and knees and fished under the edge of the spread.

This used to be Christina's room. When he was first installed here, he thought he could still sometimes smell her, but her scent had vanished with his occupation. Unbeknownst to him it had been replaced by the sweet smell of hay and leather and toil.

Reaching under the bed up to his shoulder, Jorgé pulled out a cigar box that was bound by a thick rubber band. Still kneeling on the floor, he carefully unbound the box and reverentially lifted the lid. A thing of real value was not too often visited. In the box he tucked Mayella's letter and both Wills under a yellowed envelope of apple seeds and an old postcard. He was about to close the box again, but stopped. With hesitation at first, then purpose, he pulled the leather cord from around his neck, coiled it and left it on top of the other trinkets in the box before sealing it with the rubber band.

Overhead, the attic floor creaked.

TWO MOONS OVER CEDAR HILL

Chapter 20

Stewart arrived home just hours after his mother left it. Jorgé thought, how ironic these two should always be at cross purposes.

Stewart lay on his stomach and patted the dark wood floor.

"Come on, ol' fellow. Come on out. It's me."

Beebo thumped his tail in greeting, but would not come out from under the bed.

"He's not budging." Jorgé spoke from the doorway.

"How long's he been under there?"

"Since Mayella… since your mother…."

Stewart sat up, but didn't move from the floor beside his late mother's bed. "But suicide?"

"It hardly counts, Stewart. You didn't see how ill she was… had been… for so long. She was on so much medication, I'm sure she was able to convince herself it was no weakness in taking a handful of one type of pill when daily she took as many of various kinds. I can't say I'd have tried to stop her. She had stopped eating… and you know your mother. Everything has to be… had to be… on her own terms." He had to clear his throat.

Stewart shook his head. "Did you know she called Christina? Asked her to come home? Finally. Ten years and she called yesterday. Christina's on her way."

Jorgé nodded and despite the fact that Stewart couldn't see him, he pretended nonchalance as he leaned casually against the door facing, his hands shoved deep in his pockets. "How is your sister? How have you both been?" He quickly amended.

"The same... and different." Stewart raised the bed skirt one more time and stretched his hand toward Beebo, that the dog might smell him. The dog wasn't going to move. He dropped the spread and the tasseled fringe shivered for the dog.

Beebo had been beyond his puppy years ten years ago when Stewart and Christina left, so it was no surprise that the dog no longer had any bond with Stewart. Jorgé was sure it hurt Stewart though who, like his mother, had had a special bond with the animals on the farm. It was Mayella, the grand dame, who had marched about the farm with a small pack of a dozen dogs in tow, each trying to hold her attention, hold court with her. Ironic that it was the least warm person who won the favor of the dogs. Not so ironic that Stewart, in the absence of affection from his mother found affection from the beasts that gave it freely.

Stewart pushed away from the bed. "You know Christina. At least, you know how she *was*. She's changed, Jorgé." He felt his way around the bed to stand in front of Jorgé. "She's become more and more like Mama in more ways than she likes to admit."

"In what ways?"

"Embittered."

Jorgé had to look up at the stranger who had taken over the boyish body of lean, lanky Stewart Little.

"I went away by choice. Christina was in exile."

"She left of her own choosing."

Stewart shook his head. "She was pushed. I was kind of hoping you might be able to shed some light on it." Stewart pushed his hands into his pocket, a slightly larger mirror image of Jorgé. They both cocked their head in the same direction.

"You mean our argument."

"What'd you argue about?"

Jorgé hesitated. "Cedar Hill."

Stewart waited him out.

"She thought my love for this farm was greater than my love for her... or you."

Stewart put a hand out and touched Jorgé's in the center of his chest – over his heart. "I've missed you too, Jorgé."

Jorgé grinned and threw an arm around Stewart's shoulder.

Together they walked out of the room and Jorgé gave what he thought would be one last look over his shoulder. Like the woman herself, Mayella's room was austere – almost dead. It smelled of mothballs like something held in limbo, of lavender like the ghost of Mayella, and of cleaner in preparation for a new occupant.

Mayella had never been a warm mother, her bond and loyalties tying her closer to the dogs than her own children, closer to nearly everyone and everything than to her only son.

Jorgé moved from the doorway and went to the room he had occupied for the past ten years. Stewart followed him across the passage.

The Antebellum house was arranged for conservation of heat in the winter and maximum circulation in the summer with a central hallway dividing the four upstairs bedrooms. When both of her children had been at home, Mayella and Christina occupied the two largest rooms positioned to the front of the house. It was in Christina's old room, Jorgé's adopted room, where he began packing up his things.

"What are you doing?" Stewart took up a position in the doorway.

"Moving my things out."

Stewart stepped into the room, cautiously feeling his way to the opposite side of the bed from which Jorgé filled a duffle bag.

"You moved in here to take care of her?"

Jorgé took a small stack of identical plaid flannel shirts from one of the dresser drawers and laid them in the bag.

TWO MOONS OVER CEDAR HILL

"I can stay out in the barracks… until it gets too cold."

Stewart walked around the bed, hands outstretched. "You've kept everything in the same place it was ten years ago." He touched his hand to the surface of the dresser, running his hands tentatively over the trinkets that belonged to his sister and that had not been moved since her last occupation.

Jorgé kept packing.

"What about your cottage?"

Jorgé didn't look up. "Occupied."

"Rented out?"

"Annabelle lives there." Finally, he chanced a glance at Stewart, but except for more stillness than usual, the younger man bore the news well. As if he could see, Stewart moved toward the window.

"How long?"

Jorgé stopped to give Stewart his attention. This was gonna hurt, probably worse than losing a parent. "Shortly after you and Christina left she came back. Mayella moved me in here and Annabelle moved into the cottage."

"How long?" Stewart looked up at Jorgé with an angry smirk.

"The day after you and Christina left."

The air was sucked out of the room. Stewart crossed his arms over his chest and put one hand over his eyes, squeezing his temples. He ended on a sigh and raked his hand over his head, pushing his auburn hair away from his face.

"Son-of-a-*bitch*." Stewart's epithet was surely meant in its literal sense.

There was nothing Jorgé could offer by way of apology or sympathy. Stewart had left and never tried to contact him until today. Who, but Mayella… and Stewart himself, could be blamed?

"She left, I thought forever. Mama told me she gave Annabelle a choice – me or more money than she had ever seen in her impoverished life, and she chose the money." Stewart shook his head, then seemed to reconnect with the events around him. He felt his way to the duffle bag on the foot of Christina's bed. "Don't move out to the barracks, Jorgé. You could take Mama's room."

Jorgé thought about it a moment, then nodded absently, but watched Stewart closely now.

"Are you nervous about seeing her again?" Jorgé asked.

"Huh? Who?" He finally turned his cheek toward the window, then brushed away the discomfort with a shrug of one shoulder. "Annabelle? Why would I be nervous about seeing her again?" He turned his face toward Jorgé's, then smiled. "I thought she was gone for good. I've spent the past ten years being as angry with her for leaving as I was with Mama for paying her to go."

Jorgé opened the next drawer on the bureau, a crease taking up post on his brow. He felt he should have missed Stewart more, but instead he had been too wrapped up in his own hurt like an injured animal turned in on himself to lick his wounds, like Beebo hiding under the bed.

"Yeah. I'm a little nervous, I guess."

"Stewart, there's something I should tell you...."

"Yeah, like why you never called." Changing the subject, Stewart's tone held no anger, just curiosity.

Jorgé shrugged and turned back to his packing.

Stewart answered for him. "The ol' girl wouldn't tell you where we were, would she?"

Jorgé looked up again. "The 'ol' girl' was your mother, Stewart," he scolded, "...and no, she wouldn't say."

"She treated you like shit. Why'd you stay, Jorgé?" Stewart turned his face back toward the direction of the dresser, taking in more than a sighted person. He moved back to the dresser and without hesitation, reached for and picked up the fuzzy pink and gold Avon ice cream cone powder duster from his sister's dresser. He gave it a sniff, then blew powder out of his nose with a cringe. "I couldn't get far enough away and you moved to live right under her nose." He reached out and touched the lamp that had not moved an inch in his absence. "Why stay here... right across the hall from the old battle ax?"

His blind eyes were more penetrating than any sighted person's. Jorgé focused on the mirror, to the spot where a decade old message was scrawled in lipstick: *"Meet J at 6:30 – by the lake."* Of course he hadn't erased the message. He told himself it wasn't his place.

Seventeen years ago

They were innocent playmates. Jorgé who had never had a childhood and Christina, his Chita, who was an old soul. They climbed out of the river, he reaching back to help her up the slippery embankment.

"You've almost got the hang of this swimming thing," she said.

"Nearly drowned me is what you did."

Jorgé dropped down on the side of the grassy slope and Chita dropped down beside him, twirling around on her bottom and laying her head back in his lap. That felt wrong. He pushed her out of his lap and spun himself in the opposite direction and lay back on the ground beside her, his head beside hers, but his body laying in the opposite direction so they were just watching clouds overhead.

"The whole point is to keep someone else from drowning. You're not much good to Stewart if he falls in again – someplace where the water is deeper - and you still can't swim."

That whole episode had been nearly catastrophic. Stewart had been coaxed into the water by some local kids and would have drowned had the water been any deeper. As it was, Jorgé had jumped in without considering the risks to himself and Stewart. Christina had been so upset by the prospect of losing them both, he had succumb to her insistence that he learn to swim.

"So what do I get in return for teaching you to swim?"

"Do what?" He sat up. "Now I owe you something for swimming lessons? This was your idea, Chita."

She was smiling. "I thought maybe you could teach me to drive."

Jorgé rolled his eyes. "You're thirteen."

"Yes, but I'll be sixteen in three short years and then won't it be a help to have another licensed driver you can send on errands?"

"Okay."

She was about to launch further argument, but she snapped her mouth shut.

"Okay?"

"Okay. I'll teach you."

Christina jumped up from the ground and clapped her hands. "Hot damn! I'm gonna get to drive!"

Jorgé rose from the ground more slowly. "Just on the farm, mind you. We're not taking this show on the road until you're licensed. Promise."

She bounced up, kissed his cheek, kissed his hand, and spun around in a circle."

And Jorgé laughed and shook his head. She always had had the ability to wrap him to her will.

Present day

Jorgé zipped the duffle bag before going down on his hands and knees to fish the cigar box out from under the bed.

Stewart answered his own question with dawning wonder. "You wanted to be here… when she came back?"

"Your mother was ill. She needed extra care." He rose from the floor with the cigar box in one hand. He threw it on the bedcovers. "Your mother asked me to move into the main house… from the cottage the same week you and Christina left. Didn't want to be in the house alone, she said."

Stewart shook his head in disbelief and drew a small smile from Jorgé. Jorgé wagged his finger.

"You do know you're more like your mother than perhaps *you* may wish to admit."

Stewart grinned. "And you wear this pretense of fulfilling my mother's stereotypes about you, but…." He trailed off.

Jorgé, still smiling amicably blew him off with a characteristic wave of his hand. "I should have thought you knew me well enough to know that the one thing I am *not* is a man of pretenses."

"No." Stewart shook his head. "I'm right about this. You've stayed, biding your time, waiting for her to come back, surrounding yourself with…" Stewart waved his hand around the room. "…with her," he finished, crossing his arms over his chest. "How could I have missed it all those years ago?"

Had he not been so uncomfortable with the turn of subject Jorgé might have noticed how Stewart took on his mannerisms like a son in the presence of an admired father. Jorgé was quiet a long moment before looking up at Stewart again. "Your sister was quite young when we parted. Eighteen. *Eighteen! Aie*. Impressionable." He put a hand to his chin. "She admired me in the absence of her father. That's all."

Stewart's grin broadened. "She left 'cause Mama threatened to fire you if she didn't end it with you."

Jorgé froze with his hand wrapped around a framed picture on the dresser. It was the only personal item of his there amidst the pink fuzzy ice cream cone shaped powder duster and the cheap, now petrified, tube of pink lip stick. Jorgé's single personal effect was a blurry photograph, taken of himself and Chita – Christina – in the front seat of the old pick-up truck. She had brought her camera to commemorate the event of her first driving lesson. The other artifacts on the dresser were a shrine and unaware of his actions, he reshuffled the things Stewart had picked up and touched, returning them to their original spot.

"Mama didn't approve of your relationship with Christina, did she?"

"She did not." Jorgé chuckled, but without humor and shook his head. "And I should have known better. Mayella forced me to see it for what it was… indecent…."

"And that better explains…. She thought…. No. Mama convinced her… you loved the farm… not her."

Jorgé shook his head in wonder at Stewart's ability to put it all together so quickly.

"Mayella had many faults, but lack of insight was not one of them."

"Did you? Did you love the farm more than Christina?"

Jorgé slipped the photograph into the side pocket of the duffle bag without responding.

"All this time, I thought it was because of me. I thought she left, because Mama threatened her using me in some way." Stewart shrugged, making it seem like no big deal.

"I thought she would come back before now."

TWO MOONS OVER CEDAR HILL

Stewart always surprised him with his ability to "see" inside a person's heart. Unwilling to undertake that degree of introspection, Jorgé turned away sharply, tucking the cigar box under his arm.

"All this time, I thought she gave up her home because of me, but all along...."

"...it was because of me," Jorgé finished for him, accepting full blame.

Jorgé hefted his duffle bag, strode out of the room and crossed the hall. Stewart followed.

In the other room, he dropped the bag on the foot of Mayella's bed, then turned to face Stewart who blocked the doorway.

"I want to see Christina take her proper place here at Cedar Hill. This is where she belongs – not on the coast, scraping up a living scavenging and selling junk," Stewart said.

"I hope you... and Christina... get your wish. My job is... always has been... to take care of this farm."

"Hmmm." The attic floor overhead creaked and Stewart cocked his ear toward the noise. "And Treeny? Who is she? She looks like a permanent fixture."

"She cleans the house. Has done so for the past ten years. Took care of your mother this past year."

"She come to mean something to you?"

Sofie Couch

Jorgé gave Stewart a stern look as if he could see it. "She took care of *Mayella*. I think she had become very attached to your mother."

"Is she pretty?"

"Enough, Stewart."

Stewart pointed his chin at the ceiling. "What's she doing up there anyway?"

"She offered to put your mother's room in order. She's taken some of the non-returnable medical equipment up to the attic. Before your mother… before… I think she was having Treeny inventory the attic… to put her 'house in order' so to speak, before…."

"Measuring her life's accomplishments in pounds of junk, just like Christina's been doing for the past ten years." Stewart waved a hand, almost brushing Jorgé's chest. "It's funny. Everything's changed… and yet nothing has."

Jorgé couldn't bring himself to enlighten Stewart. It wasn't his place. Everything *had* changed… and nothing. Christina was coming home – like a celestial event – twin moons rising over a single star.

TWO MOONS OVER CEDAR HILL

Chapter 21

"CEDAR HILL, c. 1850 was originally the home of Virginia State Legislator, Llewellyn Thompson, who voted against secession prior to the U.S. Civil War. Despite his divided loyalties, Thompson went on to fight in the War Between the States for the Confederacy. He was captured near the end of the war, but released six months later after agreeing to sign a letter of affiliation."

Twin stone pillars and an historical road sign marked the entrance to Cedar Hill. Christina's truck wanted to turn like a horse that guides itself back to the barn, but she held firmly to the reigns, refusing to allow the wheel to turn and drove right past it, not sure where she would stop. A familiar country market came into view less than a mile past her old home.

She pulled the truck to a stop around back like one of the men who used to park here, hiding their cars from public view, while they walked to the adjoining farm for some liquid comfort.

Christina wondered if Annabelle had ever come back to this place, her childhood home, and the secret moonshine still that was no secret to anyone local. Some things never change at the same time other things disappear forever.

The truck was half hidden by the green dumpster at the side of the store. The old paint peeling sign had been replaced by a crisp, new sign. A slow drizzle thrummed on the roof and through the market's side window was the promise of renovation to the store since the last time Christina had been here - ten years ago. Inside, incandescent lights had been replaced with halogen white bulbs that cut cleanly through the windows and overcast skies.

"Coward," she chided herself, then opened the truck door in favor of some false courage – of the chocolate variety.

As she entered the store, the clerk looked up from the newspaper she had been perusing. Recognition was instantaneous. Who could mistake the copper curls of the woman behind the counter?

"Annabelle?" A rock fell in the center of Christina's stomach.

"Christina!"

The other woman strode around the counter, lifted the hinged countertop and without reservation took her childhood friend by the hands, kissed Christina's cheek, then pulled her into a rib cracking embrace.

"I knew you'd be back soon," she chided as though Christina was only sneaking in a few hours past curfew. "Knew you'd be back, but still can't quite believe you're standing here in front of me."

Christina's stomach tightened, her only thought and concern was for Stewart who had preceded her home. Christina had wheedled at least that much out of Richard before she had left the dispirited coastal town.

Annabelle looked the same. She had filled out a little, no more the gaunt look of neglect about her. Her cheeks were full, her clothes were new, and her white apron pristine, her hair worn back from her face with a headband that fit her like the halo she should always have been adorned with. Her smile was genuine.

Christina looked from Annabelle, then gazed around the store, now converted into something more posh than the inside of the formerly named, "Watt's Market" had ever dreamed of being. "You work here?"

"I work, eat, sleep and breathe it. I own it." Her smile did more than hint at her satisfaction. Annabelle was proud of herself - finally – and it made her already pretty features glow.

"So you've been back… for a while?"

Annabelle grinned and nodded. "Mayella got over it."

Annabelle stepped forward again and hugged her, which was as well, since Christina felt her knees turning loose jointed. Annabelle's embrace lasted long enough for Christina to fix on a smile that she intended to be convincing. When Annabelle released her more suddenly than she had expected, Christina had to reach out and grab the edge of the counter for support.

"Wow. Things sure have changed." Her heart hammered and Christina saw spots of light flickering at the corners of her peripheral vision. The hum of the refrigeration units sounded as if they had moved off to some very far away place. She had never fainted before in her life, but she thought this would be as good a time as any.

"More than you know." Annabelle's sweet smile hinted at a secret.

Christina had no desire to guess at it. She needed to put her head between her knees. She tried to recall, ten years ago.

Christina locked her knees to remain in an upright position. If she went down she was going to go down hard.

"Sometimes we don't see what's right under our own nose until we put a little distance between it and ourselves. I moved away from here too, only to turn right around. I realized this was right where I was meant to be all along. I found something I might have missed otherwise," and she waved her hand around the store.

"You seem… happy."

"I am," but her smile fluttered a little. "And how are you… and Stewart?" As soon as the question was out of her mouth, Annabelle turned her back, hiding her expression, and walked back to the counter and busied herself with straightening the newspaper she had been perusing before Christina entered. She looked up from the paper only fleetingly.

"Then you… you haven't seen him? He came ahead of me. Probably beat me here by a couple of hours."

"I knew you'd both be home soon." Annabelle's lip twitched, the sure sign of discomfort in her childhood friend. "I'm sorry about your mother." Annabelle's affect was stiff.

"So, it really is serious?"

Annabelle stiffened. "You… you haven't heard?"

It was not the same easy relationship she and Annabelle had shared ten years ago, but what right, Christina wondered, did she have to expect everyone's life to have been held in limbo simply because she had chosen not to live? Christina shook her head for clarity. "Everybody heard except us. She only just called yesterday. Stewart came ahead of me."

Annabelle nodded, then looked up at the same time a truck pulled up outside.

Then it occurred to Christina, that maybe her mother had told Annabelle… and she was recovered from the truth. "You said Mama got over it. Did she talk to you? About Stewart… and you?"

Outside, a truck pulled up between the store and the gas pumps, a man whose movements were as familiar to Christina today as they had been ten years ago, opened the truck door and stepped out into the drizzle that had picked up to a steady drum. Christina stood transfixed as she watched Jorgé's figure move toward the rain spattered door.

Annabelle saw him at almost the same time, leaving Christina's cryptic question unanswered.

Neither of them spoke while Jorgé pushed open the door, took off his baseball cap and wiped his boots on the mat just inside the door. For a brief second Christina could pretend that everything and everyone had been held in limbo and that she might just take back what had been said in haste and hurt.

"Hello, Annabelle." His gaze slowly moved from Annabelle to Christina who stood partially concealed by a metal rack of local wines. "Christina." Her name came out on an exhale, as though the wind had been knocked out of him.

Her heart lightened, then briefly fell again. This could never end well.

"Hello, Jorgé."

He took two steps toward her, then stopped short, as if he also remembered.

"She told me you were coming home." His voice was gravely. "I hardly believed her."

"If Stewart hadn't come ahead of me, I'm not sure I would have come."

Jorgé's gaze flickered to Annabelle who stiffened beside Christina. "He got in about an hour ago."

"Stewart? He's here?"

Jorgé nodded. "Came ahead of Chita. Came by train, then cab."

"He drove separate. I couldn't leave until I closed up the shop." Christina turned her body slightly, trying to include Annabelle in the revelation.

In a protective gesture that both stirred Christina's heart and made her stomach lurch, Jorgé took the last step separating them and moved… to Annabelle, wrapping an arm around her shoulder. He gave her a kiss on the top of her head.

"I was just coming down to tell you," he whispered to Annabelle.

The intimacy, the shared space, the shared thoughts stirred something in Christina. She felt brief jealousy that was quickly replaced by… loss.

"And instead I found our wayward child."

"She just turned up on the doorstep." Annabelle turned under Jorgé's arm and her shell-shocked expression was replaced by a smile.

"Truant." Jorgé shook his head at Christina, then finally found his own smile.

And as though nothing had changed, as though no ten years had lapsed since last they had parted with harsh words between them, without the full understanding of Mayella's motives, Jorgé unwrapped himself from Annabelle, took a step toward Christina and gave her a chaste kiss on the forehead.

"I'll go home with Christina. You can drive my truck back when you're ready." Another intimate, psychic interchange passed between Jorgé and Annabelle before he pulled his keys from his pocket and dropped them into Annabelle's palm."

Again, Christina felt like the outsider she had allowed herself to become. With a hand on her elbow, but a last look over his shoulder to Annabelle, he ushered Christina out of the store, leaving behind her excuse of chocolate courage before what was sure to be an awkward family reunion.

"Where did you park?"

"Around back."

He kept a hand on her elbow as if she might make a break for it and bolt like a nervous filly. Not until they were at the passenger door did he release her elbow and open the door, then hold out his hand for her keys.

She hesitated just a second before pulling them out of the front pocket of the zip-front jersey jacket she was wearing. He closed her in and she felt the impending claustrophobia. Their gazes broke apart as he moved around the front of the truck, fishing through the keychain to find the one that would start the engine. He climbed in, the sound of the rain turning on and then off again as he opened, then closed the door behind him. He hesitated a moment, then started the engine.

"Ahhh," he ran his hands lovingly over the steering wheel. "I've missed you," he said to the truck.

Christina held on to the door handle, her grip tight enough to cause her muscles to spasm. The slap of wipers on wet windshield mirrored the ticking of sustained strain between them. Whereas before they had found companionability in their shared silence, now they shared awkward confinement.

Jorgé made the truck turn where she had been unable.

The driveway's crisp, hard lines of paved drive were cracked – slowly reclaimed by the earth, turned back to their pure elements. The ancient cedar trees that lined the driveway did their part with roots that pushed up the shattered pavement. Green moss filled in the gaps along the edges and down the center of the drive. Everything was exactly as it had been when she and Stewart had last left.

Jorgé drove the driveway, missing the potholes, washed clean of gravel patches that he had probably been maneuvering around for the past year.

Were it not for the pregnant silence between them, Christina would have been happy to take this drive slow, putting off the inevitable reunion with the only other woman as strong willed as herself. She drifted through an altered state, feeling one-sided in the presence of the only person who had ever made her feel whole. Apparently he had gotten over her – if there was ever anything on his part to get over. Her stomach spasmed.

She could not prevent her eye from traveling down a side gravel lane toward the small cottage that stood a little away from the barn. The cottage looked the same as ever, warm, cozy, inviting. A light burned inside. Christina recalled the warm order there, the smell of Jorgé's ethnic, though not always palatable, cooking. The moments she stole there sitting in a chair in his sitting room or studying while waiting for him to finish the day's work. She looked ahead toward her mother's house.

As they rounded the curved driveway for a view of the front of her mother's old house, she looked to the upstairs windows, half-expecting and so imagining the curtains moved. There was no greeting, no fanfare announcement from the pack of ill-bred dogs. Instead, there was only the steady drum of the rain, and silence, and Jorgé at her side pretending she meant no more to him than a distant relative that one is never surprised to see after years of separation.

She forgot her dislike of the place, however, when the front door opened and Stewart stepped out onto the porch. This is where he was meant to be. He was her anchor. And he had beat her here by a good couple of hours.

Jorgé stopped the pick-up, climbed out and before Christina could unspasm her clenched grip on the door handle, he had rounded the truck. Rain spattered the window between them. Jorgé watched her through the glass a second before pulling the door open.

The wind was knocked out of her as Jorgé crushed her in his arms and held her in delayed greeting. Christina let herself be held and be melded by the rain to his body. When next she was aware of being a separate entity, she found she had wound her arms around his neck and pressed her face into his ear, drinking in the smell of him. She pulled back slowly and ran her thumb beside his eye, pulling away tiny crow's feet that had accumulated there in the past few years. A raindrop held on to his cheek.

Recalling herself, she looked up at the upstairs windows and pushed herself away from him. "Don't, Jorgé. Mama might see."

Jorgé shook his head, his relaxed expression going dark. He stiffened and released her. "Mayella couldn't wait for you."

Christina stopped breathing. "She's... gone?"

Jorgé nodded. "This morning."

Christina stepped back and shook her head. "This morning? She called me just yesterday morning. I... I could have come sooner." She leaned back against the wet truck, pushing her moist frizzed hair away from her face and feeling a fool for clinging to Jorgé. His was a comforting embrace in preparation of the news he had just delivered. "I told her I'd be down at the weekend. Just one day later. She didn't say…."

Jorgé put his arm around her shoulder and guided her toward the house out of the steady rain. "No one could know. I'd have thought she would last longer too. But she had completed all the work she had to do on earth. And it was simply time."

"That's what Annabelle meant." At the porch, she turned to Stewart. Without preamble, she asked, "Were you with her when…?"

He shook his head. He seemed at a loss for words.

"So she died alone."

Jorgé put a strong hand on her upper arm. "She died… on her own terms."

Christina stopped at the double wooden doors that opened into the foyer. She looked over the threshold at the house's interior, unchanged in ten years. The half-painted, half-wallpapered walls were dingy, the dark wood floors darker, the brown banister oilier, but it looked as though not a single other thing had moved in the house. Familiar smells filled her senses. The house was holding its breath.

"You've seen Annabelle?" Stewart asked from the doorway.

TWO MOONS OVER CEDAR HILL

Guiltily, Christina looked from her brother to Jorgé. "Yes. She was working at the little market down the road now."

"I went down to tell her you had arrived," Jorgé volunteered. "I found Christina there."

Stewart's affect was still startled. Christina put a hand to his arm, but he shrugged off her attempt to comfort him as he gestured for her to precede him over the threshold.

"The house won't bite, Christina."

She stopped again in the foyer and looked up the dark steps. It was late in the day, the sun covered in clouds, but on the opposite side of the house dim light filtered in through the symmetric rear window at the top of the stairs. She inhaled memories, both pleasurable and painful. She could not reconcile herself to the fact that Mayella was not in the house. Christina stepped deeper into the foyer and the old oak boards creaked and popped under the threadbare rug.

"Where is she... now?"

"Funeral home. She made the arrangements... before. Now that you and Stewart are here, there's no reason to delay." His voice cracked. He cleared his throat, then added, "I'll just go out and get your things from your truck."

He left the door open behind him. Christina wanted to rush out the door like a giant exhale. When he returned, Jorgé had recovered and closing the doors behind him, he also closed off Christina's escape.

"I'll put your things upstairs." He glanced at Stewart. "…In your old room."

Again, Christina looked up the stairs with hesitancy, then blinked as a woman stepped out onto the upstairs landing. A feeling of *déjà vu* swept over her. The light was dim, so her face was in shadow, but Christina could almost imagine it was her mother. It would have been just like Mayella to meet death with enough resistance to be returned to life. Christina froze on the bottom step while Jorgé climbed and did not see the woman until he was half way along.

"Treeny, you've not met Christina yet." He stopped and turned to make the introduction.

"Hello." Christina finally found her tongue and ascended to the spot where Jorgé stood.

"Hello, Ms. Breeden." The small framed woman extended her hand. It was thin, not like her mother's brick mason hands. "I'm sorry about your mother. I hope it's some comfort to you to know that she was very ill and this is a relief to her."

Christina nodded, but felt odd receiving this intimate condolence from a stranger. The woman even looked a little like her mother, but she bore the sort of classic good looks that would age well. Not so, the Breeden women.

TWO MOONS OVER CEDAR HILL

"Treeny has kept the house running for the past nine and a half years. She's been caring for most of your mother's needs for the past year." Jorgé had to clear his throat again. "She's staying in the guest room – next to Stewart's room." He didn't say, "next to Stewart's *old* room. It was as if he fully expected them to take up their old places.

"Thank you for taking care of our mother. I'm glad she had someone to comfort her."

Treeny looked from Christina to Jorgé. "She had Mr. Lopez too. Are you sure I won't be in the way if I stay a while longer? I'd hate to impose on anyone."

Jorgé took the lead as host and shook his head. "You need time to adjust. We all do. Let's keep our lives as settled as possible." He looked to Christina to back him up.

"Of course. Whatever you and Jorgé have worked out, I'm sure it's fine."

"Thank you," the woman accepted, nodding and sliding past them on the steps.

Jorgé continued up the wide steps.

Christina ascended in his wake and tried to grasp the fact that there was no reason to leave.

"You were with her when she died?"

He stopped outside Christina's old bedroom door.

"I was… nearby." He gestured toward her old room. Christina hesitated with her hand on the knob, then stopped and turned toward her mother's room. She had to see for herself. She took that knob and stepped inside.

Everything was exactly as it had been ten years ago. Christina looked around the room taking it all in. She inhaled deeply. "She really is gone."

Jorgé nodded although she had her back to him now. Christina walked around the bed, running her hand over the throw at the foot of the bed. She hesitated, her hand freezing on the stack of men's flannel shirts on the far side.

"Oh, sorry." Jorgé rushed to pick them up, pulled open the top dresser drawer and shoved his shirts in amongst Mayella's sturdy cotton underwear.

Christina blinked hard, her gaze coming to rest on the photograph – the photo of herself and Jorgé – the framed picture taking a place of prominence front and center on Mayella's dresser.

She tasted the raw tinny taste of blood in her mouth from having bitten the inside of her cheek.

"Mayella hasn't been physically able for some time. I moved into the house shortly after you and Stewart left, but it's only been in the past two months that she's required more physical care…."

He continued speaking as Christina moved ahead of him to the master bath. His words became a dull hum. Her mother's toothbrush still rested in the toothbrush holder. A black handled toothbrush kept her mother's toothbrush company. An electric trimmer sat on the toilet tank, plugged into a GFI plug over the sink.

She turned back around, saw the same tired daisy wallpaper of ten years ago. A white chenille bedspread covered the bed, but Jorgé's boots peeked their toes under the bed, facing the same direction they had been pointing when last he had taken them off. She heard the tick of a clock on her mother's bedside table, or was that Jorgé's side of the bed, she wondered. The tick turned into a deafening hammer. She saw the light spots in her peripheral vision that changed color and spun in place. She meant to move past him, took one step forward, then everything went black.

Mayella sat at her side and with a hand to her forehead, she stroked her hair.
"*Wake up, Christina.*"
"Just five more minutes," she pleaded.
Mayella kissed her forehead.
"*It's your choice, Christina. We face our mistakes or roll over and try to ignore them. Head on you tackle them or turn tail and they'll bite you on the ass just as sure as an ill-bred dog with unpredictable temperament.*"
Her mother's face became indistinct.

A darker face descended over her and kissed her lips.
"I don't wanna go to school."

"I don't think you have school today." Jorgé spoke softly into her ear.

Christina's eyes fluttered open.

"Mama?"

"It's me, Chita."

"Jorgé?"

"You fainted."

"No."

"I'm no expert, but I'm pretty sure that was a swoon." He took his hand from her forehead and moved from the side of the bed to the bathroom. She heard water running and when he returned he was carrying a wet washcloth which he put to her forehead. He pulled up a ladder-back chair to the side of the bed.

"How long have I been….Mama? She was here."

Jorgé shook his head. "Less than a minute. We should call someone."

"She was right here." She patted the side of the bed. "She said something about a dog… biting me on the ass." There was still a divot there.

"Mayella died, Chita. That was me."

Under the bed something thumped rapidly. Christina bolted upright.

"That's the dog. He won't come out."

"Which one?" Christina swung her legs over the side of the bed, then threw her hand to her spinning head.

TWO MOONS OVER CEDAR HILL

"The only one left. Ol' Beebo."

"Beebo's a puppy." Christina leaned over, putting her head between her knees, trying to recall some conversation she had had with her mother about a dog biting her ass. With one hand, she grabbed the side of the spread and pulled it up, then made a kissing noise to call the dog out. He shuffled, but soon settled with no intention of budging.

"He'll come out soon enough. You should lay back."

But Christina sat up slowly this time and put the wash cloth to her face again.

"He is mourning her loss… like the rest of us." He stopped when he registered her altered state.

Christina held the washcloth over her eyes, but her shoulders shook.

"Christina."

She held up her hand like a shield between Jorgé and her face. She shook her head.

Jorgé left the chair and sat down beside her again, reclaiming the divot on the bed. The mattress dipped with his weight and gravity pulled her to his side. He put an arm around her shoulders, then taking her hands and the washcloth in his other hand, he tried to pull her around to face him.

She jumped up from the bed and faced the far wall. "No. Don't… just don't." She looked back to the spot beside him that had been filled by her mother only the day before. But he was only being kind. "You know me. Sympathy'll only make it worse."

More slowly, he rose from the bed, hesitated with a hand stretched toward her before he dropped it and walked to the door. "Would you be more comfortable if I called Stewart?"

"No. Just… give me a minute."

"You should lie down, Christina." He hovered, unsure which direction to turn. "Rest." He gestured her back toward the bed.

Christina sat down cautiously, stiffly.

"Take your time. I'll go downstairs. Give you a minute. Call if you need me."

She waved him out the door. He walked out and Christina felt the immediate abandonment. The horrible things she had said to him at their last parting came flooding back to her. The horrible things her mother had said to her… all confirmed true now. Hastily, she rushed to the door, her head spinning.

"Jorgé?"

He stopped at the top of the stairs and looked back.

"Have you been happy here?"

He stopped, turned and tipped his head to the side, carefully considering her question. "Yes."

"How?"

"I found that despite her many flaws, there was much to… admire in Mayella."

TWO MOONS OVER CEDAR HILL

Christina nodded, although not quite in agreement. "Did you... ever try to find me?" She could not meet his eyes, but he did not answer directly, so she looked up.

"She wouldn't tell me where you were."

"Did you try to find out?"

"At first."

"I lied, Jorgé, when we last spoke." She felt tears prick the back of her eyelids again.

"I think there was truth to what you said, Christina. You did *not* love me. At least, you didn't love me in the way I was asking you to love me... as an adult and I had no right to expect that of you." He raised his hand, gesturing toward her hair. "Look at you, Christina." He returned to her side, his hand coming up to touch the curls that shot wild from her head. "Ten years later and you're barely a grown woman now." He ran an assessing look down her front, taking in the grunge jeans, Lynrd Skynrd tee-shirt and unzipped hooded fleece jacket that had been hastily donned for the trip home. "I'm practically old enough to be your father and what I proposed then... was indecent. Mayella saw that. And I think you saw it then too - and it scared you." He dropped his hands to his sides, then stepped backward.

Christina blinked hard to clear her eyes and crossed her arms over her chest. "I wasn't afraid of you. But I was afraid of coming back. I was afraid of this." She pointed toward her mother's bed, then put her hand over her eyes again. She took a deep breath. "I was afraid I'd come back only to learn that I don't belong here."

"You do belong here."

Mayella's words to her at their last parting came back to haunt her. They had argued in this very room, in this very doorway. She shared much in common with her mother, physically. She would not sacrifice her own pride. There were some things that just were not to be passed from mother to daughter.

Ten years ago

"Think smart, girl. What do you have that he wants?"

Christina toyed with the medallion on the chain around her neck, her mother's bluntness difficult to bear.

"One thing you need to remember, Christina, is that good lookin' men always have an ulterior motive. Take your Daddy. I shoulda known he wasn't in it for love. Hell, I wasn't in it for love. I wanted heirs. I thought he did too. Weren't neither one of us spring chickens when we married. And you have to ask yourself why is George paying so much attention to you of late? Is it your looks? You took after me in the looks department, so you can figure that one out without too much trouble."

TWO MOONS OVER CEDAR HILL

"Don't reduce what Jorgé and I have to something vulgar."

Mayella sighed in exasperation. "You're embarrassing yourself and bringing this family to shame along with you."

"You make it sound indecent."

"It *is* indecent. He's old enough to be your Daddy. In fact, I'd of said he was a better Daddy to you than Stew Senior ever was, but for how the two of you have been carrying on."

And there had been a shift in her relationship with Jorgé, but it was gradual. So gradual, in fact, that it was still evolving.

"I'm warning you, Christina. If you keep on carryin' on with that man I'm gonna…."

"What, Mama? Turn me out of the house? Hurt me like you've hurt Stewart? How?"

Her mother's lips pressed into a thin line and Christina knew she had crossed a line she had never trespassed before.

"I'll turn *him* out." Mayella pointed her chin in the direction of the window and beyond – to the man who was the reason the farm was fruitful.

Christina felt a shiver run up her spine and knew her mother meant it. "That'd be cutting off your own nose to spite your face."

"I didn't give birth to you children to watch you throw yourselves away on inferior blood."

Christina turned away, leaving her mother's doorway and going to her own room. Mayella followed her like a shark that smells blood.

When Mayella spoke again, her tone was softer, more concerned. "Do you think I sent that girl away lightly? Annabelle?"

Christina whirled around. "So, it was you! You sent Annabelle away?"

Mayella raised her chin in defiance, a justification of her actions. "I paid her… to have an abortion."

Christina's eyes widened, before she turned back to stare out of the front window of her room.

"At the risk of losing him, I did it. I paid that girl to get an abortion, at the risk of Stewart finding out. And now, he's threatening to leave anyway. I don't part with my children lightly."

Christina turned to face her mother. Confronting her mother head on was something she had always been able to avoid. She knew the day they did butt heads it wouldn't go well… for either of them. "Does Stewart know? Did he know… about the baby?"

"No. And he won't. I saw to it."

"What is it you object to, Mama? Annabelle or Annabelle's parentage?" It was a small town and word got around.

In a nearly unprecedented display of physical affection, Mayella moved across the room and put her arms awkwardly around Christina. "I know more than you think, Christina. What I know, that you don't know... is that your daddy frequented the place where Annabelle grew up. Annabelle's mother's place... before Annabelle was born, and Annabelle didn't get her Jeffersonian coloring, her auburn hair and fair complexion – so much like your own brother's - from her mama's side of the family."

As the meaning sank in, Christina slowly turned and for the first time in her life, she saw an unrestrained emotion in her mother's face. Mayella's eyes glistened with unshed tears.

"Mama. No."

"That's why I couldn't let your brother carry on with her." Mayella's voice cracked. "He has to be protected." She stifled a sob.

"He will forgive you, Mama. Don't worry. If you explain it to him...."

As quickly, Mayella put her daughter away from her, the temporary weak display a blip in history. "Don't you see, Christina? He can't know. Annabelle left, because I paid her to leave. Once that money runs out, don't you know she'll be back for more?"

"Annabelle's not like that," but Mayella cut her off.

"And don't you think that child has suffered enough? She grew up in the home she did. What's it gonna do to her if she finds out she's been carrying on with her own half-brother."

Christina cringed, every nerve ending turning back in on itself until she felt her own spine curve in revulsion.

"So no, I can't tell her... or him. My best hope is to sacrifice him and hope neither one of them ever finds out."

"But, Mama, Stewart's alone. He thinks you don't care about him... or Annabelle. He's planning on leaving his home... his family....You've got to tell him."

"He's not all alone, Christina. He's got you. You've always looked out for your brother. You'll see him through this too."

Christina was beyond reasonable solutions. At barely eighteen, her world was still black and white. She wanted to see Jorgé. He had a way of putting things into perspective. As if on cue, she saw him from her vantage point at the upstairs window. He was walking across the yard toward the house, cutting a hard and purposeful path. She turned and moved toward the door, but Mayella caught her by the arm.

"Now you know that I'm not just some old woman who runs on prejudice and stereotype. I told you I had just cause for separating Stewart and Annabelle. I've got just as good a reason to want you to stay away from that man." She glanced out the window, but Jorgé was out of sight now. He could be heard stomping up the porch steps.

"He's not like that. He doesn't have a hidden agenda."

"I'm not going on gut, Christina. I know him... better than you think."

There was a loud rap on the downstairs door before they heard it open and heard Jorgé scraping his shoes on the front mat. Christina could practically see him as he roamed the downstairs rooms in search of her. "Mayella," he called out. His tone was not happy.

It was Mayella who moved away first, but she stopped at the door. "If he thought you were lost to him, don't you know he'd be pretty quick about taking up with the only other person who can give him what he wants?"

"I don't... understand."

"Christina. You and I both know the only thing George has ever wanted was this farm. He's never been closer to anybody than he is to the land. Mark me, girl. If he can't get his hands on this farm through you, he'll find another way soon enough."

Mayella turned and left Christina's room. Christina stood in the middle of her room. A hook rug separating her from the floor that she wanted to sink into. She knew it wasn't true. And what her mother said about Annabelle couldn't be true either... or could it? The twins knew their late father had another life, another family he kept separate from them. She just had never imagined it could have been Annabelle.

    She could hear Mayella descending the stairs. Christina listened. Next she heard her mother and Jorgé arguing over Stewart... and Annabelle, but her mother would stand resolute, maintaining a pretense of snobbery without telling even Jorgé about her non-selfish reason for wanting to separate Stewart from Annabelle forever. Through the floor, Christina heard her mother's raised voice. She didn't approve of Stewart's association with "that daughter of a whore." Her mother sacrificed her own reputation to protect Stewart... and Annabelle.

TWO MOONS OVER CEDAR HILL

Chapter 22

About 20 years ago

Stewart Little followed his nose to the barn – that and a rope that wove around the farm for as long as he could remember. He perked up at the sound of voices.

"Mayella in the house?" Stewart Little recognized his father's voice.

Jorgé nodded. "Si."

Stewart Little dropped behind a stack of hay bales, then poked his head up from behind the fort Jorgé had made for him of the stacks of hay. "I'm here. You lookin' for me, Daddy?"

Stew Senior looked over at his son and smiled. He was congenial, and Jorgé recognized the other man's manic moods for what they were.

Stewart Senior was an outstanding specimen among men. Tall, handsome, with thick wavy, striking, auburn hair. Only the male of his twin children had inherited the same. "I may need your help later, Stewart Little. We're going treasure hunting."

Stewart Little jumped up.

He knew his father had little time for him and even less now that he lived at the other farm with his other family – a woman and her little boy. Stewart Little had never felt at a loss, because of his blindness before, but now he worried about his father and his sighted, replacement son. Stewart Little didn't see and Stewart Senior didn't notice how Jorgé protected him from both of his austere parents. With little caution for his personal safety, as if he could see to navigate, Stewart Little climbed up on the bales of hay.

"Cool. Where's the treasure?"

His father, as much a child as his seven year old son, pointed toward the front of the estate. "Out there somewhere. There's a fortune in gold, silver, heaven knows what all. Just waiting for a couple of industrious fellows to find it. And it's all just sitting out there… somewhere."

"Hot dogs!" Stewart jumped off of the bales, confident that Jorgé would never leave anything unsafe laying around the barn. "I know where Jorgé keeps the shovel."

"You can't just go start digging higgledy piggledy. You've gotta have a hint of where it's hidden. Look at the clues first."

"What clues?"

Father and son walked out of the barn, the older man with his hand on the little boy's shoulder as he filled him with tales of a treasure buried somewhere in the family cemetery and forgotten during the Civil War.

"First, we've gotta get past the ogre who guards the treasure."

TWO MOONS OVER CEDAR HILL

"That'd be Mama," Stewart Little rightly guessed.

"That'd be your Mama, for sure." He stopped and turned Stewart Little back toward the barn. "Maybe you'd best stay out of sight while I do the talking. Your Mama might not be in a receptive mood."

Stewart nodded doubtfully. He knew for a fact that his mother was never in a very good mood when she spoke with his father. "You won't start lookin' without me, will you?"

"You're my partner."

The father took the flight of steps to the porch and walked in without knocking. Stewart Little was left at the bottom of the steps, out of reach of the nearest guide rope. Jorgé reached Stewart Little about the same time his flailing arms found the rope and with a hand on the little boy's shoulder, Jorgé led Stewart Little back to the barn. Jorgé picked up the work he had left off of - washing organic vegetables with the rain water that he collected from the barn roof. Jorgé didn't speak at first, but cast a worried look over his shoulder at the little boy who stood, blindly staring toward the house.

"Daddy's gonna take me treasure hunting." Stewart Little's tone was defiant.

"Hmm." Jorgé let a minute tick by before inviting. "You wanna help me wash vegetables?"

"Nah." Stewart Little moved toward the worktable, felt its surface, and then nimbly climbed up, his feet swinging off the end. As quickly, he jumped back down, made three laps of the open space, and then jumped back up on the table.

Jorgé turned and lifted a bushel basket of corn to the table. "You wanna help trim this up for me?"

"Nah."

Stewart jumped down again and walked to the open barn door, turning his ear to the house so he could hear his father the minute he came out again. His father came out of the house and Stewart ran up to him without stumbling. "What'd she say?"

Stew Senior just shook his head. "Maybe some other time, Stewart Little. Go play now."

Stewart Little stopped and his shoulders fell as his father cut a direct route back down the farm road that led to his own home on the adjoining property. The child made his own way back to the barn.

"Look at the size of this ear of corn, Stewart." Jorgé gave the little boy guidance through his voice. He also dropped the diminutive "Little" from his name.

And Stewart pretended to forget his disappointment, recognizing, even at that age, what Jorgé was trying to do for him.

"Hey. You didn't call me Stewart 'Little'."

Jorgé chucked him on the chin. "Do you feel little? Don't look little to me."

TWO MOONS OVER CEDAR HILL

Stewart couldn't be coaxed to smile. Stewart imagined his father out treasure hunting with the other boy – the boy who was part of his father's new family. But he did not feel "little" any more.

Present day

"Come on, you." Stewart slapped his hand to the side of his thigh and with a hand on the old dog's collar, he and Beebo moved out of the plot in the front field. He and his father never had gone treasure hunting, but a part of him wanted the man, who sat atop a backhoe, to find what his father had always suspected lay hidden under the head stones.

In the distance, across the field and on the pitted driveway, Annabelle made her way on foot toward the end of the drive where it met the state road. She would know him anywhere, but she tried not to focus too much attention on the man in the field and to keep her eyes trained on the little boy who skipped ahead of her up the road, pointing wildly to the earth moving equipment in the front field. The boy, who was small for his age, was the sort that would give his mother a run for her money. At a brisk pace, she and the boy traversed the length of the drive, avoiding a reunion with Stewart. This was not the right time.

Behind them, Christina made her own way down the drive. When she saw Stewart, she veered to the left to intercept him half way across the field.

Sofie Couch

Stewart held on to the dog's collar, having to bend at the waist in order to keep a grip on his only aide in traversing the farm. He spoke while his sister was still twenty yards away. His voice carried over the distance.

"You doin' okay?"

"Sure." She smiled. "I was… just looking for Jorgé," she seemed to decide on the moment. "Seen him around?"

Stewart shook his head. "Minding the farm, no doubt. The work doesn't stop just because someone dies." He nodded toward the backhoe operator. "I was just chatting with the man on the backhoe. He doesn't get a paycheck unless there's somebody to bury. Paid by the job, he told me. They're almost finished," and he pointed over his shoulder toward the spot where rebar tent spikes were being driven into the ground."

"Pretty certain paycheck then. I'll be glad when this is over."

"Yeah." He turned his head in the direction of the path Annabelle had taken. Like knowing his sister twenty paces away, he had known it was Annabelle who moved past without seeing him, but she had been with someone he did not recognize. A child by the sound of it. He could not fully give his blessing to her having moved on with her life while he had abandoned her as gone forever.

TWO MOONS OVER CEDAR HILL

"Me too – 'll be glad when this is over." He looked back suddenly at his sister. "And what about when it's over?"

Christina looked up at her brother. "What about it?"

"What are you going to do… about Richard? And the shop?"

She drew her chin back. "I've got a job - obligations."

"There's nothing standing in your way anymore. You and Jorgé are free to… whatever."

Christina turned away from her brother. "Too many burned bridges."

"Water *under* the bridge."

Christina smiled. "Bridge over troubled water."

"Don't burn your bridges… 'til you come to them."

"You're mixing your metaphors."

"Then let me stick my neck out on a limb here."

"Ooh. That's bad."

"I know there was something between you two – something I nearly missed ten years ago. You should stick around a while, Christina."

She wrapped her arms tighter around her own waist. "Blood is thicker than… troubled water under the bridge."

"I don't need you any more, Christina."

"You're not considering staying, are you?"

Stewart looked back toward the direction Annabelle had passed. He shrugged. "Maybe. I'll see how things play out."

"She left you, Stewart. Mama paid her to leave you… and she did."

"Looks like she came back though, doesn't it."

Christina stiffened. The dog backed up to her and sat on her foot.

Like so many other things, Stewart sensed it rather than saw it. "He does that, because he doesn't want you to go away either."

"Mangy dog." She pulled her foot out from under the dog's rear end.

"Stop a while to smell the… end of the rainbow." Stewart looked down at the dog and slapped the side of his leg. "Come on, Beebo." Obediently, the dog strained to rise and follow him.

"You can't teach an old dog… to stay put," she fumbled.

"This dirty laundry is home to roost," he called back over his shoulder, stabbing his thumb at his own chest.

"He'll never buy the cow if he thinks the eggs are free."

"What?"

"Jorgé."

Stewart scowled. "That's not very complimentary to either of you. Jorgé's not like that."

"How do you know?"

Stewart stopped and took a step back toward his sister, lowering his voice. "There've always been two constants in my life. You and Jorgé."

Impulsively, she took a step forward and put her arms around his neck and whispered into his ear with a voice that was hoarse. "You're my only constant."

Stewart stepped away from her. "I don't want to be your constant, Christina. I don't want you… or anyone…," and he looked down the road again, in the direction Annabelle and the little boy had gone, "…to be disappointed in me for the choices I make." He sighed. "But there's one thing I'm certain of and that's Jorgé. He's stayed constant. He's stayed here all along, waiting for you."

As he walked away from his sister, Stewart knew why he had come back. It wasn't to get answers from his mother or Jorgé. It had been his secret hope that he would find Annabelle here and, painful though it might be, he had a few thousand questions for her about why she left.

Chapter 23

"...a stubbornly persistent illusion."

Cedar Hill, 1863

Salter watched Grace walk away down the lane with Jack following her like a tag-along dog. He was unprepared for the sudden rush of jealousy. He imagined Grace, married to Jack. He imagined the sort of husband and father Jack would make. He tried to imagine himself in that role, but the image would not form. He had no frame of reference.

Looking down at his feet, he saw a young cedar seedling and in frustration, he swiped at it and ripped it out of the ground. Its sharp needles found the only tender spot on the inside of his hand. When he looked down, a drop of blood beaded out of the palm, between thumb and finger, the marriage between white palm and black back of hand. The seedling came out of the ground with its roots intact and Salter bent at the waist, pulled back enough hard packed clay to hold the roots again, and he patted the seedling back into place, burying with it his jealousy and anger. Things had a way of working out the way they were supposed to.

Twenty years ago

Stew Senior decided on a whim that his children needed to see more of him. He walked over from his home to check on them. They were moving away from him, walking down the cedar lined driveway where the bus would pick them up. He was walking in a leisurely fashion on foot and dressed in clothes that might have been better suited to driving, but the car did not run and he could not afford to fix it and he would not ask Mayella for money, but rather, he would pass the task on to Jorgé whose labor came free.

He waved and called out to his children, but they did not hear him and he put his hand down and looked around to see if anyone on the farm had noticed his vain attempt to get their attention.

Instead, he saw Jorgé at some distance repairing a fence gate. He looked toward the house and through the ground level kitchen window to see Mayella there. She was tackling some domestic task involving a lot of jars and steam. And he had forgotten that it was a school day and his children had no thought of him this morning.

Self-pity was his only comfort. Self-pity and the shade of a hundred-fifty year old cedar tree. He stopped in the middle of the road at 8:30 and wondered what he should be doing with his day.

Present day

Annabelle walked a young boy to the end of the drive where the bus would collect him for school, but she kept turning to look at the side of the man who stood at the fence. He was looking out across the pasture toward the cemetery that was being prepared for Mayella's final resting place.

Stewart listened to Christina's retreating steps, then to the machinery as it dug into the earth, then the men's noises as they hoisted a tent. Taking a deep breath, presumably for fortitude, Stewart let go of Beebo's collar and moved toward the driveway and the fence. He still remembered – 66 fence posts between the house and the spot where he and Christina used to catch the bus. The two other people were far enough ahead of him that he could no longer hear their footsteps in the gravel. Stewart picked up his pace and caught up with them at the highway. The boy continued to chirp at Annabelle. He was seated on or about the large stone at the end of the drive, directly under the wooden sign that gave the farm its name, "Cedar Hill", Stewart remembered the stone, the feel of it, the crack that ran along the left side, and the sign with its concave lettering that was smooth in contrast to the wood background. He could not tell at first where the second person was.

"Sheesh. I can tie my own shoes, Mom."

"Yet you never do."

"When you knot them like that, I can't get them off."

"Why do you need to get your shoes off at school anyway?"

"What if I get a rock or mulch in my shoe?" He answered in a smart tone.

"Then I guess you're stuck."

The boy paused and Stewart knew he had been noticed. The woman, the person tying the boy's shoe spun around on the gravel. Stewart could tell she was squatting in front of the boy when she spun around. But he knew so much more about her.

The kid looked up at Stewart who was well within ear shot. "Hey."

Stewart pulled away from the drive his cane at the end of the fence and listened to the sound of the gravel as he moved toward the boulder. When he was close enough, he extended his hand.

"Hey there. I'm Stewart Breeden." He nodded toward the woman who was still squatting, but who rose as he spoke. "I'm an old friend of your Mama's."

The kid looked to his mother, then slowly slid off of the rock. Hesitantly, he shoved his hand back at Stewart, then put the palm of his hand into Stewart's hand. He licked his chapped lips. "Nice to meet ya."

"And you are?" Stewart shook his hand heartily, then stuffed his hand in his tight jeans pocket and glanced in the direction of the bus that was slowing down for the pick-up.

"Stewart Breeden… number three."

The bus stopped. The younger Stewart snatched up his shoulder bag, turned his back on the speechless adult behind him and climbed on the bus.

The bus doors closed. The boy took his seat, then turned to watch his parents as the bus pulled out.

Stewart stood staring after the bus, his breath coming out like a smoker's exhale, then evaporating like every thought in his head. Slowly, he turned back toward Annabelle.

"Why - the hell - didn't you tell me?"

"By the time I got back, you had gone. Mayella wouldn't tell me where you were." She kicked the gravel in front of her toe. Her arms were wrapped tight around her middle. Her tone was unrepentant.

"She said she offered you money to go away and you took it."

"She gave me money for an abortion. Do you really think I'd take her up on that? I went away 'cause I needed time to think."

"If you weren't going away for an abortion, what was there to think about? Did you think I wouldn't want to be involved with my own…?" Stewart pressed his lips together and turned toward the fast retreating bus before it disappeared from hearing.

TWO MOONS OVER CEDAR HILL

"Stewart, you know my background. The cloud I grew up under."

Stewart knew all too well. You didn't grow up in a small community and not know who the men went to when there was no comfort at home. Only the women referred to Annabelle's mother in whispered epithets: "slut" and "whore". Everyone looked down on Annabelle with pity and fear – pity for her single parent upbringing and fear that she might be the child of their husband.

"I didn't want my child saddled with the same sort of crap. He knows who his daddy is. Always has known – unlike me."

Stewart was shaking his head. "But what kind of Daddy does that make me? Shit, Annabelle. I'm a father and I didn't even know it. Why didn't you...."

"...Tell you?" She finished for him and he knew the answer.

"You didn't know where I was."

"Nope."

"Until this week." He ran his hands through his hair and it stood on end.

"At first I tried to find you, but I was pregnant and Mayella said she'd take care of us if I didn't try to contact you. Yesterday, I didn't think marching up to tell you you've got a nine and a half year old child was quite the proper way to handle a reunion... or an introduction." She waved a hand toward the bus. "But this wasn't quite the way I had envisioned it either."

Stewart was silent a moment. "Is he small for his age?"

"Well, don't say that to his face or he'll kick your ass."

Stewart smiled. "Smart mouth too."

"Guess he comes by that honest."

"Yeah. Definitely gets that from you," and without inhibition or fear that Annabelle might kick his, he took a step toward her and reached out a hand. "How are you, Annabelle? Has it been hard?"

She took his hand, but did not close the gap between them. "No. It really hasn't been. I guess it might have been, but your mother… she's been…." She rolled her eyes. "…Mayella. Except for not letting me tell you about your son… she's been great."

"Mama?"

Annabelle nodded. "Mayella. She surprised me too. She gave me the cottage. I tried to help out around the estate where I could, but with a baby we did more by way of getting in the way than helping. And now I've got the market to run."

Stewart saw Annabelle through a new perspective – an adult perspective. No longer the completely testosterone driven male of his youth, he was only a partially testosterone driven male who was able to see something more in Annabelle.

"I guess she knew the child was mine? Does he look like me?"

Annabelle nodded, then said, "Just like."

"Did she hate me that much? That she would keep something like this from me… all these years?" He dropped Annabelle's hand and gripped the cane in both his hands.

"Your mother, the enigma."

They were silent a moment.

"Well, I've got a shop to run."

Stewart looked at his watch. "What time you open?"

"Six o'clock. I've got a fellow opens up for me. We work it together until noon until his relief comes in. She didn't show up yesterday. That's why I was working on the day Mayella…." She looked down at the gravel under her white Keds sneakers.

"And… Stewart… the other Stewart." Stewart grinned. "He help out at the market?"

"Sometimes."

"This name thing could get confusing."

"His nickname's Tomato."

"Sheesh, Annabelle. What'd you go and do a thing like that for?"

She laughed. "I know. It's awful. Jorgé came up with it."

He smiled, then sobered. "I guess Jorgé's been filling in for me while I was away?"

Annabelle cocked her head and studied his face. "He's only 'filling in' if you plan to stick around."

"What's he do when he gets off from school? Tomato. He go to the market or get off here?"

Annabelle knew where he was headed. "He gets off the bus here. Jorgé usually meets him. You wanna meet him today?"

"Yeah."

"Good. Do you both good."

"I doubt he could really kick my ass anyway."

"Watch your butt." He could not see that Annabelle gave his butt a pointed look before walking off in the direction of the market.

This explained a lot with regard to his mother's behavior, and nothing. If her goal had been to separate him from Annabelle so many years ago, to go so far as to pay for her to have an abortion, then why, later, did she take them in? But immediately, he knew the answer. Tomato was blood. He could imagine his mother justifying it in that way.

Half way along the road back to the house, Stewart stood with his hand on the fence.

His mother *was* an enigma. Mayella had done a good job of portraying herself as a racist and a snob, but why then had she kept on Jorgé and taken care of Annabelle, sending her own children away?

TWO MOONS OVER CEDAR HILL

Ahead, he heard the gray muzzled golden retriever limping down the driveway toward him.

"Beebo. Come on, boy."

The dog barely picked up his pace, but when he and Stewart reached the open gate in the fence, the dog veered off, into the pasture, back toward the site of the tent.

Stewart hesitated only briefly before pulling out the cane again and using it to help guide him toward the noise of the tent.

The tent was up. The workers had moved off and Stewart's cane struck one of the metal support poles on the tent. He felt the post, tapped his cane on the pressed grass and bent down to touch the Astroturf that surrounded the new grave.

"Careful there."

Stewart straightened and turned toward Jorgé who approached from the direction of the house.

"They took the fence down?"

"They had to get the heavy machinery in to dig your mother's... to dig the grave."

Stewart jutted his chin toward the hole. "I followed Beebo."

Jorgé casually put his hand on Stewart's elbow and the familiarity of it felt right to Stewart, like something that had been missing for ten years that was finally reunited.

He could tell Jorgé nodded toward the dog. "He's just there. In the spot where Mayella died. She came out here – sick – barely able to move – she walked all the way out here, at night, and chose this as her final resting place."

"Why here?"

Jorgé paused a long minute before answering him. "To stick it to me one last time."

"Whatdaya mean?"

He heard Jorgé's deep sigh, then followed where the older man led him. They moved toward the spot where Beebo lay. Jorgé guided Stewart around the dog, to the head of the grave and the tombstone that was there.

"Here." He guided Stewart's hand toward the stone.

Stewart gripped the edge of the stone, then ran his hand over the face of it. His fingers sought out the indentations there: G-R-A-C-E T-H-O, Stewart mouthed. "Grace Thompson?"

"And here." Jorgé put his hand to the emblem – two moons over a single star. Stewart moved his hand to the spot and felt it.

"What is it?"

"The same symbols that were on the pendant I gave Chita. The pendant Mayella told me belonged to my mother."

Stewart re-traced the lichen covered etching. If he had ever seen the pendant Christina wore, he would know it was undeniably the same symbol. He rubbed his fingers across the stone, retracing the name and the dates of birth and death.

"You don't think…."

"What?" Jorgé's voice turned toward Stewart.

"The date's too old to be…."

"My mother? No. It is no link to my past. I have no family."

Jorgé sighed. He had already mourned enough over his losses.

Chapter 24

1864

"You'll marry him."

"I won't." Grace was insistent.

"You will. You got no choice."

"Everyone has choices."

And that showed how little she knew of him and his lot in life.

"They have ways to make you marry him."

"My Daddy never would."

She did not know what her Daddy was capable of. Salter knew, had known other men like him whose intentions had been good, but who were equally stunted by the influence of society.

"Your daddy is basically a good man," he hedged.

"And he will stop Mama from making me marry Jack." Grace spun in a circle, grabbing Salter's hand and forcing him to spin her before wrapping herself in his arm like a sausage wrapped in sweet dough.

"I'd marry you if I wanted to."

Salter stopped breathing. She was breathing enough for the both of them, her small chest rising and falling between them.

"Do you… do you want to?"

She laughed and spun away from him. "Don't be silly. You're a Negro." She ran ahead of him, but when she looked back, Salter was heading in the opposite direction. She did not go after him, too great was her shame.

Instead, she turned back toward her own home down the wagon trail. She tried to find comfort in the dolls that lined the pillows on her bed. But these were a child's comforts. Eventually, she found her way to the narrow steps that led up to the attic and there in a far corner, she spied the trunk her mother had begun filling with a married woman's trinkets the day Grace was born.

Grace lifted the lid, then lifted the corner of a wool blanket her mother used to pack away a set of china with gold gilt edging. She tried to imagine herself seated at one end of the dining table downstairs, the table lain out with the china. There were faceless guests seated around the table in her imaginings, but at the head of the table was Salter. He would make a fine steward of the farm and in her childish innocence she dreamt it possible.

Present day

The attic was a time capsule – a jungle of macramé plant holders. The floor was soggy with water in puddles around discarded silk flower arrangements, wreathes and a dusty casket topper from some previous Breeden or Thompson funeral. A mid-ground of furniture, trunks, boxes and stacks of moldy books and papers blocked the path.

Sofie Couch

Christina tentatively touched a faded book that was nestled inside an old Esso oil can. The can was lined with a calico flour sack.

A splash of water dropped onto the dusty cover and Christina looked up at the raftered ceiling where the water filtered in through whatever insufficient sheathing still remained in a house over two hundred years old.

Jorgé fumbled with a latch on the sloped ceiling overhead and with a shove, he pushed the angled ceiling out and up. The roof, now a porch over the widow's perch sheltered him from the rain.

He prodded the copper walk with his foot, then once satisfied with its ability to support his weight, he stepped outside. Christina dropped the book back into the drum, looked around on the floor and found its metal lid and popped it precariously on top to protect the books and papers inside from further water damage. She followed Jorgé, matching his caution with a tentative toe before entrusting the widow's perch to her weight.

Jorgé leaned around the rooftop door to inspect the slate shingles above what would roughly correspond to the placement of the leak inside.

"I can see one broken tile. I suspect many more are cracked. This house has gone too long with too few repairs."

"Did Mama make any repairs since we've been away?"

TWO MOONS OVER CEDAR HILL

Jorgé pulled his head back under the roof awning. He was far more thorough in his inspection of her features than he had been of the roof tiles.

"Mayella would allow nothing to be done to preserve the house. She considered it the source of her unhappiness."

Christina could not hold eye contact. She looked down at the copper edging turned mint green with age.

"That's odd. Was a time, I thought this house was all she cared about... stewardship of the land... a slave to the land... preservation of our family's ties to it. If it was the source of her unhappiness, then she made it that."

Jorgé sighed and shoved his hands into his pockets. He was wearing his usual uniform of plaid shirt and jeans, a land steward's uniform.

"She came to regret her actions – her treatment of Stewart, her estrangement from you."

"She could have called us sooner."

"Chita, the telephone - it works both ways."

"I called, Jorgé. She never told you?"

Jorgé shook his head. "She meant to separate us."

"Then why ask me and Stewart to come back? Now?"

He shrugged.

Christina looked down at the floor and ran a toe through the dirt on the wood flooring that ran at a diagonal. "Why…" she began with hesitation, "…didn't you leave?" She didn't add, "With me."

"This is my home."

Christina glanced up only briefly, ashamed at herself for asking. "But life under Mama's roof? Living by Mama's rules? Were the perks adequate compensation, because the pay sure as hell wasn't."

"Mayella was who she was. She was a bitter woman, a racist at her worse, but something inspiring at her best. Mayella was family."

"Not *your* family though. You didn't have to put up with her."

"Yes, Chita. She *was* my family."

Try as she might, Christina could no longer read him.

"And Mayella loved me… in her own way."

Confirmation of any doubt she might have had gripped her heart.

"I felt no debt to her. I was here of my own will. Before she died, I think Mayella understood why I never left."

Christina grinned. "I bet."

"You remember your mother well. She was a handful — especially at the end."

"Had she been an invalid long?"

He shook his head. "Only at the end. It was my honor to be able to care for her briefly. That I didn't mind. Some things, however, I could not tolerate."

TWO MOONS OVER CEDAR HILL

Christina frowned. "Like?"

"She had it within her power to improve the conditions of a few people close to her."

"Like?"

"Like the people who worked to make her life a comfort when it would have been otherwise intolerable. Annabelle, Annabelle's son, Treeny, Stewart, you… and me."

"And now that Mama is gone?"

Jorgé sighed. "I imagine that's up to you and Stewart. What are your plans now, Chita?"

"I hadn't thought…."

"I would have believed that of the old Chita. This new Chita though," and he looked her over from head to foot appraisingly. "I don't think you came back without a plan."

Her chin jutted out defensively for having been so transparent. "I wasn't planning on Mama dying."

"My question was not intended to rile you, *querida*."

"I'm not riled. I feel… pressured."

"A great number of people are very nervous about their futures here now that Mayella is gone. I would like to be able to comfort them."

Christina looked down at her wet shoes. "Or prepare them."

"Prepare them?"

She tilted her chin up with determination. "I don't plan on staying."

"May I ask why?" His tone was steady.

"I'm not like you. This isn't my home anymore. I can't come back here and feel like I belong." In her distraction, Christina ran her hand down the edge of the roof opening where the slate touched copper. The jagged edge of the slate sliced through her finger. "Ahh." She embraced the pain and pinched closed the cut on her finger. "I wouldn't feel a loss if this farm went out of my family forever."

Jorgé took her hand and inspected the cut, then squeezed it closed. "Maybe it's not yours to sell."

Christina inhaled sharply. "What do you mean?" She imagined the scenario in which Mayella did the only thing within her power to ensure that her children were forever separated from the people she deemed unworthy of their blood attachment by disinheriting both of her children. She hoped it was true. It would settle matters for her. At the forefront of her thoughts was Jorgé holding her hand under the pretense of staunching the blood that wanted to leave her finger.

"Maybe Stewart won't want to sell. Maybe he wants to come home. Maybe this farm is your destiny too. Perhaps you're rooted to this place as firmly as the cedar trees that pepper the mountain."

TWO MOONS OVER CEDAR HILL

And he nodded toward the hill, visible from the widow's walk.

"I don't want anything this farm has to offer. You... don't understand. If you did...." She could not finish what she was about to say and fumbled for an ending. "... You'd go away from here too." She pulled her hand free of his.

"Then tell me."

Christina clenched her jaw with determination.

Jorgé threw up his hand and in a gesture that was as familiar and memory provoking as the scent of the black coffee he drank in the mornings, she knew the finality implied by the wave of his hand. It was how they had parted ten years ago.

He turned toward the widow's walk.

"Jorgé?"

He stopped and faced her, his head tipped to the side. She could read little of his expressions any more. "You could take up your mother's place here. It would be a comfort... to many."

"There are only so many things I'm willing to share with my mother. Here." She pulled the necklace out of her collar and slipped the chain over her head. "I would have sent it to you years ago, but I was afraid... Mama might intercept it. I didn't know...."

She held out the necklace to him.

"So, you've just been wearing it all this time until you had a chance to return it in person?"

She thrust it toward him. "Take it. This represents *your* family."

The expression around his mouth was hidden, but not his eyes. He was hurt.

Again, he made that gesture, the wave of a hand as if flicking away a bothersome fly.

"Keep it. It may mean more to you someday. It no longer holds meaning for me."

TWO MOONS OVER CEDAR HILL

Chapter 25

The pill bottles were gone from the bedside table. Mayella looked around the room and felt the absence of herself. Christina turned into the room and walked through her mother without the reunion due two people who had not seen each other in ten years. Instead, her expression was blank and like someone suffering from exhaustion she sat down hard on the edge of the bed. Christina stared down at a chain that spilled over the sides of her hand. With hesitation, Christina lifted the chain and slipped it back over her head. She winced and looked down at her sliced finger, then stood and made her way into the adjoining bathroom.

Mayella did not so much open the top drawer of the bedside table as insinuate it open. She was not aware of opening it or not opening it. The drawer was simply opened to expose the tube of antibiotic ointment.

Christina came out of the bathroom still holding her finger, scanned the room, then walked to the bedside table, glanced into the crack in the top drawer, then slid it open.

"Ah-ha." She took out the ointment, dabbed it on her finger and was about to return the ointment to the drawer when her attention fell to something that protruded from the side of the mattress. She ran her hand down the side of the bedspread and felt the hard corner of something that had worked its way out from between the mattress and the box spring. Christina lifted the chenille spread and saw the corner of a marble composition notebook.

Mayella left the room.

Christina pulled out the notebook and her heart spasmed with regret when she recognized her mother's handwriting.

Then she heard Jorgé's footsteps as he descended the awkward attic stairs. Hastily, she threw open the wardrobe in her mother's room, took out the first over-sized sweater she saw there, and wrapped the book. She couldn't face him again this soon. With the sweater and journal secreted under her arm, she hastily moved out of the room and headed down the stairs and out the front door.

Late October and it was already cold, not usual for this part of Virginia. Christina slipped on the sweater, then glancing over her shoulder, she slipped the journal between sweater and chest, her hand wrapped under it. Like a rote learner, she knew where she was heading for privacy, but she didn't think about it. Instead, her feet simply carried her to that spot where she had always taken herself for introspection.

She circled around behind the house where there stood the ruins of an incomplete brick Grecian temple – a folly constructed by someone long forgotten. The history of the out-of-place structure

TWO MOONS OVER CEDAR HILL

was long lost and the skeletal remains were being pulled back into the earth by vines. To those alive now, the brick structure had no purpose other than that which they gave it – the venue of the annual end of harvest party.

Twelve years ago

"I've been looking everywhere for you." Jorgé put down his drink and with a grin he held out his hand.

"What's that?" Christina looked from his hand to his face.

"What's it look like, Chita?" A bonfire blazed behind him, backlighting him and the ruins of the brick folly that stood between them and the party.

Only in Virginia could you hire a three piece bluegrass mariachi band. For the annual event held at the end of the harvest season, no expense was spared. It was the one night of celebration in which Mayella took part, although she would complain the rest of the year about the waste and expense.

"I'm going to teach you to dance."

"Nooooo." Christina walked backwards and he came toward her playfully, menacingly.

"Yes. Remember when you were a kid and tried to drown me by way of pretending to teach me to swim? I believe the phrase you used then was 'uptight'. I'll show you who's 'uptight'."

Christina ran around him, then turned again and backed into the brick structure that filled the center of the back yard. "No. Not in front of all of these people."

As one of the only half-dozen women at the end of season party, she had been the center of attention from the moment she came out of the house. Jorgé stepped between her and the mostly male, well-behaved ensemble.

"The more production you make of this the more people are going to stare." He looked around with a grin. "Now, are we gonna do this the nice way or the embarrassing way."

"You are so gonna pay for this."

Someone called, in Spanish, for a change in the music from the three piece band and a tune with a salsa rhythm began.

"Goes like this." Jorgé took her hand in his left and put his right hand on her waist, holding her away from him at a respectable distance. She hesitantly put her other hand on his shoulder. "It's a rock step. Back, middle, middle, front, middle, middle…. Watch my feet." He chucked her on the chin and pointed down."

"Wait. Wait. Do that again."

"Back, middle, middle, front…. You do the opposite. I'm front, middle, middle, back, middle, middle."

Christina caught on quickly.

TWO MOONS OVER CEDAR HILL

"Now, look up. Ouch."

"Sorry."

"Okay, look back down until you get the hang of it." Laughter was in his voice. "Back, middle, middle, front...."

She mouthed the words. He smiled. His face was clean shaven and his hair worn short and instead of his usual denim or plaid shirt, he had dressed up in a crisp, white shirt that stood out against his dark hair and skin.

"Now, who's the uptight one?"

"I'm doing really well!"

He nodded with a grin. "Very well. Now, stop counting and feel the music." He moved his hand from her waist to her back and pressed her shoulder blade, their circle becoming more intimate, yet their steps taking them in a broader counter-clockwise arc, slowly moving around the bonfire. As they moved, the heat of the fire warmed alternately her back, then her face and hands.

"Okay, show me something more."

He spun her out, keeping hold of one of her hands, then spun her back in, catching her waist again. She laughed and without inhibition, rested the side of her head against his, they being of about the same height. Slowly, her smile faded. On the far side of the bonfire they were practically alone. It only required a slight turn of her head and she could see him up close. His was the face she knew best. When had she made such a close study of him? There was nothing new about the face next to hers, and yet, every inch was new. Only she knew how he had acquired the scar on his chin. Yep. Same scar. Long ago she had commented on his eyes, how they turned up at the outside corners like a subtle smile. Yep. Same eyes. His lashes were longer and darker than hers would ever be. Her hand, the one on his shoulder, tentatively brushed the clean-cut edge of his hair. Just yesterday it had been a quarter inch longer. He must have got it cut for the party. Same hair, only shorter than yesterday. She studied his face up close and he hers and she felt the change in their relationship take place. Somehow, she had known all along they were meant to be together. Maybe he had known too, but he had been careful with her, waiting for her to grow up and to realize that he had been standing right there in front of her all along.

His dance frame went rigid and he put physical distance between them. When she met his look, he averted his eyes, looking down at his feet, as if he were the one learning the steps, but that point in their relationship was past. One song bled into another, they came full-circle, in the thick of the party, but it was as if everyone else saw the difference now too. They danced three songs straight. When they stopped dancing, she knew no one else would ask her to dance. She was meant for

TWO MOONS OVER CEDAR HILL

Jorgé, their destinies inextricably bound toward some goal as yet unknown to them.

The third song ended, and Jorgé let go her hand. It felt odd, the absence, and she rubbed her fingers against her palm in an attempt to refill that void.

Jorgé cleared his throat and took a step back. "You done good." He looked around him. "Now that you know how, I shouldn't take up every dance." He caught the arm of the nearest man, a kind old man who would leave this farm for the next on his seasonal route. "She needs more practice. Watch her though. She's got big feet."

The older man stepped up without hesitation and extended his hand to Christina. She had lost her fear of dancing. She took his proffered hand, flicked the much older man a smile, and then scanned for Jorgé over his shoulder. Jorgé was moving away, fast. He was already on the far side of the folly, away from the light of the bonfire, being swallowed by the dark.

But before he disappeared completely, Christina saw what he did. He put his hand to his cheek, his eyes closing for just a second, inhaling the scent of her.

Present day

Christina turned toward the original road that ran between the two old farms. As her path led her closer to the woods, she slowed and was swallowed by the trees, both cedar and deciduous, that narrowed in on her in a sheltering way. The track was as clear as it had been when she was a young girl and came here to get close to her confusing feelings.

  The road veered to the left and would have taken her past the charred ruinous remains of her father's old house, but Christina turned to the smaller foot path to the right and followed it to the base of the mountain range. There stood the preserved remains of an old smoke house. The building stood as sturdy as it had for probably more than two hundred years. The smokehouse door stood open and she stepped over the stone threshold that was like stepping back in time.

Ten years ago
  The threshold was a stone slab that had been worn to a curvaceous swale by the traffic of previous generations. In the month since they first danced, Jorgé had hardly spoken a dozen words to her. Today, Christina followed Jorgé to the smoke house. She inhaled deeply.

  "It smells like bacon in here."

  Jorgé looked up from his seat on the hearth. She had surprised him, lost in thought. This was the place he came to think - alone.

  "Chita."

TWO MOONS OVER CEDAR HILL

"What're you doing out here?" She looked around the house with curiosity, having followed him from the barn nearly a mile away.

He was sitting on the stone hearth, his hands folded, elbows resting on his knees. His head was down when she came in. Prayer and organized religion were a foreign construct to her, something reserved for traditional families.

"I came out here to think."

She scrunched up her nose. "Smell makes me hungry."

Without reserve, and without imagining he might want to be left alone, she crossed the brick floor and plopped down on the hearth beside him.

He stood up in the same motion.

"It's late. You shouldn't be out here alone."

"I'm not alone. Got the best guide this side of the South West Mountains." She did not budge.

"Your 'guide' just flunked the eye exam on his DMV test."

"You have to get glasses?"

"Got them. Well, got the glasses for up-close. I'll have to get a prescription for distance." He pulled a pair of black dime store reading glasses from his breast pocket. "The man at the DMV mentioned it often sneaks up on you when you get to be my age." Slipping them on, he looked toward the open shutter at the gable. "Come on. We'd better get you back."

Sofie Couch

Grace peeked in through the open door of Salter's house. It smelled like ham.

"You'd best get back to y'own house, Miss Grace."

"Don't boss me around. Everybody bosses me."

In comparison to him, she did not know what it was to be bossed.

"Did you hear something?"

Jorgé cocked his head to the side to hear something he might have missed, but he shook his head and moved toward the door.

Christina jumped up and beat him to the door. Hands on hips, feet planted firmly as though she was riding astride a horse, she barred the way.

"Plenty of time before dark." She turned to better inspect the small house. "This is real cozy. You'd think someone would be using the place for something other than smoked ham."

"It was my home."

"No way."

He nodded. "When I first came here with my mother and father. We were housed here. That was ages ago."

As was her habit, Christina scrunched her nose again. "I said it was cozy, but… it could use a little… something… before people were housed here."

"Beggars can't be choosers. And besides, it was home... a happy place."

Christina nodded. "I can feel that. It has good karma."

He chuckled. "Yeah. It does. Come on."

He moved toward the doorway, toward her, but she did not move.

"What were you thinking about? Before I came in."

He shrugged. Jorgé was always amiable. He usually wore an air of contentment, but today he seemed restless.

"Big thoughts." He moved to the side to squeeze past her.

Christina stepped sideways in front of him.

"What kind of big thoughts."

He sighed and shoved his hands into his pockets. "The meaning of life and my place in it." With his eyes he said, *now are you going to let me pass?*

"Are you happy here?"

His smile broadened, his apple cheeks rising to hide behind his new glasses frames. He nodded again. "Pretty much."

Christina's expression turned serious. "You're not thinking about leaving, are you?"

"Where'd that come from?"

She didn't answer.

"I thought you were all grown up now, Chita. That's a little girl's fear." He shrugged and moved away from her. "Besides, you're the one who'll be leaving soon."

"College isn't forever. I'm talking about the big picture. You're not going to disappear while I'm away, are you? You'll wait for me?"

"Don't be ridiculous."

"'Ridiculous' – because you're not planning on disappearing or 'ridiculous,' – you're not going to wait for me."

His smile melted. "I'm not planning on disappearing."

"And the other thing?" The smoke house grew cozy again.

He laughed without so much as a twitch of a smile. "Wait for you. What's to wait for? I'm here. You'll be back soon."

She was not blind. There had been enough awkward moments between them to raise the question in her own mind.

"And is that what you came here to think about?" She took a step closer to him until she did not think he could raise a hand between them without touching her. Her back was to the open door.

"*Si.* No." He turned away from her, shoving his hands deeper into his pockets. "You're a child, Chita. And I'm an old man." He touched the corner of his glasses frame. "It was wrong of me to think I could be…. That we could just…." He rolled his eyes as he spun around. "What I mean to say…."

"I know what you mean. Everything's different between us now."

"No, Chita. Nothing is different. At least, nothing should be different."

"Are you, of all people, worried about what the rest of the world thinks? Or are you just worried about what Mama will think?"

He chuckled. "Your *Mamá* does tend to take up an inequitable share of the world." He turned and paced the length of the stone fireplace hearth. "Yes… and no. It's not right in my own mind."

"You're comparing me, the way you are with me, to the way you are with Stewart. It's not the same, Jorgé."

"It should be the same."

"But it isn't… and it never was. Stewart grew up comparing you to Daddy. I don't think of you like that – never did. I've always admired you… in the same way I admire…," she struggled for an apt comparison, "…the landscape of this farm."

She waved her hand in the direction of the Southwest Mountains, then she let her hand drop to her side and she took a step toward him. He stopped pacing and for a second, his attention was held by a study of her lips.

"I doubt my own ability to see things clearly."

Christina grinned and, reaching up, took the black frames from his eyes.

"It's these silly things." Slowly and deliberately, she folded them, slipped them into the soft case in his breast pocket, and then let her hand slide over the pocket to the middle of his chest.

"Chita… Chita… I don't think…."

"My point exactly. You've been thinking too much."

Then she kissed him. She could not say he kissed her, because he was a frozen participant. His lips did not respond under hers and although her eyes were closed, she thought perhaps he had not closed his eyes. When she pulled away from him, she tried to exude a confidence she did not feel.

"Now you can walk me back."

And he did.

Present day

Christina inhaled deeply of the faint scent of ham mingled with the damp smell of leaf litter and decomposition. The shutter on the upper gable above the loft creaked in its frame and now the sunlight came in through the gap along with wind and rain. The elements and neglect had taken their toll on the old smoke house. She doubted Jorgé came here anymore.

Tentatively, she looked down at the dirty hearth and swiped at the debris there before taking a

seat. Pulling out the journal, she opened it to the first page.
  Mayella wrote:

I have been on the shelf for too long, so tonight when Stewart Breeden asked me to marry him for the twenty-eleventh time, I finally said yes. He seemed quite surprised, maybe even a bit dismayed, at my having accepted, but if he didn't mean it, he should not have been so persistent. He asked why I finally chose to accept him and I told him it seemed as good a time as any.

All I have to offer for dowry is history and land. The Breedens are what Mama used to call Old Virginia horse money, having made a name for themselves during the reconstruction after The War and having made a fortune in the horse trade. The Thompsons, on the other hand, are just Old Virginia – no money. All we have is the farm here at Cedar Hill – 1500 acres of it.

Stewart and I are in disagreement about where we will live after we are married. The whole point of marrying at all is to have children to whom I can pass Cedar Hill, and as this house is the more comfortable, I think it only makes sense we should live here rather than next door at River's Edge. There, the fireplaces are too large, making the house difficult to heat.

We are planning a big wedding.

Christina turned the page.

June 6th:

Sofie Couch

Tomorrow I will be a new bride at thirty-nine years old. (Stewart is younger than I – by more than five years.) We have called off the wedding no less than a half dozen times, but each time, he has shown contrition. Neither of us is in our youth anymore and we will have to settle the matter soon through compromise. We have both given on a few matters. It is finally decided that we will live here at Cedar Hill. I have conceded to his bringing that Mexican boy to live with us. He is young, not a little bit handsome, and will probably serve well for shuttling between the two estates. Stewart is not a hardship to the eye, but his little Mexican servant is very gentle on the eye. I'll not tell Stewart that. He might call off the wedding – again.

September 26th:
I am pregnant! And my husband shows more enthusiasm for this than any other matter. Now there will be a child to inherit Cedar Hill and as that was my main objective I cannot complain about the constant nausea.

February 7th:
Still-birth.

December 22nd:
I am remiss in not relating the events of the past year, but I found I had little heart for it after the death of my son. It seems inconceivable that I never had a chance to bestow a name on my little boy, but we planned to call him Stewart after his father, but as his father has played little part in my

comfort since the loss, I find I cannot think of my little one as a "Stewart".

George has proven to be a great comfort. He is a sweet boy who is given to Latin emotion. He brought flowers when he heard of the loss of the child. My husband is often away, but I am kept company by George. I think he may be the greatest asset to have been gained in my marriage to Stewart.

January 27:
Stewart has dishonored his family's name and, by association, mine. I did not know he was a gambler when we married, but he makes no effort to hide his vice now. He cannot. Our finances are a mess. Had I known the state of things, I would never have consented to marry him. My only concern at this point is in preventing Stewart from doing anything ridiculous that might jeopardize the farm.

George is my counsel. He has the unique ability to see this farm as a whole. In fact, he is more in charge than my own husband.

March 8th:
I have prevented my husband selling a large portion of timberland, George has taken over as farm manager, and my husband has accused us of having an affair....

Christina put her hand to her mouth, inadvertently smeared the antibiotic ointment from her cut finger onto her lip, wiped it with the back of her hand and turned her full attention back to the journal.

...I don't know which I find more distressing — his gambling us into the poor house or his accusing me of bedding a Mexican.
It is fortunate that I am pregnant again. Stewart has served his usefulness and now may lead his life as he likes. And George and I may lead our lives as we like.

Christina closed the book and took a deep breath. Hadn't she always known it would come to this? Hadn't this been what she feared she would return to find? She just wondered how much she had missed so many years ago.

Back at Cedar Hill in the attic, Mayella thumbed through the journals of her long departed ancestor, Grace Thompson. She only wanted Christina to know her through her own words. Sometimes, she was joined by the man in the ticking pants. At present he thumbed through one of the dusty journals in an attempt to decipher the clues that would ensure his freedom from this place. Sadly, he held the book upside-down, unable to read.
In the smoke house, Grace Thompson's sad spectral-self searched for a lost love.

TWO MOONS OVER CEDAR HILL

Chapter 26

Jorgé held his breath. Mayella walked toward him – an apparition out of the mist. How, he wondered, did one greet a ghost?

What were you thinking, would be high on his list of questions. *Thief* was one epithet he might use for having stolen from him his history. *Liar* for claiming to have fixed things only to have made them worse. *Saboteur* for ruining his only chance at happiness.

Christina, wearing one of Mayella's sweaters, might pass as her twin, separated by 40 years, life and death. Surround her with a small pack of domestic dogs and anyone who had not seen her in a while might think she had escaped the ravages of age and spite.

Christina looked up from the leaf strewn yard, her arms wrapped tight around her body. Her smile looked forced.

"Hey."

"Hey." Jorgé sat on the top step of the porch. Christina climbed, then settled down on the step beside him, watching as he packed a homemade firecracker. In answer to her inquisitive look, he held it up.

"For Mayella's funeral. Her request."

"*La dia de los meurtos?*"

"*Sí.* End of the week." He smiled and inserted a fuse.

"I'll be sorry to miss it."

Jorgé did not respond.

"Miss what?" Stewart came out onto the porch. The dog followed him, found a spot against the house where the sun hit under the porch, circled twice, then groaned as he lay down. "And where've you been hiding all day? I needed to talk to you. Tell you something pretty…," he took a deep breath, "…amazing."

Christina raised her chin in gesture toward the old wagon road that led to the older smoke house. "Went for a walk. What's the surprise?"

"You saw Annabelle?" Jorgé rightly guessed with a smile that held double meaning, although Stewart could not see it.

"Yeah." Stewart grinned. "What are you gonna miss, Christina?"

"*La Dia de los Meurtos,*" Christina supplied. "You've seen Annabelle?" There was a noticeable edge to her voice.

Stewart nonchalantly shoved his hands into his pockets and leaned back against the wall of the house. "Yeah. Why are you gonna miss the celebration."

"I've gotta get back to the shop." With decisiveness, Christina jumped up from the step. "I imagine you'll be wanting to get back too – right after the funeral." She pulled open the screen door in invitation to her brother as though he might just pick up at that moment and leave with her. Stewart did not budge. The screen door tapped Christina on the backside. "And I left Richard on one of the shop's busiest weekends. He was none too pleased."

Stewart snorted. "Don't guess he was… losing his cheap labor for a whole weekend."

Jorgé looked from Christina to Stewart, settling on Stewart. He pretended nonchalance. "Richard?"

"He… owns the antique shop where I work. Stewart and I live above the shop."

"This antique shop that Stewart mentioned to me before you arrived? You didn't mention this man… Richard."

"He's my boss."

Again, Stewart snorted. "Something a bit more, I think. At least, he'd like to be."

Jorgé did not miss the glare Christina shot at her brother, although it was lost on Stewart.

"Ahh, a boyfriend, perhaps?"

With a hand on the door knob, she answered. *"Quizá."* Christina turned the brass door knob, but Stewart moved away from the wall, his hand out stretched.

"You can't leave, Christina."

Jorgé looked over his shoulder, the firecracker held tight between his knees.

Sofie Couch

"I have to get back to work." Her voice was thick, her back to them. Jorgé thought maybe her voice cracked a little.

Jorgé jumped up from the step, pulling his own rabbit out of the clichéd hat. He pulled a bundle of papers out of his back pocket. "You can't leave, Chita."

"And why not?" She finally stopped with the oversized front door open and looked over her shoulder to the papers in Jorgé's hand.

Jorgé touched Stewart's hand that he still held outstretched to his sister.

Jorgé unfolded and handed the papers to Christina. She began reading, stopped and looked around, then took a seat again on the top step. She read through the first page and a half before she stopped.

Jorgé reclaimed his seat on the step beside Christina, then turned his attention to the second firecracker.

For just one more short minute, he wanted to preserve this moment – the smell of gun powder, the scent of Christina beside him, the hint of wood smoke on the air – a time before she read and digested the contents of her mother's Will, before she knew about her mother's cruel trick. It was like the night around the bonfire when he had felt something permanently alter in their relationship. This would be that sort of alteration.

TWO MOONS OVER CEDAR HILL

Christina read the Will to the end, then handed the document back to Jorgé without a word. Jorgé stopped wrapping a second fuse and with a hesitant hand he took the will and lifting one hip, shoved it back into the rear pocket from which he had pulled it.

"You knew about this?"

"What? What's going on," Stewart asked.

Jorgé nodded. "She had her lawyer out just two weeks ago. She was a sick woman at the end." He glanced over his shoulder at Stewart. "Christina just read your mother's will." He turned his attention back to the fire cracker still clenched between his knees.

Out of the corner of his eye, he saw Christina put her hands to her face. When she took them away she was smiling.

"I thought, when I arrived the other day, the place looked as though it had gone to the dogs. Little did I know, it literally had," and she looked behind her to the old dog curled up beside the house. Beebo thumped his tail twice for the notice he received.

For Stewart's benefit, she explained, "I have to stay and take care of him in order to inherit."

"Jorgé?"

"The dog," and Christina laughed out loud. "What did she hope to accomplish?" Christina covered her face again.

"Didn't she leave anything to Jorgé?" Stewart asked.

"I'm accounted for." Jorgé finally spoke. "I retain my position as farm manager, but you and Chita must stay and care for the dog."

"You stay to maintain what they call a 'pet trust' or the estate… and the care of Beebo… goes to the ASPCA. Only if you stay and care for him, after his natural life ends, do the two of you inherit."

Christina pushed herself up from the step.

"I want no part of it."

"But you have to. It's the only way Stewart can inherit… if you stay to care for the dog, keeping the land in your immediate family." Jorgé rose to follow her, leaving the firecrackers on the top step.

"I want no part of it." She waved her hand. "With any of it." She turned to Stewart. "We'll go back to the coast. We were comfortable there, Stewart. I have a business to run."

"Then the place goes to the dogs – quite literally."

"This is crazy. Mama would never have let the farm slip out of the family," Stewart protested.

Jorgé spoke up. "She would if she wanted to retain some control after she was gone."

Christina deflated. "I… She can't do that."

Jorgé shrugged and spoke as if it did not matter to him what she chose to do. "She can. She has. Unless you stay, the farm – everything – goes to the care of Beebo and a nice fat donation to the shelter."

"But you won't leave," Stewart answered for her. "And I'm not planning on leaving either."

In a seemingly dream state, she slowly turned to face her brother. "Why, Stewart?"

"I have to stay, Christina ...for my son."

The essence of Mayella wandered onto the porch, her vision allowing greater clarity than she had ever known in life, recognized the mistakes Christina was making. She had not seen them when she herself made those same mistakes.

"Annabelle gave birth to my son."

Christina was speechless and stood, staring at her brother, her mouth open.

Mayella understood the emotional turmoil going on within Christina and was powerless to do anything about it. She wanted to comfort her.

The blood drained from Christina's face. "Annabelle... had your baby?"

"She was pregnant when we went away. I thought Mama had paid her to leave me. Really, she paid her to have an abortion... which she refused to do. He's nine and half, nearly ten years old. I met him this morning."

Stewart was grinning and Christina felt faint. Jorgé watched – a silent observer.

"I'm going to meet him this afternoon when he gets off of the bus, try to get to know him and I know that isn't going to happen over the course of two days. Without you, and this farm, I've got no right to come, only to go. I won't have a home anymore… and if the farm passes out of our hands, neither will he and Annabelle."

Christina sank into a rocking chair on the porch. She looked to Jorgé. "Did you know?"

He nodded. "I could do the math. That, and she named the boy Stewart."

Christina covered her face with her hands, then quickly looked up again. "The child… he's alright?"

Stewart answered her. "Apparently he's known all along. Shit. What must he think of me?"

Jorgé watched Christina with curiosity. When she met his gaze, she turned away pointedly.

"I have a business to run – a life back on the coast. I can't afford to play around here looking after a dog… and this taint of a farm."

"A life back on the coast? You peddle trinkets that split up another family's history."

"It's a legitimate business."

"You sound like you're trying to convince yourself of that."

Christina pressed her lips together. Mayella understood the pain she had caused her daughter through the ten year exile.

TWO MOONS OVER CEDAR HILL

"You don't expect Beebo to last long, I know, Christina, but don't count on my going back with you when he's gone."

Christina threw an accusatory look at Jorgé before turning back on her brother. "Annabelle's done just fine without you up until now."

Stewart laughed. "You've got to be kidding. You expect me to turn my back on my own child… to live with my sister over a shop?"

"No. No. Of course not. I need time to think." She ran her hands over her face. "And what will you do here? For a living? Your job…."

"Will fare just fine without me. And while I'm here, I've got a plan."

Christina shook her head. "You've already planned this?"

"I've only had the morning, Christina. I wasn't keeping secrets from you… very long. I need to find the means to bond with my son. I'm going to initiate the treasure hunt again."

Christina rolled her eyes. "Stewart. There is no treasure. Don't drag a little boy through it like Daddy dragged you."

"I think there is a treasure, still buried out there somewhere, and if not, then I've lost nothing, and possibly built some new memories with my son. I have to stick around to try and find it, now more than ever. Dad told me during the Civil War that the family treasure was buried in a grave to hide it from the Federal Army. What's more, I'm convinced Mama found something before she died and I believe she left clues as to where it's hidden."

"Based on what evidence?"

Stewart hesitated. "Evidence. I think there was a link between Grace Thompson and the treasure."

"Who's Grace Thompson?"

"She's buried out there." He pointed in the general vicinity of the graveyard with its newly staked tent. "Are you sure we're related? Listen. The date sort of fits. It would make sense if you were trying to hide something that you'd hide it in a place where no one would think to look – someplace like a grave. Especially, a fresh grave."

"That's sick."

"Ours is a sick heritage. Our family fought for their right to *own* people. That's sick. Think of the time, Christina. Poor medical care. A family member dies. What better place to conceal the treasure than in that person's grave."

"You don't think they would have gone back to dig it up?"

"Would you go back to dig up your dead relative to retrieve something that was probably safer in the ground? What better way to safeguard your treasure. People back then didn't trust banks. Hell. I don't even know if they had banks back then."

TWO MOONS OVER CEDAR HILL

Christina laughed. "Suppose there is treasure out there somewhere, Stewart." She waved her hand in the direction of the cemetery. "It's probably all in Confederate dollars."

"No. Daddy said it was gold and silver – coin and household items made of precious metals."

"And Daddy also thought a horse by the name of Slew-Eyed Sally was a good bet. She was a long-shot for a good reason. Don't drag your… child… through this like you were." Christina was breathing fast.

Jorgé spoke. "Your future is Cedar Hill, Christina, and you know it has nothing to do with wills or birth rights – not even to do with your brother… or your nephew."

"Oh God." She ran her hands over her face again. "My nephew."

"It has everything to do with fate and we agreed a long time ago that it was your fate to live here at Cedar Hill… just as it was fate that brought me here so many years ago. Maybe that fate is directing Stewart, giving him a purpose, and a goal that will bond him to his son. It makes sense."

"None of it makes sense. That Mama invited Annabelle to live here… and all these years…." Understanding dawned. "… because of your son… who is family, regardless of…."

"My son… who will lose his home if you and I don't stay to take care of the dog."

"Your... son." She digested the words, and only she understood why it was not a cause for celebration. "But Stewart," Christina ran her hand through her hair, tousling the tight curls, "of course, you can't... a son." She paced. "I've got to think." Christina turned on Jorgé. "You had some influence over Mama. You might have prevented her ever writing that will and keeping us here."

"Annabelle was your friend too, Christina. Don't you feel any relief over this?"

Christina swung back to face her brother, the truth she and her mother had kept from him on the tip of her tongue. They were accomplices in this horrible deed that had kept Stewart from his child. She had a nephew. Or was there a different name for their relationship?

Jorgé watched Christina, puzzled by her reaction.

Christina glared at Jorgé who had been a passive observer. "You could have prevented this." She stood up. "I wish I had never received a call from Mama two days ago."

And as though she carried the weight of the world, she left the porch, encasing herself in the large old house, leaving the door open behind her. With far more reserve, Jorgé followed her. She was already at the top of the steps and before he had ascended half-way, she slammed her door in the upstairs hall. At the top of the stairs, he glanced toward the closet door that led to the attic. It was slightly ajar. He pushed it closed, then moved past it to Christina's room. He did not bother to knock, but quietly entered her room.

"Go away, Stewart."

"Stewart does not seem upset about the way things were left. He said something about phoning Annabelle, then meeting his son at the bus stop."

"Damn." Christina rose and headed toward the door. "I've got to stop him. Take him away from here. You should… get away too," she said more gently.

He shook his head. "Not likely."

She tried to move past him, but Jorgé reached out to catch her elbow.

"You have been unjust to Stewart and to Mayella's memory."

"I'm the bad guy?"

"There are no bad guys. Stewart will stay and take up his place here, with his son… and Annabelle. You accuse Mayella of being manipulative. You accuse me of aiding her. Yet, it is you who would force Stewart to do your bidding. What are you afraid of, Christina? Losing his dependency?"

She froze. "You're the second person to accuse me of that in as many days. I don't want him… them… to get hurt again." She stuttered in an attempt to clarify. "This Will – Mama's last voice – and she undoes everything."

"What is it she undoes?"

Christina pressed her lips together, tight, before slowly changing the subject. "And what about you, Jorgé? You've been here with her all these years. Is this how you expected to be treated? You're barely mentioned in her Will – and as what? You retain the right to the job you've held your entire life? Don't you feel even a little bit cheated?"

"I feel cheated, but not for the reasons you might imagine."

She dropped her shoulders in defeat.

He continued. "Mayella lied to me about something that I held more dear than anything of monetary value." He did not enlighten further, but his gaze fell to the slight bulge the necklace made under her knit shirt. When he looked up, Christina was biting her lower lip. "Stewart will stay… get to know his son. He cannot do that if you don't maintain the trust as outlined in the Will."

She hesitated. "And I don't keep Stewart as a dependent."

"Last year, did you claim him on your taxes?"

"Smart ass."

"You've changed, Chita."

"Living with Mama has changed you too."

"I hope in a good way."

"I don't know."

"Stay and find out, Chita." He took a step closer. Every nerve in his body pointed its compass toward her, so he stiffened and stopped. Old habits. "You are far more like your mother than you may wish to admit. Consider that a compliment."

She did not look flattered.

"As soon as it's possible, I'm taking Stewart away from here."

"What happened to the Christina of old?" He shook his head. "Has your life been so hard these past ten years?" She didn't respond, so he continued, "Stewart is a big boy now, but he respects you and wants your support. Support him in this, Christina, or you may lose him too. Don't let history repeat itself."

"I thought we agreed, it's all pre-destined?"

Without answering, but with full knowledge of that to which she was referring, Jorgé turned and left her room.

Twelve years ago

Christina sat on a horse saddle that was draped over a wooden saw horse, her feet in stirrups on either side, not touching the ground. Her back was straight and she pretended to canter. At sixteen, she was an accomplished rider, like her father had been before her.

"Jorgé, I think you'd be safer on horseback."

Jorgé worked on a truck that had seen a better day. It bore tags that said simply, "farm use only."

"Too high maintenance."

She muttered under her breath, "yeah, and that truck's not." Louder, she asked, "Are you happy here?"

Jorgé laughed and a sixteen year old Christina knew his answer.

"No," he answered from his position lying under the truck.

"I didn't think so." She grinned and knew he was smiling too although she couldn't see his face.

"What would I do with myself if I wasn't here extending the life of rusty engines."

"You might be married. You're old enough to be married, aren't you?"

He snorted. "It's not about age. It's about finding your soul mate."

"What characteristics would this soul mate of yours happen to have?"

"Why do *you* wanna know?" She squirmed, so he relented. Still speaking from under the truck he said, "Don't know. Haven't found her yet."

"Hm." Christina poked out her bottom lip. "Did you ever feel like somebody put you here for a reason? I feel like I'm waiting… for… something.... You ever feel like that?"

He spun around, poking his head out from under the engine block, finally making eye contact. "Yeah. Waiting for you to get down here and help me."

TWO MOONS OVER CEDAR HILL

Christina jumped off of the saw horse and handed him the wrench he was struggling to reach.

"It's called pre-destiny," he called out again from under the truck.

"What's pre-destiny?"

"It's something to do with fate - the force that puts you in the right place at the right time."

She stood beside him and the truck. "What if you find out there's no such thing as fate? You're just here… because…. And your soul mate lives in another town. Maybe another country. Maybe we're supposed to roam the planet looking for them."

"I'm not going anywhere, Christina. I've already told you that."

"You told me that when I was a little kid - trying to make me feel – not so alone. Do you ever wish you were doing something else, living someplace else?"

Jorgé narrowed his eyes and studied her in a way that made her uncomfortable. "Are you embarrassed for me?" He held up his hand. It was covered in engine oil.

Christina reached down, took his hand and helped pull him up. "'Course not."

"I'm never gonna be anything more – or less – than a farmer. You can challenge me all you want, but don't try to push me to be something I'm not. I'm proud of what I do. Don't make it something less."

Sofie Couch

"I'm proud of what you do too."

He nodded as he rose, but without conviction. He turned his back on her and his attention to the top side of the truck's motor looking down through it and trying to reach that inaccessible belt.

"It's just…," stalling for time, she spit on her finger and rubbed at the truck's rust red primer coat. She put her hand on the truck's dirty fender, then pulled it away with a grimace. "…at school, they keep pushing college in everybody's face. Junior year is when everyone starts looking at schools. Applications have to be in by next December. William and Mary is closest, but…."

"You should go away to college." His response was quick.

"I could do community college – live at home."

But Jorgé put down the wrench he was holding, wiped his hands on an oily rag, and then leaned casually against the side of the truck, giving her his full attention. "You need to go away for college. Don't stick around here just because… just because."

Christina moved back around the truck and stopped right at his side. She did not take her eyes from his. "You *want* me to go away?"

"Yes."

"You want me to live away from home?"

"Yes."

TWO MOONS OVER CEDAR HILL

"You want me to meet other... people?"

"Yes." His eyes dropped to her neckline and the necklace that she had never taken off in the year since he had given it to her. He reached out, almost touched the necklace, and then put his hand down at his side.

"Yes. Go away to college, Christina."

"Then what was the point of your being here, Jorgé?"

He laughed. "Maybe it has nothing to do with you."

"You think I'm egocentric?"

"You're *Americana,* aren't you," but he was still smiling.

Just then, without warning, there was a shudder beside them. Jorgé pushed Christina hard, throwing her sideways. She fell into the saw horse, then toppled over it. The force of pushing her sent him crashing in the opposite direction. They both landed well away from the truck as it glided, in slow motion, off of the jack. The frame hit the cinderblocks Jorgé had planted under it just in case of such an accident, then one block cracked, split and the whole truck came down on the ground. Without tires, it hit the soft earth in the barn and sank almost level with the dirt.

Christina slowly picked herself up from the heap she had landed in six feet away from the near disaster.

"Christina? Are you okay?"

She was bruised and scraped, but as soon as she was up, she rushed to where Jorgé was still laying on the ground. He was unscathed too.

"You could have been crushed," she managed to mumble through her shock.

Jorgé looked at the truck and swore. "Ah, mierde." He picked himself up from the ground, went to Christina and put his hands to her shoulders to assure himself she was in one piece. He swiped the dirt from Christina's backside and pulled hay from her hair. "You okay?" He asked again, unconvinced.

"Yeah. You?"

"Si. Not so your truck."

"*My* truck?"

"You don't think I'd be caught dead driving an eye sore like that, do you?"

Christina giggled, a nervous, post-near death experience sort of laugh.

"You see? Fate." His tone was serious.

Christina knew it was fate too.

For no reason that she was aware of, Christina popped a kiss on his cheek, then flounced out of the barn. He reached up and wiped his cheek, leaving an oil smudge, marking the spot.

TWO MOONS OVER CEDAR HILL

Chapter 27

Present day

 Change is the one constant… and yet nothing had changed. Stewart sat on the stone at the end of the driveway, looking up, and then standing when he heard the school bus round the curve in the road and start to slow. He was thirteen years old again and waiting for his own bus to collect him and his sister for school.

 But everything had changed.

 With dramatic *panache,* he re-folded his red-tipped cane and thrust it into his back pocket. The windows on the bus were down, so he could easily hear the conversation on the bus, the small collective and disjointed, "ahhh. Cool. Did you see that?" in response to his kung fu style flourish of his cane, then Tomato's cool, "yeah. That's my Dad. He's got some crazy skills. He's like a blind ninja."

 And suddenly, it was very important to Stewart that he not disappoint this kid.

 "Hey," said Tomato. Something clunked down the bus steps as he disembarked.

 "Need a hand?" Stewart extended his hand and Tomato put a stick into his hand. Stewart ran his hands over the stick to the ends to determine what it was. "Hmm. Lacrosse. You any good at it?"

"I'm okay. I wanted to play junior football, but Mama won't let me. How'd you know I was carrying extra stuff?"

"Crazy blind ninja skills." He smiled to let Tomato know that he wasn't upset about the label. He could sometimes tell when the person he was talking to was nodding or making some other cue that required vision.

"Cool," Tomato said once he recalled that his father could not see him nod.

Stewart used the lacrosse stick in place of his cane to navigate the distance to the grassy embankment beside the driveway and the fence that ran alongside. He heard Tomato pause, then move to that side of the driveway to be near his father.

"Tell me. Is Mrs. Blankenship still teaching math at your school?"

"I don't think so. I've got Mr. Davis for math. Mrs. Davis teaches English. They're married. It's weird."

"Yep. That would seem weird when you're nine years old."

"I'll be ten next month. Are you and Mama married?"

So this was what it was like to be a parent. "No. I'm afraid we didn't get around to that."

"Jorgé's not married either. Grammy said the reason neither one of you married was because of outside interference. I think it was because of Grammy. 'Zat right?"

"Grammy…" Stewart paused. He had never thought of his mother as being a "Grammy", but then he had never thought of himself as being a father. "…she can bear the blame for interfering, but at some point, we have to accept responsibility for our own actions… or inaction."

Tomato was walking on top of the cobble stone edging along the driveway, listening, processing the adult discussion before answering. "You talk like Jorgé."

"Jorgé was kind of like my Dad when I was a kid."

"Why? Didn't you have a real Dad either?"

That cut him in a way Tomato had not intended. "My father, your grandfather, wasn't really around a lot." The irony was not lost on him. "He had another family… and another little boy that I thought kept him occupied. In truth, he probably wasn't around much for his other family either."

Stewart heard Tomato stop walking, so he stopped as well and turned back to the last place he heard Tomato.

"Do you have another family?" Tomato finally asked.

"What? No! No way." Stewart took a step away from the fence. "And until this morning, I didn't know I had this family – you and your Mama. No, Tomato. You're my only… my only son."

He heard one more footfall on the gravel drive before a small hand slipped into his.

"'Zat's what I thought."

Mayella recognized that semi-omniscience was heartbreaking, joyful, and boring. There were few surprises for her anymore. She knew how things would play themselves out and the overriding feeling was tedious. She wanted to go on to a better place, knew she *would* eventually go on, but there was a task yet to complete. She was to escort one more soul from this place.

Jorgé lit the fuse and with a tremendous boom the fire cracker exploded. The dog ran for shelter.

Mayella was a silent, invisible observer from the widow's walk.

"Won't be seeing him for a while." Christina joined Stewart and Jorgé late. They stood in the open field where there would be little danger of a rogue spark setting anything on fire.

"I should have locked him in the house first." Jorgé watched the dog round the bend in the road and high tail it toward the barn.

Christina walked up from behind, her arms crossed over her chest. Mayella recognized her own sweater on Christina's thinner frame. It made her spirit smile.

"That one was for Mayella."

Mayella felt regret.

Stewart draped his arm around Christina's shoulder and she smiled up at him. "Decided to stick around a little longer?"

She shrugged and he dropped his arm. "I've gotta get back soon."

"Beebo was lookin' pretty spry. I don't think he's going anywhere anytime soon."

Jorgé took up another fire cracker and lit the fuse. It sputtered, he stepped back to stand beside Christina, and then it went off with another tremendous explosion. The sound echoed off of the mountains in the distance.

"And who was that one for?"

"That one was for my father." Jorgé wore a contented expression.

He lit the third fire cracker. It exploded.

"And that one was for my *Mama*."

No one knew better than Mayella, the tragic story of Jorgé's parents, how they had come to the U.S. as undocumented migrant workers, finding seasonal work at River's Edge farm next door, long before she and the senior Stewart were married. She knew how the migrant couple had died within a few weeks of each other leaving Jorgé, still just a child, alone in a country with no relatives to claim him.

Because he was also illegal and because Mayella's Stewart had employed them illegally, no effort was made to find his family. Instead, he was kept on to work at the farm. Mayella knew she had much to answer for in the hereafter.

"Do you ever wonder about your family?" Stewart asked.

"*En Cielo, me presumir.*"

"I meant, your extended family."

He nodded. "Sometimes."

"Have you ever considered going back? Trying to find them?"

"Go back where? I wouldn't know where to look. No. This is the home and family fate has assigned to me... us."

"I don't put as much stock in fate as you do," Christina said.

Before Jorgé could protest, a car was heard coming up the drive and they all turned to see who it was.

Stewart spoke. "I'd say fate was playing us all a pretty nasty blow." He knew the sound of that car before anyone else had identified its driver.

The car stopped, the driver switched off the engine and Richard stepped out. Mayella drifted off to sift through the attic vignettes of her life. A woman was already there rifling through her things. She was not a spirit. Treeny wore a pink cardigan, pushed up at the elbows and in a hasty, secretive way, she combed through a box of papers, pocketing some items. Her mouth was set in a hard expression. She might have been pretty if she smiled. Mayella watched her for a few minutes, then drifted from the attic to the temple ruins out back. She knew what Treeny was looking for and she knew she would not find it in the attic.

"Richard?" Christina strode to the side of his car, her hands on her hips. "Who's looking after the shop?"

The territorial invasion was complete when he took her in his arms and kissed her on the mouth. Richard let her go and she took a step back.

"I put up the closed sign, added a note about a death in the family and that you'd be back in a few days." Before she could protest, he cut her off. "No one's going to fall apart for the inability to purchase a blue willow plate or a dog-eared first edition."

"We can't afford to close up for days on end. I'm going to have to get back."

Richard turned an appraising eye toward the house in front of which they all stood. "It doesn't look as though that's going to be a great concern for you anymore, Christina."

Christina turned toward the house, seeing it through Richard's eyes. It was Stewart who brought her attention to Jorgé. Stewart put a hand to Jorgé's arm and Christina saw as Stewart had intuited, the jealousy and territorial set of his hips and shoulders.

"Richard, let me introduce you to… the rest of my family."

Christina propelled Richard toward the front steps of the house. "Jorgé Lopez, this is Richard Lyons, my… our… land lord."

Jorgé took two steps down and Richard took three strides forward leaving a gap too large for either man to shake hands. It was Jorgé who made the added effort and took two more steps down the front steps, forcing him to stand a head shorter than the man from the waterfront town six hours down the coast. He tipped his chin up defiantly.

"Thank you for… looking out for Christina since she's been away. We've missed her."

Richard shook his hand briefly, then turned his attention back to the house. "I'm not sure I've kept her in the manner she's been accustomed."

"I've enjoyed my life these past ten years just fine. And as I earn my keep, you'll excuse me if I don't exactly feel as though I've been 'kept.' I like that the terms were always on the table."

Jorgé nodded, understanding that Christina did not want there to be any confusion over how she had been able to sustain herself for the past ten years.

Jorgé bowed his chin. "Yet nothing comes free, does it?"

TWO MOONS OVER CEDAR HILL

Christina could still feel the burn of Richard's kiss on her lips. She pressed them together hard.

"Richard, what are you doing here?" She turned on him, not intending to sound as peeved as she was.

Richard turned his address to Christina. "I've had this secret fear that once you were home, you might decide not to come back."

"I hope to convince her to stay," Jorgé said.

Richard let that sink in. "I think, Christina, Mr. Lopez has some influence over you. You didn't tell me you had attachments here."

"Christina has always been free to do as she pleases."

Stewart chuckled. "Oh, this is gonna be fun."

"Shut up, Stewart," Christina snapped and turned her back on them all to stomp up to the porch.

"Richard, you're not from this coastal town, I think?" Jorgé asked.

"No?"

"Your accent."

"And you're not from Virginia, I think."

Jorgé laughed, but Christina knew him well enough to know it was not genuine. "No."

Stewart turned to ascend the porch steps, leaving the two competing men to follow in his wake. He reached Christina's side before she made it through the double front door and he whispered. "If there's one thing the blind man knows, it's that if you take a pissing match inside, it's gonna get messy." He didn't need vision to know that his sister glared at him.

TWO MOONS OVER CEDAR HILL

Chapter 28

Jorgé sat behind a beaten up desk in the barn's tack room. One drawer held tools, another, bits of leather and metal retrieved from the riding ring years ago. The top drawer held the farm accounts and it was in this Jorgé attempted to distract himself. But the specter of jealousy kept wafting under his nose.

As he wrote the last check he realized his chest was still puffed. He let out a calming breath, then with a conscious effort, he let out the stomach he had been holding in check – probably since Christina's arrival. It pressed against his belt buckle.

Jealous old fool, he scolded himself. Christina was not an impressionable girl. She made informed decisions about who she chose for friends. For years, Mayella had been telling him that Christina's temporary interest in him was the result of her isolation here on the farm, the absence of a father figure in her life, and to spite a mother whose prejudice was a source of embarrassment.

But Richard Lyons's face was just too pretty to be ignored and he hoped he did not delude himself in believing he was jealous of what the man possessed by way of flashy car and Italian shoes. There was something in his manner that was a façade.

Jorgé returned the checkbook and tickler folder of bills to the top drawer. His stomach rumbled, he supposed aided by his efforts to hold it in, and he headed back to the house for lunch.

The sports car was still in the drive where the younger man had left it. It was too much to hope, he supposed, for Richard Lyons to have left as he had only just arrived a short hour ago. As he walked past, Jorgé looked inside the car through the windows. Clean, waxed and polished – like the man.

In the foyer, he heard their voices coming from the parlor. Christina popped her head around the door facing and unconscious of the effort, Jorgé pulled in his stomach again before turning around.

"Treeny's already started lunch. She just announced it'll be ready in fifteen." She wore a smile and Jorgé wondered if Richard was making her smile or if it was for him.

"I'm just going up to wash. I'll be ready in ten." He took the steps two at a time.

Had he been attentive he might have heard the shuffle in his room. Instead, his thoughts were on Christina. The game was afoot and he had, unconsciously, made himself a contestant. That's why it took him off guard when he opened his door to find he had company. Treeny was seated on his bed.

Beside her, the cigar box was open and in her hand, she held Mayella's second Will. She held it up to him, undaunted by the fact that he had discovered her sifting through his things.

"When were you gonna tell us about this?"

He walked to the side of the bed, his bed for the present, and took the Will from her hand.

"No one need ever know."

"You're gonna let everything be left to the dog?"

"It will go to Chita and her brother – the rightful heirs."

"She left it all to you."

"She left me a choice. Keep it," and he nodded toward the Will, which he began to fold, "or make sure it went to the family."

"You could have kept it and saw that it was equitably distributed!"

"It will be. Mayella's children will inherit."

Treeny snorted. "You'll excuse me if I don't exactly trust her children to see to it the rest of us have some security and keep our home."

"Maybe it was never our home." He shoved the paper into his back pocket. "You don't need to worry about Christina and Stewart. They'll do what's best – what needs to be done."

Chapter 29

  Mayella hovered over the assemblage, taking in the tears shed by her estranged daughter, the lump in Jorgé's throat and the pounding of Stewart's chest.
  Christina did not speak at the funeral. Instead, she sat stiff in a folding chair planted close to the casket.
  Jorgé spoke with difficulty at first, then with strength and assurance, drawing parallels between Mayella's life and its interconnectivity with Cedar Hill. On the whole, Mayella thought his eulogy accurate. When he was finished, he took the vacant seat between Christina and Stewart. Christina looked at him, studying the side of his face as though his was the face of a stranger whose lines she had to learn anew.
  Annabelle sat next to Mayella's grandson. The boy sat between his parents, as he should.
  Mayella drifted off, away from the funeral that was taking place under an outdoor tent. She returned to the house and found herself in the attic. The boards creaked and groaned. There was a man pacing at the top of the attic steps. He was not of this life, yet he hung in limbo, somewhere between living and dead. He looked at her and she understood they were both waiting for some resolution to occur in this time. Mayella smiled and nodded a greeting. He somberly returned her nod of

a greeting before he turned his attention back to the steps. She understood that he was afraid of heights in life, so she walked over to him, took his hand and invited him to sit beside her on the top step. His pants were made of sturdy blue and white striped fabric – like a pillow lining and he was made of hard sinew – when he was alive. Even the fingers in his hands were honed muscle like someone who was used to hard physical labor.

Mayella patted the back of his black hand with her white hand and he leaned closer and put an arm around her shoulder… and together they waited.

In another corner of the attic, Treeny, unaware of her spectral witnesses, sifted through a box. She paused to make a note in a notebook to which she kept referring, then moved on to inspect the next item, again, making another note in her book of notes. Her movements were jittery with nervousness and she occasionally stopped to touch the gold band on her left ring finger as if that was the one thing that kept her grounded.

Twenty-one years ago
Seven year old Stewart slid on his tummy with undulating sides like a snake. It was hard to make your body move forward without using hands or feet and the grass slowed him down, but Jorgé had explained that this was how a snake moved. He had

never seen one before, only felt the one Jorgé gave him to explore.

"Stewart. This isn't a safe game to play here." Jorgé scolded him from the barn. "Come give me a hand."

Jorgé did not scold in the way his mother or father would have scolded him – because it was bad enough to be blind, but to be a blind kid who slithered would have been too weird. Jorgé scolded, because he was concerned for his safety.

Stewart didn't like the smell of tractor oil. "Can I play snake on your porch?"

"That would be safer."

Stewart dragged his body with his hands – no feet – and slithered and pulled himself up the two wooden porch steps, then across the porch of Jorgé's cottage. He wondered how a snake would open a door. He pushed it with his head and the door swung open. Still in slither mode, he squirmed over the floor, through the sitting room and into the bedroom.

Jorgé's house was clean. Stewart moved across the floor and when his head bumped the bed frame, he ducked and like a snake, buried beneath the bed. His hand touched something. A box under Jorgé's bed was intriguing in that it was the only thing under it and that gave it some importance. Stewart pulled it out.

TWO MOONS OVER CEDAR HILL

Stewart Little's Daddy had taken him to see INDIANA JONES last weekend. Cautiously, Stewart raised the lid. "'Ah, asps. You go first, Indie....'"

He sucked air between his teeth as he opened the lid to discover by touch....

Some folded papers of no interest to a little boy who could not see them. He lifted out a crucifix, without knowing what it was called, then a necklace. This was something of value. He felt the ceramic pendant feeling and memorizing the symbol on it. It was strung on... he felt the squareness of it and ran his fingers around the circumference... a piece of raw hide. Stewart tapped the ceramic pendant to his teeth, then touched it with his tongue, like a snake.

"Stewart."

He nearly dropped it.

"Jorgé. You scared me."

"What are you doing there?"

Stewart held up the necklace triumphantly. "I found treasure."

Jorgé walked across the wooden floor, wiping his motor oil stained hands on the front of his jeans as he crossed the room, then the floor creaked as he squatted down beside Stewart Little. Jorgé took the necklace from Stewart, holding it up for inspection.

"It *is* a treasure." He lowered it back into the old cigar box. "But of no value other than sentimental." He closed the lid, took out an oversized rubber band from his breast pocket, and then sealed it shut.

"Is it Mexican?"

"It belonged to my mother."

"Old."

Jorgé slid the cigar box back under his bed. "You can play in my house, but please do not disturb my treasure box."

He stood and moved toward the door.

"Is it really a treasure box?"

"I keep all my most prized possessions there."

"So I found a real live treasure?"

Jorgé nodded. "Sí."

"Cool."

Present day

The space under his mother's bed was clear except for the cigar box. Stewart reached under, pulled it out, snapped off the rubber band fastening, and then lifted the lid off. The original cigar box had been replaced by numerous successors and the paper hinge on this one had long since ripped. The papers that once seemed so unimportant took on new meaning. Stewart pulled them out one at a time for hasty inspection.

A bundle of papers. He took them out, still bound with a rubber band, and put them inside his shirt. His computer optical recognition software would be able to interpret all, but a child's drawing of a horse, signed "Stewart Breeden". He was looking for something concrete that would validate his suspicions with regard to Jorgé's attachment to this farm – and his family.

The next set of papers was newer, attached at the top corner with a staple. He put the papers to his nose and smelled the scent of his mother. As scent often does, it conjured for him a time, ten years ago, when his mother had filled this room, and this house, and this farm.

Because he was intent on remembering his mother, he did not hear the footsteps out in the hall and barely heard the door open behind him.

He knew an instant of guilt when Jorgé cleared his throat.

"I really am going to have to put a lock on my things."

Stewart took the pages away from his nose and held it up by the stapled corner.

"What's this?"

Jorgé quietly closed the gap between them and took the Will from Stewart's hand. Rather than hide it from him again, he sat down on the edge of the bed, fanned the pages, and read them – the letter from Mayella, and the Will – the one leaving the farm, in its entirety, to him.

"You didn't have to share that."

"I did. Treeny found it. Mayella manipulates us from the grave."

"You love her… or you wouldn't have hidden this."

Jorgé shrugged. "I've always loved Chita, but she left anyway."

"You loved her, but just not enough to come after her."

"I would have… if I had known where the two of you were. As it was, I had no choice but to wait for her to return."

"When were you planning on dropping this little bomb?" He took the document from Jorgé's hand and the older man did nothing to stop him.

Jorgé closed the door behind him.

"She might never have known."

"You might have had it all. She left… everything… to you."

"It's not mine. Mayella left two wills. She told me to choose which I would put forward as her last Will, so I left the one, leaving the estate in trust to Christina." He moved toward Stewart and held out his hand for the Will. "This one, I secreted away. I should have destroyed it."

Stewart did not relinquish the Will. Instead, he turned it over in his hands. "You pick the one leaving the entire estate to the damn dog?" Both Wills were notarized, but the one leaving everything to Jorgé was dated a day later. It would take precedence.

TWO MOONS OVER CEDAR HILL

"I thought it preferable that you and Christina retain something of your birthright."

"Christina doesn't think of it like that. Not like it's her due or something."

"I know she doesn't." Angrily, Jorgé strode over to the bed and swept the other baubles that lay on the chenille spread and dumped them back into the cigar box. He hesitated a moment, then dropped the whole box into the bedside trash can.

Understanding finally dawned on Stewart. "You <u>do</u> know her pretty well. You knew she would never stay knowing that the farm wasn't hers to claim. You knew she wouldn't stay unless she had some obligation – even if the obligation is to care for a dog standing on his last leg."

Jorgé said nothing.

"And you, Stewart. She'll stay to share the estate with you… and your son. She doesn't believe in a buried treasure any more than I do, but when the dog is gone, the estate will be hers and yours."

"And you?"

"This is your birthright – yours and Christina's."

"I could never care for this farm in the same way you do, Jorgé."

But Jorgé was shaking his head. "It used to be my home. I cannot stay here… and Mayella has shown me that."

"How? What do you mean?"

Sofie Couch

Jorgé threw up his hands. "And this Richard downstairs? I recall the way he greeted Chita when he arrived and I feel a knife in my stomach, like some old jealous…."

Stewart shook his head. "…like someone who loves her?"

"Did you know I asked her to marry me? Shortly before she left."

"I didn't know. She never said."

"No. She wouldn't have said. She was embarrassed by my offer."

Stewart hesitated, then shook his head. "No. That's not like Christina. She wouldn't be pushed out of her home. She had to be… blackmailed… somehow."

"By your mother… who knew it was wrong."

"I'm not sure." Stewart shrugged. "She always claimed she left, because Mama threatened to fire you if we didn't take over the farm – which is kinda crazy. If we took over the farm, there'd be no reason to keep you on as farm manager. Call me crazy, but I think it had something to do… with Tomato."

Jorgé shook his head. "Christina was as surprised to learn about the child as anyone. I don't think she knew Annabelle was pregnant."

"She didn't know Annabelle was pregnant, but she wanted me away from here for some reason."

"You love Christina," Stewart continued, "but you would risk the farm… everything… just for the chance to keep her from going away again?"

He hesitated just a moment. "Sí."

A grin split Stewart's face. "And they say I took after my daddy, the gambler."

At the same time, they both heard Christina's voice out in the hallway. Jorgé spoke hurriedly in a low voice.

"Will you give me the Will?" He pointed to the document in Stewart's hand.

Stewart folded the paper in quarters, then slipped it into his own back pocket. "No."

"No?"

There was a knock on a door down the hall and Christina called. "Stewart. Are you in there?"

He rose from the bed and poked his head out of the doorway of his mother's old room. "Down here."

"Oh."

Stewart stepped out into the hall and Jorgé followed him, to the visible surprise of Christina and Richard who was on her heels.

"Stewart, do you mind bunking up with Richard tonight?"

Stewart moved ahead of his sister and slapped Richard on the back. "Sure thing, Dick. You bunk up with me. It'll be like a big ol' frat party."

Jorgé stepped out into the hall.

Sofie Couch

"What are you two up to?" Christina asked, looking from her brother to Jorgé.

Stewart patted the papers in his back pocket and answered for him. "Just clearing up a few details with Jorgé. I think we may have found some evidence pointing to the location of the buried treasure."

"Buried treasure?" Richard, who pretended bland indifference, but who took in everything with calculation, lit up.

"Who's up for a treasure hunt?"

TWO MOONS OVER CEDAR HILL

Chapter 30

1862

Llewellyn Thompson half-heartedly joined in the Southern cause. He was to leave for duty within the week. His disgrace would soon be common knowledge and then it would begin to affect the rest of the family. He had voted against secession and that view was becoming almost as popular as freed Negroes in the south. Grace, against her mother's wishes, was to be sent to the girl's boarding school twelve miles away in Charlottesville to separate her from her family's potential disgrace. The other alternative was, of course, to marry her off, but as her father was opposed to that, a compromise was struck. She would return to school through the fall and winter, and be married in the spring. Her father considered this a possibility. Her mother considered it a certainty.

So it simply became common knowledge that in the spring, Grace Thompson would betroth herself to Jack Lyons. This she was able to ignore, but school, and separation from the man she was finding more interesting by the day seemed a punishment.

Grace watched from an upstairs window as her father observed from outside and Salter Lyons supervised the small community of dependents in the annual sorghum molasses production. Everyone came to help and everyone would share in the end product – although not equal to their effort. She felt her attention, her pride in and her smile for Salter turn to him again and again.

He spoke little, but directed the entire operation. In a systematic fashion, the wagon was brought in with the fresh cut sorghum. The stalks were run through a press that was turned by a mule and the sweet juice was collected at the bottom. The children involved were greedy for the juice before it was cooked, but Salter made them wait, showing them, instead, how to gnaw on the crushed canes for remnants of sweet juice.

The cooking pan, the width of a full grown man and the length of two wagons, was positioned on stacks of bricks arranged to give it a slight slope. A low fire was built under the pan and had to be tended carefully to prevent the molasses from burning. The sorghum juice would run back and forth across ridges in the pan, slow cooking all the way to the bottom where it was bottled in salt glazed pottery that had been made and cured in the kiln at the Lyons brick yard.

Grace watched from her upstairs window, noticing for the first time, the cleanliness of the entire process. There was no waste - the cane to be fed to the pigs and when the weather turned cold enough, the same community process to begin again with the slaughter of those same pigs.

TWO MOONS OVER CEDAR HILL

Jack Lyons strode up to stand beside her father. Grace's father was a large man and Jack was dwarfed beside him, like a sorghum cane growing next to corn. She looked for some sign in her father of discontent with Jack, but was disappointed to find none. Her father was amiable enough.

She wondered if amiability was enough to sustain a married couple. Her mother and father were amiable toward one another. She had little experience of and had never witnessed true love. The love in literature seemed to her artificial, so her reading tendencies usually turned more toward the sciences and politics, although if her mother knew what she was reading, she guessed it would have been forbidden.

She had just consumed a treatise on the inability of Negroes to comprehend and the stress that learning would place on their brains and through her indignation she knew the author to have used something less than scientific method to arrive at his conclusions. Salter was a man of unparalleled brilliance. He was an artisan whose circumstances allowed him to build the cathedral, but prevented his preaching from the pulpit. She held her father in the highest esteem, yet he owned slaves. Her loyalty argued that there were "good" slave owners, but her heart knew different.

Grace pulled a wrap from the trunk at the foot of her bed and threw it around her shoulders.

Outside, Jack spoke solemnly to her father, then looked up when Grace came out of the house.

"We will discuss this later," her father answered with a pointed look toward Grace. "And here is my young scholar now."

Since the death of his eldest son at the beginning of the war, Llewellyn Thompson lavished all his affection in his daughter. She was strong and would be the steward to care for the estate when he was dead and buried.

"Mr. Lyons and I were just discussing the merits of tobacco over sorghum. What is your opinion, Grace?"

Grace did not imagine they were only asking her opinion to cover up the fact that they had been discussing her, so she turned her honest attention to the question.

"I confess, I have been watching this process from my window." She turned and cast her gaze upon her upstairs window. When she looked back, she noticed that Salter was looking toward her window too. He quickly bent his head back to the task of scraping the ridges of the sorghum pan with a rounded stick. "I've been marveling over the cleanliness of the process."

Jack laughed. "How genteel of you, Miss Grace, to consider the process and how it relates to the preservation of a fine frock."

TWO MOONS OVER CEDAR HILL

    Grace did not smile and Jack's sudden interest in her frock, especially the bodice, made her self-conscious and uncomfortable. "You are mistaken, Mr. Lyons, on two counts. I am neither genteel nor concerned with the preservation of my frock. I was referring to the process and the economy of both effort, cost and waste. The sorghum harvest and molasses preparation result in maximum yield for minimal effort, virtually none on the part of the land owners," and she looked pointedly at both Jack Lyons and her father. "The yield, if memory serves, is considerable, supplying two homes with enough molasses to see us through the year as well as supplying the laborers with a good ration and more than a little to sell. It is virtually waste free in that the expended cane will be used to feed the pigs which will in turn feed us." She turned toward Salter, who was inconspicuously listening between tending the fire under the pan and scraping the ridges of the pan to keep the molasses from burning. "I would defer to Mr. Salter with regard to whether or not the drain on the land and intensity of the labor is more or less than tobacco."

    Salter looked up, took a tentative step away from the fire, and then cleared his throat. "Less, if you use the pig waste to feed the field. Tobacco work will kill a strong man and drain the land."

    Jack laughed, but without humor. "And there you have it, Mr. Thompson. If we leave the direction of this country to the women and slaves, we'll be swimming in molasses and shiftless Negroes."

Grace stiffened. "I was asked my opinion, Mr. Lyons. I regret drawing Mr. Salter into what has become an ethics debate." She turned on her heel and marched back toward the house.

Back inside, she ran to her window again and could practically hear Jack Lyons as he tried to back his way out of the mire he had just created for himself. Her opinion of him had altered little, but he had answered one question for her. If there was an illiterate among the men in the back yard, she would place her bet on it being Jack Lyons.

Throughout the morning, she found herself returning to the window where she took great pleasure in watching Salter at work. Toward him, she could acknowledge a feeling of great… amiability.

Present day

Richard put his ear to the door and waited until all of the upstairs traffic descended the stairs for lunch. When he was certain he was alone upstairs, he hastily moved across the room, pulled back the curtain at the window and looked out.

A dose of adrenalin surged through his body when he saw it. In a low section of the front field stood a cemetery, its walls guarded by a small iron fence.

TWO MOONS OVER CEDAR HILL

Richard dropped the curtain to fall back over the window and looked around the room in something like panic. At random, he walked to the fireplace mantle and tapped on the trim. His taps were loud and he stopped as quickly, looking to the closed door.

"Think. Slow down." He whispered to himself, knowing they would be expecting him downstairs. He couldn't poke about now… and he, they, had waited a long time for this. There was no rush.

There was a light tap at his door and hastily, Richard tucked his shirt tight into his waist band, took a deep breath, and pulled open the door.

Outside the door, Treeny handed him a notebook. She opened the cover and dropped her index finger to the first line on the first page.

Christina called up the stairs. "Richard? Will you join us for lunch?"

"Starved," he called to Christina, but nodded to the housekeeper, taking the book from her hand. He slid the notebook under one of the two twin mattress, pulled the cover down over it, then turned back to the woman. She was gone.

So Richard left the room casting a look of longing back over his shoulder toward the room that he was going to have to share with Stewart.

Sofie Couch

Chapter 31

The table was pulled out with an extra leaf added to accommodate the holiday proportions seated around it. Christina expected to sit opposite Jorgé at the head of the table which made it more noticeable to her when Richard came in and made himself comfortable at the head. Jorgé entered behind him and did not hesitate to draw out the chair opposite and invite Christina to sit, pushing her chair in for her in a gentlemanly way that was both formal and comfortable. He sat down beside her and she smiled.

Stewart, Tomato, and Annabelle took up an odd number of chairs along one side of the table and on the opposite side, a seventh, odd chair sat empty to Richard's right. This place was set, but Treeny bustled back and forth between the kitchen and the dining room for the extras that had been forgotten. Christina had, over the past ten years, imagined holidays at her mother's as quiet and lacking with only Jorgé and her mother sitting in silence, eating left overs. It somehow made her exile more bearable. She never imagined the family that had grown about them in her absence. What she and Stewart had missed made her stomach feel hollow.

Christina kept a nervous eye on the complete family made up of her brother, her nephew and her…. She had no digestible title for Annabelle other than childhood friend. Tomato was the center of their attention, as it should be, but there was always the potential for Stewart to rekindle his affection for Annabelle. They had a very real bond, literally, between them.

Finally, Treeny was seated. Christina reached for her fork, but Jorgé discreetly put his hand over hers.

Tomato bowed his head and gave a simple offering of thanks. "…and thanks to my Gama for bringing my whole family together."

"Amen." Jorgé, Treeny, and Annabelle repeated in unison. The other three adults sat dumb, then waited for Jorgé to set the pace by taking up the ladle and dishing soup from a tureen into Christina's bowl.

"Daddy's gonna help me start my school project tomorrow," Tomato began, oblivious to the awkward moment.

"Really? So you finally decided on a project for your unit on Egyptology?" his mother asked.

"Well, Daddy helped me come up with an idea. We're going to launch a real archaeological dig."

His mother looked around her son at Stewart and gave him a smile. Christina felt herself begin to squirm. Jorgé wore his pleasure on his contented face.

"Just make sure *you* do the actual work, not your... Daddy."

"That's an excellent project, Tomato," Jorgé encouraged. "This farm is full to bursting with history that's buried just below the surface. Mayella once told me a full regiment of Federal infantrymen camped around the house. They surely left behind some artifacts.

"I've always been interested in that ruined Grecian temple out back. What's the history of that, I wonder," Treeny added to the conversation.

"Daddy told me," Stewart began, "that the temple was started as an example of craftsmanship – a sort of salesman's sample – a selling tool for the skilled masons over at the adjoining farm where they ran a brick yard. The temple was to have a brick lain vaulted ceiling, but the war prevented its completion."

"Do you think there might be something interesting buried around there?" Tomato asked the question of his father.

"Probably more building debris than anything else. Nah. If you want to find some good stuff, we'd do better to look for an old privy or well." He glanced at his sister. "...Or grave."

"A privy? You mean an old outhouse? I don't think I'd wanna dig up anything we'd find down there."

TWO MOONS OVER CEDAR HILL

"Lovely dinner conversation," Christina reprimanded her brother.

The wine, bottled by their cousins who might hope to someday inherit the very table at which they sat, was passed from Jorgé to Christina, to Annabelle, over the head of Tomato, to Stewart, (although he kept his glass close to Tomato with a conspiratorial wink,) Richard, and finally Treeny who seemed to be a settled fixture in the house despite her mother's passing. And for a brief moment Christina thought, to someone standing outside looking in, they might almost look like a normal family. But she knew better.

It was an oddly eclectic grouping for her mother's household that had been ruled by prejudice and a code of Virginian aristocratic snobbery. If ever there was a concrete example of fate having dumped a bunch of inhomogeneous people under one roof, then this was it.

Richard, who was possibly the only person who looked as though he fit at the head of the table in this setting raised his glass.

"If I may be bold…."

Christina thought, even his accent was beginning to fit. She thought she detected a hint of a Virginia drawl. Everyone looked to Richard.

"I believe Tomato was correct in giving thanks to his grandmother - the person who is to credit for bringing us all together. Sadly, I never had the opportunity to meet your grandmother," and here he tipped his glass toward Christina, "but it seems like a wholly democratic and distinctly Virginian atmosphere that I find myself a part of." He bowed his head toward Jorgé as though to point him out as a guest who was lucky to be seated at the table rather than out in the barn.

Christina picked up her glass hastily and raised it. "To my mother's outstanding taste in the company she kept." Christina nodded to Treeny, hoping she felt no slight.

For the first time Christina thought there might be a chance of unifying this family. Then her attention was caught by Stewart who looked over Tomato's head to Annabelle. Annabelle looked back to him and smiled over the rim of her wine glass. Tomato looked from his mother to his father and a smile flickered across his childish face. Christina felt her stomach churn.

TWO MOONS OVER CEDAR HILL

Chapter 32

Mayella felt almost comfortable as she curled up on the bed beside Christina and read over her shoulder. She luxuriated in the feel of the familiar words as they were revealed to her daughter for the first time. She wanted Christina to know her – to understand the motivation behind her actions.

Christina settled deeper into the pillow and pulled the book closer. She was eager for insight and long overdue hard evidence.

There was a knock on the bedroom door and Mayella rose to hover somewhere between the bed and the ceiling. Christina put her hand between the pages of her mother's journal like a book mark and slipped it beside her under the covers. She felt like a voyeur for reading the intimate details of her mother's life, but how else would she ever reconcile herself with the memory of the woman and the hurt she had caused. How else to learn her mother's motivation for sending Stewart away, then inviting him to come back when a threat still existed?

"Come in. It's open."

Jorgé pushed open the door and looked around the corner.

"Is your guest settled for the night?"

Surreptitiously, Christina slipped her hand out of the book and pulled the covers up to her waist to further conceal it.

"He's settled… in with Stewart," she clarified.

Jorgé nodded. "There is no easy way to broach it. I would like to know, Christina, if this arrangement," and he gestured toward her now open door, "is awkward for you… and Richard."

"What's to feel awkward about," she rushed.

"You were away a long time. I wasn't so foolish as to think you might not have made… other attachments."

"Richard and I are not attached."

Jorgé nodded, but looked unconvinced. "He would seem to think otherwise."

"You're referring to dinner. I'm sorry. That was a snotty thing for Richard to say".

Jorgé shrugged. "I *am* the hired help."

Mayella pushed the corner of a straight back chair out from the wall an extra inch. Jorgé looked around, spotted the side chair and made himself comfortable there.

"Hardly."

"Technically."

Christina shifted, sitting up higher in the bed and pulling the covers up with her. When she looked at him again, he was staring out the night black window.

"I saw the orchard today. It's beautiful."

Jorgé looked back and smiled. "Mayella called them our children."

"Hmmm." Christina ran her finger along the creases in the blanket bunched at her waist. She wondered if she and Jorgé would ever find the easy affection they had known before they parted. "You know, Richard just feels... threatened by you."

His mouth turned up at one corner. It was a playful smile that Mayella had seen infrequently and Christina hadn't seen in over a decade.

"It must be my good looks..."

Christina smiled.

"He sounds like a jealous lover."

"He's not, you know. A lover, I mean."

"It's none of my business."

"He's not."

"It's just that, since he arrived, you've seemed uneasy."

"Yeah, well, Richard has that sort of effect on me."

"Ah." Jorgé nodded.

"No. Not 'ah'."

Mayella felt the need to intercede, but at that moment, the dark skinned man from the attic came down the steps. On his shoulders he carried a large steamer trunk.

"Where are you going with that?" Mayella called after him, but he didn't answer. He glanced over his shoulder and looked right through her. "I'm talkin' to you!"

The man kept moving, so Mayella followed, although she suspected she knew where he was going with it.

"It's good... healthy... for you to have... made friends while you were away."

"I didn't make friends," she refuted.

"Then that's just sad," and again, that playful grin tugged at the corner of his mouth.

Christina smiled and looked down at her hands that were now folded in her lap. "And you?"

"Me?"

"Did you... make friends... while I was away?" In her absence life had gone on. She had been the only one caught in the ten year emotional time warp. In her absence he had been able to form an attachment with her mother, despite her blatant prejudice, and with the housekeeper, who seemed very comfortable throughout dinner sitting on his left side. He had a familial relationship with Tomato and treated Annabelle like a daughter.

"When you were away, the heart left this house."

"Lucky thing you had Mama... and she had you."

Jorgé nodded. "Mayella's heart was broken... too."

"Is that my fault?"

TWO MOONS OVER CEDAR HILL

He tilted his chin up as though he was fortifying himself to argue a point. "I asked you to marry me once, but for the wrong reason. I blame only myself. I won't make that mistake again."

Christina dipped her chin in thought. That it was a "mistake" was all she heard

Ten years ago

"Why are you going away, Chita?"

"Stewart's going away. Mama's sending him away. He needs someone."

"That's between your mother and Stewart."

"I need him."

Jorgé grabbed her by her upper arms. "*I need you.*"

Christina backed away from him and he let her go. "You don't need me. You need this farm. You want this farm."

"That's crap Mayella's been feeding you."

"Then come away with me."

His expression faltered. Longing turned to something like panic. He shook his head. "Leave our home? Christina, this argument is between your mother and your brother. Don't let them pull you into it."

"I'm all he has now. Mama sent Annabelle away – paid her off and she took the money over Stewart. Now Mama's cut him off."

"He's a big boy. He can take care of himself and don't you see? If you stay here you can make her come around. But if you leave with him, Stewart's got no reason to come back. This family can't be broken apart." He sounded desperate.

"Then you won't come with me?"

"Marry me."

Christina caught her breath.

"I know. I'm too old for you."

Christina found her smile and stepped into his arms. He held her stiffly, awkwardly. She wrapped her arms around his waist and it didn't matter if her mother saw them or not. She had threatened to fire Jorgé so often her threat no longer held any water. She could feel her mother watching them from an upstairs window.

"I've been asking *you* to marry *me*… for a year."

"And I've been telling you for years that I'm too old for you. My marrying you would be for all the wrong reasons but I give up. Marry me. Your mother can't write off both of her children at once." He waited.

Christina, with her face buried in his chest, held her breath a moment.

With hesitation, she whispered. "You would do that… rather than leave Cedar Hill? You'd do that to save Mama being left alone… even though it's by her own doing?" Her heart froze.

TWO MOONS OVER CEDAR HILL

"I'd marry you... if it kept you here... and prevented this family being split up." He held her tight as though she might slip away.

"You'd make that... sacrifice?" Slowly, she took her arms from around his waist and he, more slowly, loosened his hold on her too.

When he looked at her face, the outward expression of realization came slowly as he pieced together what he had said and how she had interpreted it. He shook his head. "That's not what I meant, Christina."

But she shook her head and took another step back. "You look after Mama... and this farm." She took a second and a third step back. "I'll look after Stewart."

Present day

"I don't blame you for leaving... anymore."

Christina fidgeted and traced the crazy quilt design covering her lap. "I had to leave. I had to make sure Stewart didn't come back."

"Why? And why are you trying to get him to leave with you now?"

"I... can't... tell you... yet."

He sighed. "And I won't push."

"You were happy here though? With Mama?"

He startled her by throwing a hand into the air and rolling his eyes to the ceiling. "Mayella. She had changed little... until the end. She looked the same, probably, as she did ten years ago when you left, but her heart changed." He shrugged and leaned back, pushing the chair back on two legs against the wall. "Your mother began to throw off her air of untouchability. I think she had learned that keeping everyone at a distance hurt her the most. She began to let people in… a little."

"She let you in?"

"She began to show her pretty side."

Christina found her smile and looked up at him. "Did you think she was pretty?" Christina crossed her arms over her chest feeling suddenly like an exposed ugly duckling.

"Mayella?"

"Did you find Mama attractive?"

Jorgé opened his eyes wide. With one arm across his chest, he rested his other elbow on his arm and rubbed his chin pensively.

"Beauty lies within."

"Yeah, yeah. You're avoiding the question. Did you find her attractive?"

He was smiling behind his hand. "Attractive? Yes. Like a puddle of stagnant water is attractive to a mosquito. Beautiful? No."

Christina nodded, no longer looking at him, but down at her folded arms. "I've always been told that I look like Mama. And I'm okay with that, but I won't *be* like her."

TWO MOONS OVER CEDAR HILL

"You don't look like Mayella." He was adamant. "Well, okay, there is a similarity."

"And you've never been a purveyor of false flattery. I was constantly told how much we looked alike."

He scowled. "You are… easy on the eye… as your mother would have said."

As her mother *had* said, about him. Christina rolled her eyes. "I'm not trawling for compliments, either."

"You *are* different from both your mother and your father – on the inside. What made you think such a thing? You bear a strong physical resemblance to your *mamá*, but where she allowed suspicion and deception to tarnish her outward appearance, yours glows."

He was sitting back in the chair, tipping it back on two legs, but suddenly, he let the chair tip forward at the same time coming out of it and he kissed her on the forehead, then he laughed, shook his head and kissed her again, this time on the mouth. "Majo cara."

As suddenly, he turned and left, closing the door quietly behind him.

Christina stared after him until she heard his door across the hall close. Her hand went to her mouth and behind her fingers, her mouth turned up into a smile – probably for the first time in ten years.

Sofie Couch

Mayella stood at her bedside, looking down on her daughter, incapable of offering advice or encouragement. It was because of her misrepresentation of the facts that Christina had left and no one knew better than Mayella what her daughter had sacrificed by leaving. Now, it was time to make amends.

TWO MOONS OVER CEDAR HILL

Chapter 33

Treeny pinched her nose, stifling a sneeze as dust drifted out of the packet of old postcards and letters. She knew more about this family's history than her own. Indeed, it should have been her own. Her name should have been Breeden, but for Mayella's pig headedness over granting her late husband a divorce.

The impulse to sneeze passed and she released her nose, using both hands to hastily sort through the papers. Behind her were the boxes, crates and barrels she had already sifted through. Half the attic sorted, the other half to go.

But the going would be easier now that she had Richard here to help her. She couldn't bear the possibility of not finding some evidence here in the attic and she was certain, before her passing, Mayella had found something.

She put the postcards into the box behind her and reached for the notebook at her side. A yellowed, brittle piece of paper fell from the book.

Receipt for Taxes pd. (1859)
2 Horses   *$4*
3 casks Whiskey   *$3*
5 negroes (3 men, 2 women)   *$2.50*

The attic floor boards directly over Christina's bed creaked and groaned. She had slept poorly the entire night, so waking at dawn was little inconvenience. She sat up, listened, then pulled on a sweater over her gown and quietly padded out of the room. She looked in through the open door of her mother's room where Jorgé had slept. The bed was made. He was always up early.

The attic door also stood open at the end of the hall and Christina only hesitated a moment before padding up the dusty steps.

On the other side of a box full of artificial Christmas tree, she saw the top of a head.

"Stewart? What are you doing up this early?"

He jumped and yelled. "Sheesh, Christina. You nearly scared the life out of me. What are *you* doing up this early?"

"You're rioting directly over my head. You sound like a herd of elephants."

Stewart felt around the floor boards, picked up a bundle of papers that were tied up with packing string, and handed them to Christina. "There could be answers right here, in my hands and I wouldn't know it. Did Mama throw away anything?"

She heard frustration in her brother's voice, and the one thing he never did, was to display frustration over his visual impairment.

Christina untied the thick string that was around the bundle. It snapped with a little dusty poof before it came undone. Christina glanced at the first three papers, then stopped with the third in her hand.

"Holy sh…. Look at this, Stewart."

"Yeah. Put that closer to my face so I can see that, will ya?"

Christina frowned. This was not the Stewart she knew. She read the receipt aloud. "Receipt for Taxes. '"Whiskey', with a capital 'W', '…$3. slaves…' with a lower case 's', '…$2.50.'" Gently, Christina passed the receipt to the back of the pile and filtered through the rest of the 19th Century household accounts. She found a bill of sale. "'Sold to Mr. C.D. Lyons, 1-female, African, in exchange for wagon of bricks.'" The signature at the bottom was illegible.

Christina sat down on the floor mindless of the dusty destruction to the seat of her gown.

"I wonder… how many people were enslaved here."

Christina was pensive.

"Did you know, it's only been since Jorgé that the farm has been profitable? When Mama married Daddy, they put both farms in both of their names, but it's been Jorgé who made them a success."

Her mind was on Jorgé and her mother and the legal bond that might have been when she supplied without thought, "River's Edge and Cedar Hill."

Sofie Couch

"What do you remember of the stories about the family treasure?"

Christina sighed, laying down the bundle of sad evidence of a less than laudable history. She drew up her knees and wrapped her arms around them. "Probably less than you do. I remember Mama and Daddy arguing about it. Mama didn't like to tell it, because Daddy would tease that he was going to dig up the family plot. The story goes that during the Civil War, homes were being raided and relieved of their valuables by the Union Army. So when the family heard of the imminent invasion of River's Edge, they buried everything of value out in the cemetery. The expectation being that no one would dig up a fresh grave. After the end of the war, no one could remember where the stuff had been buried… if you believe that."

"Why shouldn't I believe it?"

"You really believe they would just lose track of where it was buried? Either, one," she held up a finger, "someone dug it up long ago and two, it was of no value or three, it's long gone – spent, or four, there never was a treasure buried and it's been a great story to tell children before they fall asleep."

"Or five," Stewart continued, "it was buried, but whoever buried it died in the war before it was recovered or before he could tell anyone else where he buried it."

TWO MOONS OVER CEDAR HILL

"Well, you can rest certain it wasn't buried in the cemetery. Someone would have found it by now."

"Do you remember anyone ever looking for it? I mean *really* looking?"

"What would they do, Stewart? Dig up all of our ancestors? I recall Daddy saying one time he went out with a metal detector, but everything out there set it off. It's damp, so they planted the two old willows, then ferns grew up underneath. He said the ferns that are growing out there likely have a high lead content that sets off the metal detector as soon as you switch the thing on."

"Yeah. I remember going out there with Daddy and his metal detector. I think he did it to annoy Mama."

"More than likely. He had no intention of digging it up. He was just entertaining you and pissing her off at the same time."

Footsteps could be heard coming up the attic steps and Christina looked up while Stewart cocked his ear in that direction. It was Richard's head that rose out of the floor.

"I thought perhaps the house was haunted."

"Sorry. Hope we didn't wake you."

Richard ascended the remaining steps, then looking around, he gave a long low whistle. "Jackpot."

Sofie Couch

Christina looked around the attic, this time with Richard's perspective.

"Plug me in to E-bay. You're sitting on a fortune."

Like a protective mother, she slipped the bundle of receipts under the hem of her gown. It was her history, her past, and like it or not, she wouldn't see it, like the people it represented, sold for profit.

TWO MOONS OVER CEDAR HILL

Chapter 34

Their voices filtered across the frost covered soy bean stubble. "You're sitting on a small fortune, just in antiques, Christina. With my help we could have this stuff sorted and sold in no time. You can be rid of it all that much faster and return home." Richard looked back to the Southwest Mountain Range. "And that's not even counting the sizeable fortune in timber."

Jorgé, hands shoved deep in his pockets as he moved from the barn back toward the house where others were just beginning to stir, felt his jaw tighten. He had to consciously relax. "You're looking at one of the largest stands of old growth forest in the state of Virginia," he called over amiably.

Richard waited until he was within a few feet before responding. "Old growth doesn't pay the bills – unless it's cut and milled."

Jorgé smiled. "It would be short-sighted to clear cut. Stew Senior wanted to do that for fast cash, but I was able to convince Mayella of the benefit of keeping the forest intact, but prudently selling select trees."

"She seems to have put quite a bit of faith in you."

"We fought – often." But the smile on his lips intimated that it was not always unpleasant.

Stewart, having just come out of the house, caught up with the conversation. "Jorgé is family. We trust his judgment where the land is concerned." Christina came within hearing and he turned to her. "Tomato and I are going to start looking for the treasure today when he gets off the bus."

"Are you gonna drag Tomato around this farm like Daddy dragged you, hoping to turn up a treasure?"

"You don't need to believe in me, Christina. You just need to satisfy the terms of Mama's will so I can keep looking."

She turned on Jorgé. "And you're not helping matters – indulging him."

Jorgé threw up his hands, eyes wide in innocence. "It's a great way to bond with his son."

"Mama's still manipulating us."

"I don't think so, Christina. I think we'll all eventually see that it's about her love for you and Stewart."

"Is this how she was showing her love for you? By leaving everything to the dog?" Christina looked over at the dog, who had taken up his old role of following Stewart around the farm.

Jorgé took a deep breath, very conscious of the fact that Christina's boyfriend was taking in every word of their ongoing family squabble. He was about to respond when Stewart cut him off.

"I have proof that the treasure is real."

TWO MOONS OVER CEDAR HILL

She stopped and turned. Richard too was all ears.

Stewart made his way down the steps where Jorgé stood at the bottom. "Follow me." He popped open his red-tipped cane and moved, almost faster than Christina was comfortable walking, and headed off down the driveway.

At the gate, he pulled off the chain, then moved out, across the now crushed stubble where mourners had paid their respects just the day before, and he led his sister, Richard, and Jorgé back out to the iron gated cemetery. There, he opened the rusty gate and moved around the stones, feeling them with his cane until he stopped at the last stone in a line of pock marked headstones.

"Does this look familiar to anyone?"

Although he spoke to Christina, he tipped his head toward Jorgé. Jorgé swallowed the sudden lump in his throat. Was it familiar? The double moon, single star design was imprinted upon his own heart and on the pendant that Christina wore over her own heart.

Chapter 35

As Jorgé had done the first time he saw the tombstone, Christina fell to her knees and lay her hand on the stone. From the stone, she looked up at Stewart, then Jorgé.

"Does it look familiar?" Stewart asked.

From the neck of her blouse, she fumbled for the chain, then pulled out the medallion with its matching design.

"It matches, doesn't it? Mama made the connection."

"What *does* this mean?" But her question was directed at Jorgé.

Richard stepped forward to better see the pendant. "Hey, it's the same."

Christina looked down at the necklace, then dropped it back inside her blouse. "Yes. It's the same." Then to herself, "how could I have missed this?" She ran her hand across the stone again. "It's been here all these years."

"Your mother told me, it was from my mother. She gave it to me, she said, to return it to its rightful home."

"And you, in turn, gave it to me, as a sign of trust."

"It was going back to its rightful home, only I didn't know it represented your family, rather than mine."

TWO MOONS OVER CEDAR HILL

Richard moved around them to study the design on the stone. "It looks – odd. It's not a traditional gravestone design. It looks... African."

"... Not Mexican," Christina supplied.

"No. It's definitely African. Look." Richard knelt on the ground beside her, taking the medallion into his hand, draping the other arm across her shoulders. He ran his thumb over the primitive design. "The moon is masculine. The star feminine. Two moons and one star – two men, one woman."

Stewart tipped his hat to Richard with uncommon respect. "You know more stuff."

Richard shrugged. "Yeah. It's what I do. Stuff." He rose from his friendly position next to Christina.

Stewart snapped his fingers. "Of course. That makes sense." And he knelt down beside the grave again. "The family wouldn't desecrate the grave of a family member to hide the treasure. But they might dig up the grave of a slave."

"Was Grace Thompson a slave?" Christina asked.

"It could be a false grave," Jorgé finally contributed.

"And plant a phony head stone," Christina whispered. "With a phony name and a phony design." She met Jorgé's eyes, looked down at the medallion in her hand, and then tucked it back inside her blouse. She rose and headed out of the graveyard.

Although Stewart was excited by the discovery and more excited by vocalizing his hypothesis and meeting with consensus, he did not lose sight of what this could mean to Christina who seemed to have no love for this place."

"You had better go after her," Stewart said to Jorgé.

Richard seemed suddenly disinterested in Christina.

"Why did you do this, Stewart?"

"She was going to find out sooner or later."

"Later would have been better – after I'd had a chance to try and explain it to her."

"Maybe you could explain it to me, Jorgé."

"I didn't know."

Stewart took Jorgé's elbow. In a softer tone, he asked, "how could you not know that the necklace you gave my sister was actually one of our own family heirlooms?"

Jorgé took a deep breath. "I didn't know, because Mayella lied to me about its origin. *She* gave me the necklace, a few years after I came here. She told me it was my mother's – that my mother had given it to her as a token of appreciation when she worked here as a housekeeper. Mayella said, after my parents died and I was left here, an illegal immigrant with no papers and no family, that it should be returned to me. It was the only link to my family – my heritage – that I possessed, so it had a value beyond money. I had no idea it had no connection to my own past."

Stewart ran his hand over his unshaven chin. "How long have you known."

"Only since the day Mayella died. I found her – there." He pointed to Grace Thompson's grave.

Stewart looked him in the eye, his mouth falling open and his hand falling from his chin. "Wait. Mama died here? In the cemetery?"

"On this very grave."

"Somehow, she walked or crawled from the house to this spot. She died there. Here she took her own life before it could be taken from her." He looked back toward the grave. "On that very spot."

As if she were still lying there, a chill ran up Jorgé's spine.

"I had to tell Christina, Jorgé. Richard's been working on her – trying to talk her into selling the place. She'd lose everything. I'd lose everything. But now she'll stay."

"I'm not sure, Stewart."

Stewart nodded toward the house. "You go on. Talk to her. Tell her about the necklace – how it came into your possession. She'll stay."

Jorgé started toward the house, then stopped and turned back toward Stewart. "I won't let her leave again. I'll go away myself before I let that happen again." He moved off toward the house.

And Stewart knew he had done the right thing.

TWO MOONS OVER CEDAR HILL

Chapter 36

1864

Grace hiked up her skirt and goose stepped over the bramble and down a steep embankment. She had had to sneak out of the house in order to get into the woods without proper undergarment, but cumbersome clothing and dense vegetation went at odds with one another.

She heard the spade striking wet slurpy clay from the top of the hill and her heart swelled. For two days, she had been looking for an opportunity to meet Salter on his own and today was her last chance as she would be leaving shortly. She slowed down when she reached the edge of the clay pit. Salter had his back to her and his shirt off. Muscle rippled across his shoulders with each thrust of his spade. She cleared her throat.

Salter whirled around.

"Grace. What are you doing out here?"

He rushed to pull on his shirt and she averted her eyes until he had finished covering himself.

"Looking for rabbit. What do you think I'm doing out here? I came to see you."

He wiped his muddy hands on a tuft of grass that was growing on the embankment, then wiped them down the legs of his pants. They were rusty red with clay.

"How'd you know I'd be here?" He walked toward her, stopping a respectable distance.

"I saw the smoke from the kiln yesterday. The fire was out today, so I figured it must be time to start a new batch of brick."

He looked over his shoulder. "I got most of a load." A sturdy looking cart was half loaded and another large canvas bucket sat full on the hillside, ready for dumping onto the cart. A scrawny mule stood at the front of the cart, content to wait for his turn at toil.

"You mighta missed me."

"I'm going away soon," she said.

"I know."

She took a step closer to him, closing the gap of decency, although that gap had been breached the moment she came into the woods.

"You know? How?"

"I got ears. Jack been trying to talk your daddy out of sending you."

Grace clenched her jaw. "Just 'cause he's got no use for school…."

"My Mama used to tell me, regrets are for fools who didn't try. That's one thing I'm sorry I never got a chance to try."

"You'd have made a good scholar."

He smiled. "But how can I regret doing something that mighta taken me away from my home."

Grace did not understand. "You wouldn't have liked going to school?"

"I like working the land." He tipped his head toward the clay pit. "Not digging holes in it, nor cutting it down to run a brick oven. I like when it all evens out."

Grace smiled. "Like Daddy. He doesn't like what Jack is doing to his farm."

Salter shrugged. "Ain't but one man. He can't do but so much damage, then the land will heal itself."

"It's ten men. Four slaves, six white servants."

"'id you know it was my family that started all this?" Salter looked around the woods, as though he could see a long way off.

"How so?" Grace looked around, then tucked her skirt under and sat down on the leaves.

"They come here knowing how to make bricks. When they was brought here – bought - they had to build their own house. I was told, where they come from, 'twas all dirt. Nothing but clay to work with, so that's what the houses was made out of. Well," he looked slyly at Grace and grinned. "That and cow shit."

"Cow...." She laughed, putting a hand over her mouth.

"Yeah. They used to mix it with the dirt, dry grass, and water. They'd bake it in the sun a couple days, then cook it in a big ol' oven they'd made out of the same stuff. I guess you could say they lived in a brick shit house."

Grace's laughter rang through the trees. Salter chuckled alongside her, finally making himself comfortable on the ground beside her. Slowly, she sobered again.

"Are you afraid of going off to school, Grace?" He did not call her, "Miss Grace" and the informality suited them both.

She nodded. "A little."

"I'd be afraid if it was me having to leave home."

"You would? I wondered if you meant to run away and join the Yankees."

Salter smiled again as if she had told a joke. "It's cold up there."

"So you won't go away and leave me?"

His smile vanished. "I ain't going nowhere."

"You don't seem overly happy about staying."

He looked her in the eye. "I'd be happy if things was different. Everybody's restless."

"We're at war."

"That might have something to do with it."

"What else could it be?"

He looked her in the eye. "You."

"Me?"

"Coming out here, on your own, for no better reason than to sit in the leaves and talk about looking for rabbits."

TWO MOONS OVER CEDAR HILL

"I told you, I wasn't really looking for rabbits. I came looking for you."

"Yeah. You coming out here on your own... looking for me."

"You don't want me to come see you?"

He was silent.

"I can go away." She jumped up and brushed the leaves off of her skirt, but with no desire to leave.

He stood up more slowly.

"That'd probably be best."

She spun back around. "I don't want to go away."

"I don't want you to go away."

Neither one moved.

"Then where do I go from here?"

He felt himself being drawn to her and cared little for what he might do afterwards, but in that instant, he wanted only to kiss her. For once, he ignored years of caution.

Grace leaned toward him, turning her face up at an angle to match his descending face and somewhere in the middle, their lips met and touched. It was soft, almost non-contact, yet it exploded in her body like nothing she had ever felt before. Waves of sensation rolled through her chest and stomach... and beyond.

She opened her eyes only to see Salter starring off into the woods.

Sofie Couch

Grace spun around to see what he had seen. "What? What is it?"

Salter put his finger to her lips. She closed her eyes again.

"Don't know. Thought I heard something." He put his hand to his heart. "Lord. That scared me." He laughed, then looked back down at her.

"It sure didn't scare me," she whispered up at him.

He took a step back. "I'll give you a ten minute head start out of the woods. You can't be seen coming out with me."

Grace furrowed her brow, but nodded.

"I won't see you for a long while after today."

He nodded. "I know. I'll keep an eye on your window though. I'll know when you're back from school."

Grace stood on her toes, and planted another soft kiss at the side of his mouth. He tasted of sweat and mud. She licked her lips, turned and started up the hill without him.

"Wait a minute."

She stopped and turned. Salter was taking something out of his shirt. It was a necklace – crude – made of a strip of leather knotted at the ends with a clay medallion hanging from it.

He handed it to Grace.

"I don't know what it means. My mama gave it to me. She said her Granny's mama brought it with her…. It's come with her from Africa, so it's old."

Reverentially, Grace took the necklace from him, kissed it, then slipped it over her head.

Salter closed the gap between them and with equal reverence, wrapped his large hand around the leather strip, closing it tight around her neck. With his other hand, he ran his finger across her collar bone and tucked his finger inside the neck of her blouse.

Grace gasped. He looked her in the eye, then dropped the medallion down her blouse. He brushed the neckline closed, tucked the leather cord inside her collar behind her neck, then took a step back.

"I think that's what I was supposed to do with that necklace."

Grace put her hand to her blouse, feeling the molded shape of the rough kiln dried clay beneath. She turned away before Salter could see her cry.

From the top of the ridge, Jack Lyons pressed his back into the tree where he had found cover. He had imagined catching up with Grace when he saw her slip into the woods. His fantasy was dashed and replaced by jealousy when her unfaltering steps took her directly to the clay pit where Salter was working. Jealousy was replaced with hatred when she and Salter kissed.

Chapter 37

Present day

Whether due to the precarious arrangement of a stack of papers that had been left in the attic, or the settling of an old house or the unsettling of old spirits, the crate that was balanced on top of an old oil drum tilted. The papers on top slid off with a rush, then the crate itself followed suit resulting in a dust disturbing crash on the old, pine, attic floor boards.

Christina, already on her way upstairs, heard the disturbance. She looked briefly toward the attic door. She would have gone on to her room, but the sound of someone coming into the house below made her rush toward the attic door. She knew it was Jorgé and she couldn't face him now, knowing what she knew.

"Christina?" Jorgé called from below.

She did not answer, but closed the attic door behind her and tip toed up the steep steps. The treads creaked and popped with each step, giving her away.

Dust motes rose up in front of the small semi-circular windows at two of the four gables. Mayella sat on the floor beside the tumble of papers. With palms up like a "ta-da" girl on a game show, she presented the mess to Christina.

TWO MOONS OVER CEDAR HILL

Christina stopped to listen to Jorgé ascending the main stairs below, then busied herself with re-stacking the papers on top of the crate. The door at the base of the attic steps groaned open.

"Christina. Come down, please."

She continued re-stacking, making a messy job of it, then picked up the metal lid to the oil drum as Jorgé reached the top of the attic steps.

"Let me explain."

Christina shook her head. She put the lid back on the oil drum, hammered it on tight with her fist, and then saw a book she had neglected to return. She picked it up and held it like a shield.

Mayella smiled.

"That's why you didn't want it back?"

Jorgé laughed and the sound rang hollow against the eaves. "Your *Mamá* gave me that necklace, but her motives she took with her to her grave. She told me what I, in turn, told you. That it was my mother's, left to her keeping."

"I had my reasons," Mayella whispered.

"But you weren't surprised when Stewart found the image on the stone. You knew."

"I've known now… since the day Mayella died."

Christina shook her head and turned away from him. "But surely you know why she gave it to you?"

"Mayella had motives I'm not sure any of us will ever understand. I remember the day she gave me the necklace. I was just a boy. You and your brother were little, barely more than babies, your father was living at the other house – before it was destroyed in the fire."

"How old were you?"

He shrugged. "Teenager? I was driving. Didn't have a license, of course." He grinned and looked at her, then sobered. "I was still undocumented in this country." Moving around the attic, he paused to pick up an old bundle of papers, then replace them. He ran his hand along the angled ceiling overhead. "I had accepted this place as my home. I no longer missed my family. But out of the blue one day, Mayella presented me with the necklace. She said my mother who used to clean the house, had given it to her for safe keeping. She said it had been handed down through my family for generations and that it should be given to me as a link to my own heritage." He turned back to Christina. "I thought at the time it was a very big gesture on Mayella's behalf considering her blatant bigotry."

Christina wrapped her arms around herself.

"You're biting your lip. What do you know?"

Christina unclenched her top teeth from her lip. Only slowly did she look him in the eye. "I know about you… and Mama."

TWO MOONS OVER CEDAR HILL

Jorgé smiled. "Yeah. That would explain it." When she did not answer, he sobered, shaking his head. "You're not serious."

"If it was mutual… you don't have to keep secrets from me, Jorgé. I'm not a child."

Jorgé shoved one hand in his pocket, a gesture reserved for those infrequent times when he felt uncomfortable.

"What are you talking about, Christina? Me and Mayella?"

"I guess I've always known she was in love with you. And what are any of us supposed to think, Jorgé? I come back after ten years and you're living in the house, in her old room. You've been taking care of her, physically, for months prior to her death…."

He was not dumbstruck any more. He was angry and his voice rose to reflect it.

"How can you, of all people, think such a thing, Christina? And based on… what? Proximity? I made my feelings for you clear before you left – against all good reason - and still you did leave… without a word of where you were for ten long years. For ten years, I've waited for you to grow up - to throw off whatever control Mayella had over you. And now that you're back, this is what I learn you've thought of me all this time?"

"You asked me to marry you once. You'd rather do that than leave this farm. How am I supposed to know what you'd do to keep your home?"

Jorgé's jaw opened, then he snapped it shut. He had to take a deep breath before he could continue. "*Our* relationship was *not* indecent." He wagged a hand back and forth between them. "This thought of me and Mayella though? *That's* indecent."

The messily stacked papers on the crate slipped and half of them slid onto the floor again.

"Careful, Mama didn't like that."

In an unprecedented fit of pique, Jorgé smacked the rest of the stack with the back of his hand, sending them raining down on the attic floor. He turned and noisily descended the attic stairs.

Christina stood with the book still clenched in her hands. She was shaken and she began to doubt what she previously thought was a given – that her mother's motivation for sending her away with Stewart was so she and Jorgé might be left alone together. Had her mother been more jealous of her attachment to Jorgé than prejudiced?

Holding the book at her chest, Christina rushed down the attic steps after him.

"Jorgé. I'm sorry."

He would not answer, but was in the front hall and slammed out of the front door almost before she had maneuvered the last awkward attic step.

TWO MOONS OVER CEDAR HILL

Deflated, she turned to her room, remembered the book she was still holding and tossed it on the small hall table by the attic door.

Sofie Couch

Chapter 38

Richard looked both ways in the upstairs hall, then picked up the old journal laying on the table by the attic door. He flipped the pages and guessed it might bring a couple bucks on E-bay. He took the book back to his room, then measured the minutes until the house was quiet, when everyone would be asleep.

March 18:
I have seen the Union officers below my very window. Martha Stalwart says I have behaved poorly and there are sure to be repercussions, but I found myself unable to contain my anger. One officer in particular goaded the crowd that gathered on the street below. It was a peaceful surrender of the town, but even so, the officer in question tore down our flag and waved it in a jeering fashion as he rode by. I was so overcome with outrage, that I did raise the window of my room and shake my fist at him.
I have told no one here at school about the fate of my dear father, yet everyone seems to know that he has been taken prisoner. He is held pending his signing a letter of affiliation. Father refuses, thank goodness, but I pray he is being well treated. Certainly, his political activities are a point of record and he will be kindly treated because of his refusal to vote in favor of secession. I pray.

TWO MOONS OVER CEDAR HILL

Richard looked again at the outside cover of the book. It was old and old diaries could bring some nice coin to a collector through the internet. Diaries that discussed daily life during the Civil War were often worth more than a little coin if they exposed something of historical significance.

He heard the toilet down the hall flush, so he still had some time to kill before everyone was asleep. In the bed next to him, Stewart snored. Richard turned back to the pages of the book.

March 19:
Margaret Stalwart was sent to stay in another room. I am on disciplinary probation pending further action. The horrible Union officer did mention my misconduct to the minister, who instructed his wife to pay a visit to our headmistress. I feel the insult acutely. I am persecuted because of my father's situation. The minister has suggested, through his wife, that I be sent home before I bring greater shame to the girls' school.

April 3rd:
Do I add to my family's shame? I cannot resist the pull of this man. He insists that there is little hope of our ever being happy – such a union never finding a home, but I cannot agree. Is it love that makes me unrealistically optimistic? I see myself, someday, as mistress of my home. Certainly, then, we might find some happy balance.

Sofie Couch

I am an evil child, unfaithful daughter. My happiness rests on the prospect of the eventual demise of my dear parents. Yet, where else could Salter and I ever find happiness? A foreign island, perhaps? I could not take him away from this place. It is his devotion to the land that I find most compelling yet it is this home, this society that separates us. I move between overwhelming elation, discontent and weeping. I am overwhelmed with joy when I think of him. I am discontent with current circumstances that force us to hide our love. I weep when I consider the improbable outcome of our attraction.

Instead, I turn to prayer.

The house was still and quiet. Richard tossed the journal onto the bed, and cautiously undressed. He slipped his shoes into their flannel draw-string travel bag, donned a pair of crisp new jeans and tied on a pair of new, oiled work boots. A folding military issue shovel was in the trunk of his car. After all, how difficult could it be to dig up the treasure buried beneath Grace Thompson's tombstone?

1864

Evelyn Thompson considered herself the matriarchal leader of her family. With no sons to carry on the family name, her husband's fate uncertain, it would be Grace's husband who would inherit Cedar Hill and be its steward. Evelyn considered her own husband weak. He was no land

TWO MOONS OVER CEDAR HILL

steward, having let the farm go to seed, unlike the productive enterprise at River's Edge next door. Jack Lyons would make a good husband for Grace. He would tame her and see to the welfare of both estates into the next generation.

A canary twittered in a cage in the center of the parlor. No proper lady would be found at home without the little extravagance and Evelyn Thompson comforted herself with the fantasy of being overrun by Yankees, yet never being caught outside a state of genteel grace. She moved from the cage to her chair positioned close to one of the front windows. It was not so close her toes grew numb from the cold seeping through the glass.

Jack Thompson had made his intentions clear enough last summer, so this spring there could be no question of his engagement to Grace. But now that her own husband was indisposed in this scandalous fashion and her only child sent home from school in disgrace, there was little else to do but marry off the girl.

Grace's father could make no objection from prison.

Had he been a sensible man, he might have done, as most of their neighbors had done, and paid servants to engage in any actual fighting. But his conscience had not allowed for that. He had been weak and sentimental in attempting to appease the distress he had caused in his cowardly affiliations.

Sofie Couch

And Grace was nervous. The mother watched her daughter from the window as she walked down the lane. Grace wore a wrap about her small hunched shoulders and moved away from the house toward the wood. Evelyn Thompson decided against stopping the child from wandering. Grace had much to consider with regard to her inappropriate behavior while away at school.

This was the mother's thoughts as she watched her only surviving child until she was almost out of sight. Almost out of sight.

She saw a man in the shadow of the trees where the lane took a bend. Grace stopped. The man took her hands in his. They both looked around subversively. They kissed. Then Evelyn Thompson realized the man was not standing in shadow.

Richard sat on the edge of his bed and read while the house grew quiet.

August 4th:
I know he is dead. I cannot believe, as Mother would suggest, that my Salter has runaway to a free state. The servants whisper of a wife who is with child. This I know to be untrue. Salter told me of the "wife" who was purchased for him.

TWO MOONS OVER CEDAR HILL

Richard put the book aside. Salter was a slave. This would bring very good coin in an on-line auction.

...He would not treat her as he has been treated so many years – without respect.

September 15th:
I have no words to express my grief.

September 30th:
It is confirmed. Salter is dead. My unfaithful mother meant to tear us apart – knew of our alliance – and meant to separate us by sending him away. She gave him the task of burying our valuables in the family cemetery, but when he was noticed missing, she supposed he had left, taking the treasure with him. I know him to be incapable of leaving his home or the deceit she suspects of him. I have found and wept over his grave. The question remains as to who killed, then buried my heart.

Present day
In the hallway a door opened, then closed. Richard swore, not quite under his breath, then pressed his lips tight closed. He looked over at Stewart who lay on his bed, one hand off the bed, dangling down. His sleep was sound. It was past one o'clock in the morning, but still someone was awake. He slipped the journal under his pillow and switched

off his bedside lamp. He could see a light coming in under the door.

Richard suspected Jorgé was probably paying Christina a midnight visit, yet there was no stir of jealousy in him. He would have married her if it had meant ensuring he receive his rightful share of what was not exactly his birth right, but his due. But with the journal that was tucked under his pillow, he hoped to save himself that unsavory bit of inconvenience.

Finally, there was a whisper soft tap at his own door and he eased himself up from the bed. The springs creaked, but Stewart did not stir. He stepped around the door. He made no noise, nor did his companion as he followed her shadowy figure down the steps. He doubted whether Christina and her Latin Lover would have heard them had they made a noise. He preferred digging around attics to digging around graveyards, but the time to strike was when the iron was hot.

TWO MOONS OVER CEDAR HILL

Chapter 39

Jorgé would have fallen asleep early, as he did most nights after a full, satisfying day's work, but something nagged at him. If the treasure was buried beneath the tombstone marked Grace Thompson, why hadn't Mayella simply dug it up? Or rather, have him dig it up? He tossed in bed, unable to settle.

Finally, he could not get comfortable and rose from his bed, Mayella's old bed. He was used to sleeping in the smaller bed, across the hall. This one had a large divot on the right side that made either side uncomfortable for him. One side, you roll into the hole. The other side, he felt bent-up in a too small nest.

He jerked the covers off of the bed. He heard footsteps out in the hall, then a light tap at door. Jealousy pierced his gut. He had no doubt it was a midnight rendezvous between Chita and her Richard.

With fierceness, he grabbed the mattress by both elastic handles on the one side and flipped it over.

And a marble composition notebook fell open on the floor.

Jorgé recognized Mayella's spidery handwriting immediately. He picked it up, at once forgetting about the source of his jealousy across the hall, and he sat on the unmade mattress and started reading.

Outside his room, Christina slept, Stewart prowled, and two others toiled.

Jorgé put the journal away from him. He still could not believe the words he read were true. Certainly, there was some other tired old Mexican Mayella tortured. He adjusted his black reading glasses, then turned back to the book.

…Shamefully, I am jealous of the attention he showers on my Christina. George dotes on her like a father, but per age, she would make a far better attachment. I am jealous of a child.

Jorgé flipped back, nearer the beginning of the journal.

April 3rd,
My husband has taken up with yet another woman. I fear that his socially unacceptable behavior has in some way rubbed off on Christina. She is so like him in both appearance and disposition. She has become wild and head strong. I think it is unlikely that she could ever care for this farm in the way I would hope.
George comes to the house each evening to check on the children – hardly children any more. He sees more of them than their own father.

TWO MOONS OVER CEDAR HILL

It goes against my nature that I can find nothing socially inappropriate to say about the intermixing of the races that is stronger than my jealousy of the notion of George forming a romantic attachment to my child.

Jorgé put the book aside, removed his glasses and rubbed the bridge of his nose. He turned to the end of the journal – documentation of the time shortly before Christina and Stewart left.

September 5th,
I see the way George looks at her. I cannot bear it. Christina is as plain as I am. I am a wicked parent to say so of my own child.
However, this attachment cannot be borne. If only we were left alone here, he might begin to see me in my true light.

Jorgé put the book aside. It was like a piece of fiction written about fictional characters – certainly not the hard woman he had known for so many years. He thought he knew her better. He thought she knew him better.

Richard raised the lid on the trunk of his car and pulled out a brand new shovel purchased at an Army surplus store on his way to Cedar Hill. The woman at his side looked greedily toward the family cemetery. She held a shovel that she had salvaged from the attic. It had been repaired with black electrical tape where the handle was split.

"Hurry up."

"Shhh," Richard shushed her and looked cautiously toward the upstairs windows of the house. They were dark. "Patience, woman."

"I've been patient. I've waited decades and I'm not waiting any longer. That," and she pointed toward the plot, "is my due." She hustled ahead of Richard, taking the driveway to the pasture gate.

Richard followed her with less conviction, but he knew it was useless to argue with her. After reading the journal, he had every confidence they *would* find the treasure tonight.

Inside the plot, they located the grave in question, the one with the conspicuous groundhog hole in its center.

"Look-a-there. Some rodent's done half the work for us already."

"Half the work for 'us'. Remember you said that." Richard planted the point of the shovel and pressed it into the soft ground with his squeaky new leather work boot.

"You won't be complaining when we're dividing the treasure."

Richard felt his hands already chaff against the slick aluminum shovel handle. Six inches in he hit shale. Another two inches down and the shovel snapped. Richard's hands blistered.

TWO MOONS OVER CEDAR HILL

Chapter 40

Jorgé stood atop a step ladder to reach the grout line he was pointing. In the distance, Stewart was walking Tomato down the driveway with Annabelle on the boy's other side. The resemblance was uncanny. Annabelle and her auburn hair matching Tomato's and Stewart providing the other set of genes. They shared a common bond and now, Stewart had a familial interest to share with his son.

When Christina came out carrying coffee for them both, he rested his trowel and looked down.

He mumbled his thanks, only hesitatingly making eye contact.

"How are you?"

"Okay." He put down the scraper, came down the ladder and took the cup she held up to him.

"You sleep alright?"

"Not really," he mumbled, then took a sip and winced. Jorgé smiled. "Your mother makes me appreciate the fact that I was orphaned." He nodded toward the front field, ready to change the subject. "Today is the big day."

Christina followed his gaze to the front field and the small graveyard. "They haven't begun yet?"

"No. Stewart's waiting until Tomato gets home from school… so they can share the adventure."

"Fantasy."

"You're still unconvinced?"

Christina took a sip of coffee and turned her back on Jorgé.

"I don't want Stewart to look like a fool… in front of his son."

"There seems to be compelling evidence."

"I'd have thought you'd have had objections – ripping holes in your farm?"

Jorgé put down the cup, then came to stand beside Christina, both of them facing the field now. "It's *your* farm. Your home too. I don't believe it is going to be so easy to find, but that doesn't mean I don't believe in Stewart."

Christina sighed. "You think he's going to find something today?"

He considered a moment. "What sort of shoes are you wearing?" He asked while looking down at her feet. "Good. Are you feeling up to a little hike this morning?"

She waved toward the field. "We might miss something."

"The big moment is yet to come. Follow me."

Christina hesitated just a moment, then set her own coffee cup next to Jorgé's and took large steps to catch up to him.

Ten years ago

TWO MOONS OVER CEDAR HILL

Christina took large steps in an attempt to catch up with Jorgé. He had a five minute lead, but she was fairly certain she knew where he was heading. She knew his habits and she made her way through the field, down an old dirt road to the old homestead. It was there Jorgé always went when he was in a black mood. The ghostly brick shell was all that was left, some foundation and most of the chimneys. This was where her father lived until his death. An accidental fire had taken away the man and the home. She saw Jorgé's shadowy figure beyond the house, just inside the arched door inside the old brick kiln.

Her steps slowed. Her mother would not tell what she and Jorgé had argued about. It was a quiet argument, which meant it was not good. Mayella never spared her volume unless it was meant not to be heard by her or Stewart. Jorgé had walked out of the house, slamming the door behind him, and cut a path to the other side of the conjoined estates.

The kiln was shaped like a giant adobe igloo with a curvaceous chimney out of its top and three small "doors" evenly spaced around it. The brick it was made of was probably some of the best that had been produced in the yard, because it still stood as solid as it had two hundred years ago. Jorgé paced inside the kiln, back lit by the setting sun that streamed in through the door opposite. Christina sat down on a section of the houses foundation and watched him.

Jorgé paced, sometimes stopping to pick up a bit of rubble from the floor and hurl it at the inside wall of the kiln. He was muttering to himself, or perhaps praying. His spiritual ties were with nature.

Finally, he seemed to have come to some decision. The sun was fully set and he came out of the kiln, not expecting to see anyone, so he stopped in his tracks when he saw Christina sitting there on the foundation wall waiting for him.

"Have you worked it out?"

"In my own mind."

"Care to use me as a sounding board?"

He walked to where she was still seated, then looked down at her. She could sense his inner struggle over whether to confide or not.

"It concerns you."

Her heartbeat quickened and with naïve innocence, she suddenly understood what Jorgé's argument with her mother had been about.

"My friendship with you is none of Mama's concern."

"An innocent friendship would be of no concern to me either."

She could not meet his gaze, so she looked down to her lap and clenched her hands there. "But you're more than that. You're my best friend."

TWO MOONS OVER CEDAR HILL

He sat down beside her, but faced the kiln and kept a respectable two feet between them.

"Ours is an odd sort of friendship. No?"

Christina nodded, then looked his way with a smile on her lips. "We're an odd couple." She leaned sideways, bumping her shoulder into his.

Jorgé sighed. "This is the thing about which your mamá and I argued. She believes the attention I pay you is… indecent."

Christina gestured toward the kiln. "You seemed to be putting up quite an argument with yourself in there."

"Hmm." Jorgé grunted.

"Well," she turned to face him and took one of his hands in both of hers. "Which side won?"

Jorgé looked into her eyes with an intensity that would make anyone with fewer feelings for him turn away. Christina held his gaze.

"The jury is still out."

Christina squeezed his hand. "Stupid jury," and she grinned.

They stayed like that, holding hands sitting on the brick wall, staring at the last of the orange glow in the sky over the south-west hill. When all color was gone, they stood and Jorgé walked her home, never letting go her hand. She never imagined that in a few short weeks, she would give up everything she held dear and willingly separate herself from Jorgé and Cedar Hill.

Sofie Couch

Present day

They moved past the old foundation of the home where her father had lived separate from her mother for most of her childhood, but Jorgé passed the ruins with no more than a glance. Neither did they stop at the old kiln. Instead, he led her past its hulking smokestack and into the woods beyond.

"Where are we going?"

"Do you remember the smoke house?"

How could she forget? "I have a vague recollection."

He glanced her way, saw she was smiling, then turned his attention back to the weedy road ahead of them.

"Well, there's something there I did not show you."

He pushed ahead, smashing down the worst of the blackberry bramble and holding tree limbs to prevent them smacking her in the face until they reached the overgrown structure that was the former smoke house.

The door's leather hinges had long since been replaced with metal strap hinges that had been there long enough to rust. Jorgé turned the rectangular block of wood that served as a latch and the door swung hesitantly in and open.

They both had to duck their heads under the wooden lintel, it having been constructed either for a smaller stature or to cut down on the possible smoke outlets. Inside, the house still smelled of bacon and the smell eliciting an emotion in Christina that she had not felt in ten years, since the last time she had come here with Jorgé, and Christina inhaled gingerly.

"This place is a testament to the preservative qualities of salt and smoke."

"Lucky for us." Jorgé pointed up to the loft.

"What's up there?"

Before answering, Jorgé reached over head and grasped the edge of the loft floor, then to Christina's surprise, planted a foot on a timber in the wall, the other foot on a jutting stone in the chimney, and launched his torso onto the loft. With a wriggle, he was lying face down on the loft looking over the edge at Christina.

"A time capsule."

He extended his hand down to her.

"You're crazy." She took his hand.

"Was it ever a question?"

Christina found the same jutting stone, the "V" in the tenon frame and with an added pull from Jorgé, she found herself lying on her stomach with her rear end dangling over the side. Jorgé grabbed her waist band and helped her pull the rest of her body up.

Christina looked down at her sweater front. The damage would be irreparable. "You asked what type of *shoes* I had on. You didn't say anything about my sweater."

"Here it is. He pointed to the center post that rose from the dirt floor, through the center of the loft and to the ridge of the roof. "Have a look at this."

Christina squinted her eyes, unable to really see the thing at which he was pointing.

"Here." He crawled to the gable end and pulled open the shutter over the window hole. Light filtered in through oaks with tenacious brown curled leaves and billowed a light show over dust motes.

Christina ran her finger over the timber, then squinted to make out the notches in the beam.

"G.T. + S.B.... G.T.?" She whirled on her haunches to face Jorgé. "What does this mean?"

He reached out to grab her arm. "Long way down." He looked over the edge of the loft. "You don't put chimneys in smoke houses. You light the fire in the middle of the floor, close it up tight and let things - smoke. This house has a chimney – nicely built – but not of brick. The stone was salvaged from the creek a mile away, meaning it was someone's home. Probably a slave – S.L."

"Plus G. T. – Grace Thompson. You don't think...."

Jorgé shrugged. "Mayella was very weak at the end. She required constant care, yet she found the strength to leave the relative comfort of her sick bed, walk to the family cemetery and lay herself down upon the grave of Grace Thompson. She was as much as telling me that she had lied about the origin of the necklace that I had, in turn, given to you." His gaze moved to Christina's neckline. "Check the initials on the back. They are the same."

"I know they are – but the 'L" in 'S.L.' – doesn't it stand for your name – Lopez?"

"No." He shook his head sadly. "Still, I will be very much surprised if the mystery ends at the grave of Grace Thompson."

"Stewart… and Tomato. They'll be so disappointed."

Jorgé smiled. "You know it's a good idea – Stewart staying and bonding with his son."

She shook her head. "I'm not sure anymore."

"In the face of such evidence?"

"You don't seem to believe it."

"I knew Mayella." He hesitated, looked Christina in the eye, and then corrected. "I *thought* I knew Mayella. Nothing was easy with her."

"And for Stewart… and Annabelle, nothing has come easy. I don't want either of them to be short-changed… again. I don't want Stewart to squander his life searching for buried treasure that may not exist. I don't want Annabelle to be hurt… again. And now there's Tomato to consider."

"While you, on the other hand, refuse to allow yourself to dream."

"I have dreams, Jorgé."

"But you put them on hold for the past ten years. You are as much a slave to Mayella as the man who once lived here."

"Just because I didn't defy her? Because I didn't throw convention to the wind and marry you against her wishes?"

"Is that why you turned down my offer?"

She couldn't meet his direct stare. "No."

"Why, then?"

"I didn't want to have your name only."

He narrowed his eyes as if that would enable him to read her thoughts.

Christina shook her head and Jorgé threw up his hand in defeat.

"You allowed Mayella to separate you from your home for ten years. You spent those same years peddling the histories of others and taking care of a brother who is well past the age of maturity. You're still metaphorically tucking him in at night."

Christina swung her feet over the side of the loft.

"How am I supposed to get down from here?"

"Why did you leave ten years ago, Christina?"

"I told you."

"You didn't leave because of any threats made by Mayella and you didn't leave because you thought my offer disingenuous."

TWO MOONS OVER CEDAR HILL

"I explained all this to you then."

"You've explained nothing. We know now why your mother wanted you to go away. I don't know why she wanted Stewart out of the picture – why you're still trying to convince him to leave."

Christina winced. "There were Mama's feelings to consider."

"You... knew? How she felt about me?"

Christina scrubbed her face with her hands. "It's complicated, Jorgé. I love...." She stopped. "I love Stewart and Annabelle. I don't want to see either one of them get hurt."

"How? How can this possibly injure Stewart or Annabelle?"

"You wouldn't understand."

"I can't read minds!"

"He can't stay here."

"Why?"

"I can't say. No one can ever know... and yet, if he stays, I'll have to tell him, tell her!"

"Why, Christina?"

A tear leaked over the rim of her eye. "It's too awful."

"Why?" He took her by the shoulders. "Why did you leave? Why do you still want to get away?"

Christina shook her head. "Stewart was in love with Annabelle."

"I know your mother didn't approve. Annabelle was not acceptable – her background, her mother, but what difference does any of that make now?"

"No, she didn't approve." Her response was vehement. "Neither would you."

"I would. I do. Stewart and Annabelle can work around any present difficulties. Their only obstacle is gone. Mayella is gone. Stewart was never affected by your mother's prejudice."

Christina blinked and tears ran down her cheeks. "She couldn't let them continue. Neither can I."

His eyes narrowed.

Christina continued, unable to hold his gaze. "Annabelle's mother…."

"This is a small community, but no one thinks worse of Annabelle because of her mother's reputation. That doesn't matter to Stewart."

"It would… if he knew… Daddy was Annabelle's father."

Suddenly, Jorgé was deflated. "Mierde."

Jorgé reached out to her, cupping her cheek in his hand and she pressed her face into it. More slowly, she turned to face him and more slowly, he crushed her to his chest.

In that same instant, she only wanted to wallow in the sensation of his touch and kisses – long overdue. Yet the reason for leaving still remained.

TWO MOONS OVER CEDAR HILL

Her eyes flew open and Christina tried to push herself away from him.

"What?"

Christina shook her head, but was having difficulty recovering from the fog that had descended about her.

"I don't love you," she was finally able to eek out.

He kissed her, softly at first, then with ten years of pent up passion and longing.

With greater emotional effort she pushed him away.

Christina swallowed hard, and lifted her chin in a stoic gesture. "And you can't tell Stewart that you love me either… if I'm going to get him to leave this place. Don't you see? Now there's Tomato to consider. He can't know.… He would suffer even more than Annabelle suffered as a child. I know. I was her best friend and what she didn't tell me, I was witness to. You can't imagine how horribly she was treated at school when kids found out who her mother was… what her mother was. And if Tomato ever finds out his own parentage.… Promise me you won't tell him."

In the distance, there was a tremendous boom and the ground below them shook – enough to cause dust to shimmer down from the ceiling.

"What the?" Jorgé hesitated but a moment before jumping down from the loft. He kept his footing, but stayed on the ground with knees and hips bent while he assessed if he might have done any damage, then he straightened and held a hand up to Christina.

"It's a big leap. I suggest something less fool hearty than jumping."

She rolled over onto her stomach, scooted backwards until her legs and hips dangled off the edge of the loft. Jorgé put his hand to her backside and she dropped, knocking him backwards, but again, keeping his footing.

"Ouch." She rubbed her chaffed stomach.

"Come on." He was the first one out the door, but Christina quickly passed him in her run back to the house – in the direction of the explosion - while Jorgé limped slowly behind.

TWO MOONS OVER CEDAR HILL

Chapter 41

Jorgé reached the field just before the second explosion, and Beebo, the old dog, ran like the hounds of hell were chasing him. Christina ran ahead and reached the cemetery before him. She turned toward him to explain the explosion.

"Richard decided to help move things along by using dynamite to speed the dig."

"Not dynamite, Christina. A couple of your farm manager's left over fireworks. They really pack a punch." Richard reached down, taking a canvas bucket of dirt and handing it up to her. Stewart arrived about the same time as Jorgé, having heard the explosion from the end of the drive where he was seeing Tomato off to school.

The dog took to his hiding place in the barn.

Jorgé looked at the devastating hole in one end of the family cemetery, then in the direction the dog had run.

Richard looked every bit the overseer of the operation.

Jorgé turned on him. "Was this your idea?"

"It was our idea," Stewart defended. Richard and I were talking about this last night. We just envisioned this giving us a good head start. Those firecrackers of yours pack a more powerful punch than we anticipated."

Sofie Couch

"That's one hell of a punch." Jorgé waved his arm at the gaping hole. "Just how many did you use?"

Richard shrugged. "Six… maybe seven."

Jorgé threw his hands into the air and turned away as if the sight of the gaping hole in his farm was more than he could take.

"You do realize that just two of them carry the strength of a stick of dynamite? You could have blown up someone."

Stewart crouched down, feeling the edge of the crater. "Won't have to do much digging by hand."

Jorgé smacked his forehead. "Look around you, Stewart." He pointed in the direction of the adjacent grave, from which a foot of dirt was missing and the stone cracked in half and lying on the ground. "If you continue in this way, there won't be anything left of this farm. Just one, big, giant crater."

"Really, Jorgé, you're behaving as if we just desecrated *your* family grave."

"This farm is my home and you're my family. It is your home too. Yours and Tomato's and Annabelle's and Christina's. I don't want you to blow yourself up looking for your pot of gold. You're sitting on the gold."

Jorgé limped away in the direction of the barn, his jaw clenched, and his back straight.

TWO MOONS OVER CEDAR HILL

Christina looked at the hole, her hand covering her mouth. Through her hand, she mumbled, "we should never have come back."

Stewart's eyes narrowed. "Where were you two anyway?"

"Finding evidence."

"Of...."

"Of the existence of the treasure. That's what."

"I thought you didn't believe in the treasure."

"Maybe I've had a change of heart."

"And a change of heart about Jorgé?"

Christina looked sheepishly toward Richard who was listening with interest.

"No."

"So, you *still* love him."

"Stewart!" She looked from her brother to Richard.

"What's this?"

"Oh yeah. Sorry ol' man. You never really stood a chance with Christina. You see, she's been carrying a torch for Jorgé all these years."

He pointed a finger in the direction Jorgé had headed. "You're in love with that old man?"

"Shut up, Stewart." She turned to Richard. "And he's not an old man. There's little more than a dozen years separating...."

"Fifteen to be exact," Stewart added.

"Age has nothing to do with it." Christina glared at her brother. "Once you've found the treasure, I'm leaving. We were happy on the coast, Stewart, Richard? We can be again."

"You can't. The Will...."

"That Will holds about as much water as a sieve. I've been doing my homework, Stewart. It's called a pet trust or monitored pet care and the Commonwealth of Virginia doesn't recognize it. When Beebo...." She found she could not voice the inevitable. "I don't have to wait until the dog is gone. It was a good excuse to stick around and see if maybe..., But.... I can have the Will overridden and we can dispense with the property. Leave it to Jorgé and see that Annabelle and Tomato are provided for."

She turned away from them and headed toward the house with Richard and Stewart staring after her. "I don't plan on staying, Stewart. As soon as you and Tomato find the treasure...."

"Well, ol' man. I guess you know where you stand."

"You never did like me, did you, Stewart."

Stewart considered his words for a moment.

"Nope." Then he too walked away from the crater and headed toward the barn.

He whistled for the dog, listened, and then headed toward the office at the back of the barn.

Jorgé was seated at a swivel chair. The computer in front of him was running, but Jorgé only stared blankly at the screen in front of him. He heard Stewart though.

"Why did you hide that Will, Jorgé?"

He turned on the swivel, facing the younger man. "You need even ask?"

"Mama left you everything."

But Jorgé was shaking his head. "Mayella's motives were not philanthropic. She wanted to manipulate me."

"By giving you everything you've ever wanted?"

"Is that what you really think, Stewart? That this farm means more to me than Christina… or you? Is that why you think I've stayed here all this time?"

"Why did you stick around?"

"You know why." His voice rose, so he checked it, looking toward the outer barn door. Finally, he rose and closed the office door. "Mayella had a strange way of showing her affection. She could never give all of herself – not to your father, not to you and Christina, not to me. So she attached strings to everything. She wanted to ensure Christina and I never married. So she wrote two Wills, one leaving me the farm in case that was all I was after and another leaving everything to Christina in case I did love her, so she would not be obligated to marry *me* in order to keep her home." Jorgé paced. "Si, Mayella's jealousy was part of her motivation, but her bigotry was another part of it. She could not bear the thought of the intermingling of the races. She'd do anything to preserve the purity of your blood lines."

"And do you think Christina believes that? 'Cause if you do, you can just…."

"Of course not… no more than I believe you really expect to find the treasure in your ancestor's grave, do you?"

Stewart grinned. "No. Especially not now that it's been blown practically blown to bits."

Jorgé closed his eyes in relief and smiled. "Then why did you and Richard decide to use dynamite?"

Stewart felt his way into the barn office and sat back against the desk. "My entire childhood was spent wanting to spend time with my father. He would launch a promise of something – a father-son trip that would never happen, a gift that would never materialize, a search for buried treasure. It never mattered to me what we did. I just wanted to spend time with him. I want this treasure hunt with Tomato. I don't care if we never find anything buried out there. I just want to give him time."

Jorgé reached forward and squeezed his knee. "Don't desecrate any more graves on my behalf, Stewart."

TWO MOONS OVER CEDAR HILL

"There's only one question remaining," Stewart said.

"Si?"

"If you love Christina and she loves you, why is she leaving?"

Jorgé took a deep breath remembering Christina's assertion about Stewart's unnatural connection to Annabelle. He rose from his chair, put a hand on Stewart's shoulder, and then pointed him to take the seat he had just vacated. "Stewart, son, we have some plain talk to wade through."

Chapter 42

Richard nonchalantly poked at the blasted earth with the tip of a spade. From the corner of his eye, he watched until Stewart was out of sight, then Treeny – it appealed to his love of drama to refer to her as his accomplice - crept around the corner of the house. She had been watching the excavation from there.

"Anything?" She asked when she was within speaking distance.

"Nothing."

She walked to the edge of the crater and looked down. "I can't believe… all this time… all this waiting… and nothing. Nothing to come of this."

With sympathy, Richard put his arm around the woman's shoulder.

She looked at him like he was crazy, then cast a secretive look toward the barn and the house and took a step away from him. "Don't just stand there. See if you can get to it before they come back."

Richard looked at her with incredulity. "I can't just take up a shovel at this point. Someone might come back and see."

"Or you could dig one foot deeper and find it."

Shaking his head, Richard squatted, then lowered himself into the crater. Halfheartedly he threw his weight behind the spade. He never knew digging was such hard work and it took him several attempts before he realized it might work better if he planted his foot on the spade to help cut into the red clay and shale.

It was not long before his hands were red again and he had rubbed raw the soft skin between his thumb and forefinger. He was about to call it quits when his shovel struck something with a sound that was different than the sound it made against shale and quartz.

"It's here." He was more surprised than elated. He tapped the shovel blade against the spot again and was rewarded with another metallic thunk. "I'll be damned. It really is here." He went down on his knees to ineffectually scrape at the earth with his fingers. He grabbed up the spade again and cut at the dirt where the metal box peeked out.

Her lifelong ambition realized, the woman went down on her knees and reached out for the box. Richard pulled out the box, tears coming to his eyes as he passed the thing she believed would level out all the inequities in her life up to this point.

And what of the inequities in his own life? Richard suddenly felt the loss. It had always been his other children – blood relatives - that Stewart Breeden, Sr. had talked about and in whom he had invested his paternal love. For Richard, the child of his mistress, there were a few short lived fun moments at a race track until the money ran out. There were promises of the things he would buy him when he struck it rich. And there had always been his favorite story about the lost buried treasure, still hidden somewhere on Cedar Hill.

And yet, the woman who knelt on the ground above claimed it as her own. It was the only thing she cared about and Richard suddenly felt the full extent of his abandonment. He didn't care about the box. He would prefer she toss it back into the hole and they left together. He had money enough for them both. He wasn't hurting – at least, not in the pocket book.

"You should take it inside. Do the thing right."

But thirty years of waiting, plotting and biding her time for what she felt was her due was long enough. She pulled at the corroded box lid.

"Gimme your keys."

He pulled his car keys out of his pocket. He thought twice about it, then selected the large key to Christina's apartment and handed it up to her. Treeny ran it around the corroded lip. The sharp minerals sliced her hand and she swore. Still determined, she flipped the box upside down on the dirt.

"Hand me the shovel."

TWO MOONS OVER CEDAR HILL

Richard did as he was instructed and handed up the spade. She inserted the blade of the shovel at the lip, put her foot on it and gave a shove.

The lid remained sealed tight. Sanity left her as she sat on the edge of the crater and cried. "I can't get it open."

"Shhh, sh, sh." Richard hushed her as he climbed out, then on the surface, he sat beside her and put his arm back around her shoulder. This time, she did not pull away.

"It's mine. Stew said when he found the treasure it was gonna be mine."

"Hush." He glanced cautiously over his shoulder. "Listen. You take the box. Take it back to my place. There you'll be able to do the thing right. Buy the proper tools. Here." He reached to the wallet he was sitting on, retrieved it from his back pocket and handed her a wad of bills. "That's more than enough to get you there. I'll be along soon to help."

The woman looked up at his face like a trusting child. "You're so good to me."

He bent and kissed her on the forehead. "I love you."

She rose clutching the dirt encrusted box to her clean pink cardigan, then ran for her car.

Chapter 43

1864

Salter felt knots in his stomach. He wasn't able to keep his food down and although no one else had noticed, he was certain he was losing weight. And all for love.

He watched from a distance as Mrs. Thompson threw her only child at Jack Lyons. Since Grace's expulsion from school, Mrs. Thompson was more determined than ever to see the two united and it ate at Salter's heart. The mountain behind him, his home, comfort, kin, gave him little solace anymore, for he knew with certainty he was as bound to Grace as the South West Mountains and that their future together was doomed. He worried, premonition perhaps, that his bond with his home might someday be severed too.

"Damned if you do. Damned if you don't," he muttered as he stacked the third full cart of cross-cut and split fire wood. He found a rare stick of lightwood and set it aside for his own hearth.

"That'll be your second load?" Jack Lyons surprised him by rounding the corner of the barn.

"Third."

"Good. Mrs. Thompson asked if you'd come over to her place and give her a hand with something she's got to get moved down from the attic."

TWO MOONS OVER CEDAR HILL

There was something about Jack's tone that made him look up making eye contact. Jack Lyons waited, hands on hips, for Salter to comply, as if he was expecting him to refuse. Salter only nodded. As an afterthought, he gathered up an armload of wood to take to the Thompsons. It was this sort of quiet diplomacy that kept him in the good graces of his oppressors. It was this same diplomacy that earned him a backlash from his fellow victims of oppression.

His step never slowed in the mile trek to the Thompson home, but he could feel the weight of the wood by the time he arrived. That, more than anything, hinted to Salter that he was love sick and that he must overcome it. To leave Grace, or any of the women on the two farms, was unthinkable. They were vulnerable with most of the men gone off to fight. Salter was deemed too valuable to spare, Old Peter was too old, and Mr. Jack too wealthy and powerful to risk. Jack had taken on the task of overseeing the security of the two estates which at least made him feel as though he was making a contribution.

When Salter reached Grace's home, Mrs. Thompson was waiting at the rear door where he was expected. She turned away from him and spoke over her shoulder.

"Follow me."

Sofie Couch

    She did not acknowledge his gift of firewood and unobtrusively, Salter put it on the nearest hearth.

    The Thompsons were modern in that they kept kitchen here, on the ground floor under the same roof in which they lived. So, it was probably not so unusual for Mrs. Thompson to have seen the kitchen before, but he supposed it was not often. It was a more common sight to her, no doubt, than was the upstairs of a white man's home to him.

    He had scarce had reason to enter the Thompson's home and never Grace's room. He knew, from seeing her in her window, on which floor she slept. He had dreamt of it often, but he had only ever imagined what it must look like.

    With quiet padded steps, he followed Mrs. Thompson up the stairs, from the English basement to the second floor. Theirs was what was called a four over four, only truth be known, it was a four over four over four. Salter inspected surreptitiously, the opulence of Grace's home compared to his own tired old house. There he had started the carving of their initials in one of the beams. He doubted anyone had ever carved anything into the woodwork here. It was clean, smooth, and painted white.

    One flight of steps turned to a hall, through which they passed and Salter looked into the room that held a piano. Another room held more books than he had ever seen in his whole life – a full shelf that must have run four foot wide and equally high.

TWO MOONS OVER CEDAR HILL

Mrs. Thompson turned into the door at the end of the hall, and Salter was amazed to find another flight of stairs there that must lead, he realized, to the family's sleeping area. His heart raced. He knew she would be there and he would see her, for the first time, in her own environment.

Mrs. Thompson turned at the top of the stairs, a delicate thin rail separating her from the steps, and with eyes wide, Salter followed, clutching tight to the rail. He was not used to these sorts of dizzying heights unless it was from the safety of a scaffold.

But then he saw his reward for having made it. There, through one of the doorways toward the back of the house, sat Grace. She was perched lightly, elegantly on a low stool. Her hair was down and she toiled at a knot with a tortoise shell comb. He put his hand to his own close cut hair. The thought of running a comb through it would never have occurred to him and it would have hurt like hell.

Grace saw him through the reflection in her mirror, caught her breath and turned on the stool. With eyes intense with sudden fear, he shook his head, then turned his eyes to the floor.

With hesitation and while Mrs. Thompson fumbled with a latch of some sort between Grace's room and one other, he looked into the other room, that of the late brother, Jamie Thompson. He remembered seeing that child with his wooden boat tucked under his arm. The boat was fixed under a glass box in the center of the fireplace mantle.

Mrs. Thompson, without a word, ran her hand over the paneling between the two doorways, pulled up on a little ring, then pulled and the panel swung open. Behind this was another stair, but this like none Salter had ever seen before. The treads were each cut big enough to accommodate only one foot and rose at alternating double height, requiring one to lead with the right foot and end with the left at the attic floor. Mrs. Thompson stood back from the doorway.

"You go first."

Salter looked up the steps warily, then, ducking his head through the door, he climbed like a child, holding the higher steps with his hands while his feet ascended from behind. At the top, he made no pretense of bravery and climbed onto the floor on his hands and knees. Cautiously, he glanced over head. The house was tall with high ceilings on the other floors, but the attic was cavernous. Its hipped roof soared up into a peak at the center. The rafters overhead looked more like an inverted boat. Arched windows let in sunlight from two of the four gables, giving plenty of light for Salter to see more of an attic than he ever wanted to.

He looked down in surprise when he heard Mrs. Thompson fairly skipping up those treacherous steps behind him. She came just far enough to pop her head above the attic floor.

"That one. There. Bring it down with you." She pointed to a large trunk in a far corner of the near empty attic.

Salter crawled toward the corner, then holding onto the trunk, he slowly rose until he was standing, crouched, beside the trunk. He gave another nervous and cautious look around the attic. He felt sorry for Grace who must have been frightened as a child sleeping under such a room.

He inspected the trunk, found a leather strap handle on one end, and then went back down on his knees, dragging the trunk behind him.

He could not bear to look at the steps below him, so he tried to convince himself he was just climbing down a steep hill. He pulled the trunk, letting it come down end first and rest on his shoulder as he closed his eyes and felt with his feet for the step below until he was at the bottom. There, he opened his eyes again, stunned by the comparative brightness of the hallway, and relieved by the solid feel of the third story floor beneath his feet.

Mrs. Thompson lovingly ran her hand across the top of the trunk, then flipped the latches on the front and began raising the lid.

"That be all you needin' me for, Mrs. Thompson, I'll be getting back to…."

"Wait."

Salter held his tongue and watched and Mrs. Thompson lifted the lid. Inside was the most beautiful thing he had ever seen. Mrs. Thompson lifted off of the top, a ladies' dress that was made of the finest worm web he had ever seen. It was transparent and had a design of roses woven into it. Mrs. Thompson lifted it reverentially, then held it up to her own bosom.

"This was my wedding dress. Belgian lace is what it's made of. I bet mine was the first gown in Virginia made of Belgian lace."

Salter, having nothing conversationally required of him, held his tongue and watched.

Mrs. Thompson walked into the late Jamie's room and lovingly laid the dress across her dead son's bed, then returned to the trunk. She pulled out more fabric. "These are the linens I had made for Grace for her wedding bed."

Salter felt his heart constrict.

"See the fine white embroidery?" She held it out as if actually showing it to him, but her eyes never left the linens and then this too she solemnly folded and lay across the bed beside the dress. Below that and packed in more feed sack than he had worn over the course of his entire life, Mrs. Thompson began unwrapping china.

Grace sauntered out into the hallway to watch her mother. Salter spared her the briefest of glances.

TWO MOONS OVER CEDAR HILL

"This is not your everyday tableware, mind you. Grace's Daddy bought this straight off of a boat that come from France by way of Boston Harbor." Each piece, she unwrapped and began stacking on the floor beside the wall. "Heaven knows, I should probably hide this too, but the Yankees won't care a smidge about china made in France, except to smash it. It won't be used against us to support their war effort – not like the gold and silver would."

When he looked up, Mrs. Lyons seemed to come out of her reverie. She snapped at Grace.

"To your room, girl. And shut the door. You've got no sense of decency." She might have referred to Grace coming out with her hair down… or something else.

The unwrapping of china took a very long time, but Salter stood by without offering to add to the older woman's rambling. At last, the trunk was empty.

"You wait here."

Mrs. Thompson left him standing in the hall again and Salter feared he could feel the very floor of the house sway in the wind. While she was away… and Grace's door closed behind her, he chanced to move into Jamie's room and take a glance out of one of the windows. He moved hastily back toward the center of the room.

When Mrs. Thompson returned, Salter watched in shock as she dumped the largest pile of gold and silver metal he had ever seen onto the center of Jamie's bed covers.

A tea set on a massive tray and a bag of coin rattled together in the center.

"There's more."

She left again to return with more coin, gold pen tips and sewing needles. When she left the third time, she entered Grace's room without knocking, then he heard Mrs. Thompson speaking to Grace. He caught his breath when Grace appeared in the doorway again behind her mother.

Silently, Grace lowered an armload of silver onto the middle of the bed – the tortoise shell comb she had been using earlier was set in a silver spine. The silver spine and hairbrush and mirror handles were taken from them and put into the pile along with the silver lids from various jars and bottles. While her mother's back was turned Grace took a step toward him, her hand fluttering out to him, then nervously coming home to rest on her breast.

Mrs. Thompson apparently forgot Grace's "indecent" state and left the room. When Grace made a move toward him, Salter shook his head slightly and looked to the door.

"She's gone downstairs to Daddy's library," Grace whispered.

"She ain't right in the head."

Grace put her fingers to her mouth to stifle a sob. "What... what has she asked you to do?"

TWO MOONS OVER CEDAR HILL

He shrugged. "Ain't asked nothing of me yet. I was to help haul this down from the upstairs," and with revulsion, he looked back toward the narrow staircase behind its hidden panel door. "It's pretty high up."

Grace glanced at the door to the hall, then quickly launched herself at Salter, wrapping her arms around his waist and burying her face in his chest. She inhaled deeply.

"I just know something awful's about to happen."

"It's the war. This business up to your school. Your Daddy being held…. That's what's got everybody on edge." He tried to put her away from him, but she clung to him like hoochie-koochie vine.

"Don't leave me," she whispered into his chest.

"Grace. Look at me." He finally pried her away enough to look down into her green-gray eyes. "You know there ain't no hope for this. We ain't never gonna be… together."

"We could. Someday."

But he kept shaking his head. "And you with all that education." He finally was able to put her firmly away from himself. "You know, there ain't no place on this earth where we could be together. Not here. Not on the other side of the world."

"Then after."

"In the hereafter," he agreed.

Sofie Couch

They both heard Mrs. Thompson's ascent from the lower stairs, so his words were hurried.

"And in the spring, you gonna marry Mr. Jack."

"I won't do that."

"You gonna do that, Grace." He blinked hard, but smiled.

"You're gonna marry someone else too."

"Jack already brought her up from Richmond. She's got no family."

Mrs. Thompson rounded the corner and Salter turned his gaze back to the floor. In her skirt, she held a last load of precious metal.

Mrs. Thompson gave Grace a pinch on the arm and Grace, with her hair still down around her waist, rushed out of the room.

The trunk lay empty and open at the side of the bed and Mrs. Thompson grabbed two corners of the quilted bed spread, then nodded for Salter to do the same from the other side. With a great clatter of metal, they lifted the spread, then carried it to the trunk and lowered it in. It was Salter who tucked the ends of the spread around the precious cargo. Mrs. Thompson gave it little care.

He quietly closed the trunk lid, fastened the metal clasps, sealed the latch and pulled the leather straps over the front. He knew what she was going to have him do with it.

TWO MOONS OVER CEDAR HILL

With a mighty heave, Salter lifted the trunk to the bed, then onto his back. It was a greater load than he was used to carrying, but he would not falter in his duty – for the sake of Grace.

They passed Grace's doorway where she stood watching silently. Down the treacherous steps Salter glanced back over the rail at Grace and they knew nothing would ever be the same again.

Downstairs, Mrs. Thompson opened the rear kitchen door and spoke in hushed tones.

"Set it down there. Stack some wood on top of it. Then you come back tonight."

"Where you want me to hide it?"

She was staring toward the field where a small family plot had begun with the previous generation. "You put it out there. Put it in the ground with my Jamie. Yankees won't think to dig up a fresh grave."

"Mrs. Thompson…." He almost protested, but her sharp look stopped him.

She stared him in the eye and he did not blink or look away.

"You know what this trunk is?"

He shook his head.

"It's Grace's hope chest." She dug inside a small leather bag that hung from a silk cord at her waist. From it, she pulled out two gold coins, felt their weight, and then pulled out another. These, she handed over to Salter. "I want you to bury her hope chest… then I want you to take this coin," her voice cracked and she thrust it into his hand, "…and I want you to leave here."

"Ma'am?"

"I want you to leave here, Salter. 'Cause so long as you're around, my Grace ain't *got* no hope."

His eyes widened.

"Come back tonight… and bury her dowry with my Jamie."

TWO MOONS OVER CEDAR HILL

Chapter 44

Present day

The explosion shook the earth, and old Beebo, as deaf and arthritic as he was, wasted no time in running away from the graveyard.

He made a beeline for safe refuge, blasting past Christina who ran toward the scene of unrest, then past Jorgé who limped along behind. The dog's heart pounded in its rib cage, then spasmed. He made it to the barn before falling limp on his side. A whimper from his gray muzzle was his last testament to a dog's life of leisure.

Inside the house, Mayella roamed the upstairs hall, not quite understanding the nature of limbo. All she really understood was that she felt better than she had in months. She no longer felt jealousy, the emotion she had lived with for most of her adult life.

Ten years ago

"What did you say to her, Mayella?"

"I didn't have to say anything. She knows it's wrong. What'd she tell you?"

"Lies."

"Was it lies or things you just didn't wanna hear?" Mayella held her breath as she waited for Jorgé's response.

Jorgé's eyes narrowed with suspicion. "She said she didn't love me. She said she didn't think it…

appropriate that she should involve herself with a man… my age… and my station."

Mayella snorted. "And here I thought she wasn't listening to me all these years."

"You told her to say that, Mayella! You've done something to force her to lie about how she really feels."

"I told her she wasn't gonna marry no damn Mexican. She's grown up now and you know she makes her own decisions. Christina's gonna marry who she damn well pleases and it just so happens, that marrying you isn't what she pleases."

"To hell with marrying anyone. She's leaving her home. Why?"

"Stewart was takin' up with that girl, so I've sent her packing. He blames me for sending Annabelle away, but I say, if the girl had truly loved him, she'd have stuck around. Christina – she just chose to look after Stewart over being with you."

"*You* threatened her somehow. You threatened to disinherit Stewart unless she and I stopped seeing each other?"

"I've made that threat a million times. I'm blue in the face from making that threat and she knows it's an empty one. She'd give the boy everything she has, so I had to threaten to disinherit them both. I told her she'd see how much you loved her if there was no hope of ever gettin' your hands on this farm."

TWO MOONS OVER CEDAR HILL

Jorgé paced back and forth across the front porch and Mayella watched him with a wildly racing heart. He was enamored by Christina's youth. She shared her daughter's spirit. To some degree, her daughter's looks — after the effects of gravity. Why hadn't he looked at her the way he looked at Christina?

"Tell me where they've gone."

"I will do no such thing."

"To hell with this. I'm going after them." He started down the steps only to stop at the bottom.

"Where you gonna look, George? Your best bet is to wait around here until she decides to come back. If she loves you — really loves you — nothing I say will stop her from coming home… sooner or later."

He looked back up the stairs at her. "Why are you doing this, Mayella?"

There was a flash of regret behind her steel gray, wrinkled eyes, but she squashed a painful desire to tell him how she felt and raised her chin. "You know I wouldn't do anything to hurt you. I'm really quite fond of you, George."

He shook his head. "Then show it."

He stormed off in the direction of the barn and Mayella watched him until he was out of sight. She was to be left alone with Jorgé, but at what cost? He hated her now and that was a poor beginning for her life with the only man she had ever loved.

Sofie Couch

Present day

    The instant the dog died, she remembered all that she had done, she forgave herself and she knew she had done all that she could for those she would soon be leaving behind.

    The dog's over-long claws clicked on the wooden steps as he ascended to be with Mayella, the sound only audible to someone in a receptive frame of mind.

    "Come on, Ol' Beebo. We've done all we can here." The dog pressed his muzzle against her thigh, pushed his head under her hand and enjoyed a good twitch behind his ears.

    The man whom she now recognized as kin wandered the upstairs hall. He was still waiting for someone, but finally, he acknowledged Mayella through the floor with a gentlemanly nod of his head. Then she and Beebo left by way of the slate roofed widow's walk.

TWO MOONS OVER CEDAR HILL

Chapter 45

Somewhere between the rock and the hard place had been Jorgé's life-long address. His thoughts were scattered and he stopped in the center of the open barn and he looked around in distraction, trying to remember what he had been about.

Had he not been scattered, he might have walked out with purpose and missed the golden paw that jutted up from behind a bale of fencing wire in the corner.

His heart plummeted as he moved to the side of the room, already knowing what he would find there.

Beebo lay on his side, one paw frozen in rigor where the dog had lain, then rolled over in death. Jorgé remembered seeing the dog fly past him after the explosion in the cemetery. The exertion must have killed him.

With gentle hands, Jorgé knelt beside the old dog's body, then with tears in his eyes, lifted the stiff, furry form into his arms and pressed his face to his side.

Beebo smelled like dog and hay and earth. Jorgé rose with the dog and carried him out the back door of the barn to that spot near the edge of the woods where such things were taken care of, where a legion of family pets had been lain to rest over the years.

Sixteen years ago

Christina held Stewart's dead cat, laying its still warm body in a box. She curled its body into a "C" and draped it with an old towel, then sealed the box and wrapped it in a trash bag.

"I'm sorry about the cat," Jorgé consoled.

Christina did not cry. "He was just an old barn cat."

"He was very old."

Christina put the box under one arm and took up a shovel from the barn wall with the other hand. "I can't bury him out in the family plot. Stewart might see us."

"No. There is a special place for the burial of pets and animals." Jorgé preceded her, taking the shovel from her hands and led the way out the back of the barn to the edge of the woods. Silently, Jorgé dug the hole and Christina put the boxed cat into the grave. With her hands, she pulled the dirt back over the hole until there was a little mound over the cat, then she wiped her hands on the leg of her jeans.

"Well, I guess that's it."

"I'll tell Stewart if you prefer."

Christina, who was all of twelve years old at the time took a deep breath, a characteristic Jorgé was used to seeing in one so young who had shouldered way more responsibility in her childhood than she should have.

"That's okay. I'll tell him. He won't want to cry in front of you. He won't mind so much with me. It'll take him a full two days before he finds another cat."

Jorgé put his heavy arm around her shoulder and gave her a squeeze which she returned.

"Where do you think we go when we die?" She startled him in a way she often did by doing the unexpected. She stopped and laid down on the ground. "And don't say heaven." Christina patted the ground beside her in invitation.

"Why can't I say heaven?" He sat down beside her and craned his neck to see the sky above them. It wasn't even a pretty sky. Gray clouds clumped together and it looked like rain unless the temperature fell another ten degrees, then it would snow.

She smiled and turned her shielded eyes to him. "Because this is heaven, silly."

He leaned back until he was lying beside her, trying to capture her perspective. His eyes adjusted to the gray overhead and he unshielded his eyes, but squinted.

"Guess you haven't seen too much of the world."

"Don't need to. You're *here*."

Sofie Couch

Present day

  Beebo was average size for a golden retriever, but the dog's grave took on mammoth proportions. Jorgé was certain he had sprained his ankle earlier and now he had to press the spade into the earth with his left foot. With the hole dug, Jorgé went back to the barn for a feed sack in which to drape the dog's body for no reason other than it felt right to have the body covered in something before covering it in dirt. Then he lowered the dog into the hole, and began covering it. He couldn't keep it a secret forever and according to Stewart, Christina intended to leave regardless. Like so many years ago, he doubted Christina would shed a tear over the loss of the dog and he doubted whether his own tears were due to the loss of an old friend. He knew that this poor animal's death would have jarring repercussions that had more to do with Mayella's bequeath than the loss of a beloved pet.

  When he stood back, looking down at the mound of dirt, Jorgé saw into his own future. Where would they bury *his* tired old body when the time came? In the family plot? In some county graveyard? Somewhere between the family plot and the pet cemetery – the resting place of tired old Mexicans who didn't belong? He didn't know where his own parents were buried and maybe he would go the same way – in an unmarked grave somewhere on the estate. It was preferable to being sent back to a country he had never known. This was his home and this was where he wanted to spend the remainder of his days - with Christina – his family.

He returned the shovel to its hook on the barn wall and strode out of the front of the barn toward the house with purpose.

Chapter 46

1864

Without the benefit of light other than that given by the moon, Salter found his way back to the Thompson's back door and quietly unloaded the stack of wood he had put on top of the trunk as a disguise.

It was no surprise when Mrs. Thompson herself opened the rear door and stepped out in her dressing gown. Her hair lay in a long thin braid over her shoulder. She looked self-conscious at first, then straightened as though realizing that he, Salter, was no one to notice.

"You know what to do with it?"

"Yes ma'am."

"Then you know what to do with yourself?"

He nodded, unable to make eye contact.

There was no need for more discussion. He had his orders. He would follow them… or Grace would pay the consequences.

Shouldering the load for the second time that day, he shifted the weight of the trunk to fit the center of his back, then took halting steps away from the rear door.

Twice he glanced back, certain he could no longer be seen from the house. For the last time, he looked up at Grace's window. Whether by some trick of the moonlight or not, he thought he saw her shadow there, her hand pressed to the glass.

Salter wept.

Turning his back on the house, he proceeded to do as he had been told.

With tears blurring his vision, Salter traveled half the distance to the Thompson family plot before stopping to rest. The magnitude of what he was about to do was still unreal, but taken in small chunks, the first task, that of digging up the young Jamie's grave and laying the trunk in it, was in itself unthinkable.

Footsteps pounded the earth. He froze. Someone was coming toward him and his first thought was for Grace. Was it a messenger coming ahead to warn of the Yankees? He strained to see through the dark.

Grace ran straight at him and threw her arms around him. She was easily visible in the dark in her white gown and light flesh.

"What are you doing here?" He put her away from him.

"You're gonna leave. I know it."

"I'm gonna leave."

"You can't leave me. I'll die."

He shook her, not too gently. "You will not die." He looked her over from head to toe. "Unless it's from consumption."

"I hope I do."

"You're talking fool."

"I do," she challenged.

"Then you're talking like a child." He sighed and took her into his arms and promised himself this would be the last time.

"You're gonna go on back to the house, Grace." He spoke into the top of her head and inhaled deep. "You're gonna go on back and get to bed and wake up in the morning and be surprised when you hear that I've gone. You're gonna look out on this field and know that your future is safe, that your dowry is hidden and if the Yankees show up here, y'all are gonna open the door to them and be hospitable and treat them like they was your long-lost kin – which, more'n likely, they is."

"I won't. Because it was them that separated me from you."

"And you and I both know, they're not the cause nor the cure for what's ailing us."

They were both silent a long while and Grace clung to him and he knew she would keep on clinging until he ended it.

"You got my necklace still?"

She dug into her neckline and pulled it out on its leather strap.

"That's the only thing I had worth giving you. Think of me when you wear it." His voice cracked.

"There's something more you could give me."

He waited for her to enlighten him.

TWO MOONS OVER CEDAR HILL

Slowly, Grace put her hands to his cheeks and pulled his face down to hers and she kissed him.

Salter was a rational man. He believed in life's harsh realities. He knew the land and nature, how animals coupled and bore their young, but nothing prepared him for the sharing of souls.

He knew there were things that he could not explain, and he watched Grace as she firmly, resolutely walked away from him across the pitch dark field as if it did not hurt her to separate herself from him like it tore at his own heart.

He looked to the family plot just a few feet off from the spot where he had lain Grace. He had seen a ghost before. Once, minutes after his mother's death, he saw her take the hand of another ghost – one so white, he was almost fog. His own mother, what he could remember of her, was full of stories of spirits that ruled the skies and the land. A burial ground was a sacred place, but it was also a frightening place, where the spirits of the dead who did not go to heaven, roamed, especially at night and where those same spirits witnessed his bonding with Grace.

Digging up the grave of a child simply was not done – and the boy's grave would have to be disturbed twice – once now and once when the treasure was to be retrieved. Salter looked from the graveyard to the trunk. The graveyard consisted of no more than three gray headstones jutting out of the earth. He looked back toward the place he called home.

Past the new brick work skeleton of the folly, past the stand of trees that separated the two estates, on the other side of the brick yard and kiln, stood the smoke house that Salter called home. Beyond that, up a narrow path in a spot cleared by lightning strike seven years ago was another burial ground.

This one did not bear the trace remains marked by polished headstones. A slab of slate stood at attention over his mother's grave. The other graves of his oppressed people received far less stately a memorial. The four corners of this sacred place were marked by four cedar trees, transplanted as saplings that now struggled for prehistoric dominance.

This was the more acceptable hiding place for what would eventually be Grace's inheritance, her dowry to another man, and the sustenance of her children. With determination, Salter turned, shouldered the weight of the trunk and made his way there.

He would not, as he had been instructed to do, be leaving his home. Grace might need him now... or shortly in the future. And who else would be about to retrieve the treasure. Besides, now that he had changed the hiding place, no one would know where it was - beside the grave of his own mother.

    At the smoke house, Salter lowered the trunk outside the door. He would need a moment to rest and he would need a light to see himself through the dark woods to the sacred spot. He knew a spiritual calm when he remembered the unfinished carving of initials in the loft beam. He'd finish that one testimonial to his love.

Chapter 47

Present day

Richard slipped a crisp folded shirt into his bag.

"Why don't you let me drive you home, Christina," Richard offered half-heartedly.

But she shook her head. "I'm not sure… but I think I *am* home." Her attention fell to the old journal on his bedside table. "What's this?"

"Part of that treasure trove in your attic. Listen, when you decide to clear some of this clutter, give me a call. Don't throw anything out. Here." He handed her the attic inventory that Treeny had been compiling over the past year. She had logged most of the contents in looking for clues to the location of the treasure.

"I wouldn't dream of throwing any of it away."

They heard heavy footsteps ascending the stairs and Christina moved toward the door, selfishly clutching the journal to her breast.

"That'll be Jorgé. I should go find Treeny about lunch."

But something about his demeanor, when he rounded the corner at the top of the steps preempted her attempt to solve the awkwardness with food.

TWO MOONS OVER CEDAR HILL

"Ah. There you are." His gaze merely glanced off of Richard and his packed bag. "Is Stewart in the house?"

"Downstairs."

Ignoring Richard, Jorgé walked directly to Christina and took her hand in his.

"I'm afraid I have some sad news."

She caught her breath.

"I was just out in the barn. I caught sight of something out of the corner of my eye. It was old Beebo."

He did not need to say more. Christina melted into his arms, allowing her head to slide down to rest on his shoulder and linked her arms around his waist. Jorgé wrapped his arms around her shoulders and held her for a long while. Over her shoulder, Richard returned to the task of filling his open suitcase.

"Where is he? We should bury him… before Stewart stumbles over him… or Tomato sees him."

Jorgé pulled away and wiped the corner of his eye. "That was exactly my thought, so I took care of it already."

"Excuse me," Richard interrupted. "We are talking about that ancient, arthritic dog?"

Christina pulled away and breathed deeply. "He was a part of the family."

"You know what this means?" Richard sounded almost joyous over the news.

Christina could only look to Jorgé with distress.

Jorgé answered Richard's question. "It means the farm is Chita and Stewart's... to do with as they please." He smiled wanly.

No one heard Stewart as he came up the stairs behind them. "Well, we know that won't happen for a while." Coming in late, Stewart had only heard the last bit.

"Stewart. I didn't hear you."

"Are we having a sendoff party for Dick?"

Christina glared at her brother. "No. Listen Stewart." She softened and put a hand on his arm. "There's something we have to tell you." She looked to Jorgé, then back at her brother. "Something's happened. It's about Beebo."

The color drained from Stewart's face. "No."

"Listen, old man. He was an old dog."

"I just placed an order for some elk antler velvet. It's going to help his arthritis."

Jorgé shook his head. "He's not going to need it, Stewart."

Stewart appeared to be far more rattled by the dog's passing than Christina would ever have imagined. He took a step away from them.

"Wait. Wait there just a minute." Turning, Stewart ran to his room. He came out a minute later holding a piece of paper. "Look, Christina. You can't split up or sell the farm. It's not ours to sell."

Jorgé reached out for the paper, but Stewart pulled it away. "You can't let her do this, Jorgé." He thrust the paper at Christina, who took it with hesitation.

"That's the Will. That's Mama's Last Will and Testament. She left it to Jorgé to decide which he would put forward. He put forward the stupid one that left everything to the damn dog rather than the one that left him everything."

"Stewart. *Madre de Dios*. What are you doing to me?"

"I'm putting it out there for you, Jorgé. You see, Christina? He's been hanging around here all these years just waiting for you to come back. Mama was hanging around all these years waiting for Jorgé to fall in love with her, and you've been playing the martyr all these years, trying to keep me from the supposed truth about Annabelle."

"Annabelle. You know…?"

"That she's my half-sister? Of course not, you idiot. Don't you think I'd have known if we were related? Gross."

"Stewart, you are. That's why Mama wanted us to go away. She found out you were having an affair with Annabelle and she didn't want you to suffer when you found out she was Daddy's…."

"What? Daddy's Bastard child? She is no more related to us than Richard here, or Jorgé."

Christina was shaking her head. "But Mama was so certain. The red hair – just like Daddy's side of the family, her mother's history…."

"And that's all the evidence you had to base it on?" Stewart shook his head. "Before Jorgé told me why you were trying to keep me away, I talked to Annabelle. A few years back there was a big to do in these parts over a local politician passing away. You remember? That's when Annabelle found out who her real father is – a man related to us now by marriage, but not blood. Her Daddy, turned over a new leaf, from moonshiner to vintner to give Annabelle a respectable home life. He is her father – and no blood relation to us."

"That's how she came to be proprietor of the market. It's part of her father's estate."

"Mama told me… she was so certain. It ate her up inside to think of you and Annabelle… and your possible off-spring."

"Mayella allowed her anger at your father to determine paternity." Jorgé finally offered.

"But now… your inheritance…." Christina looked from the Will held limp in Stewart's hand to her brother's face, then, with regret to Jorgé. "Of course, I'm happy for you, Jorgé. It's what I would have done with the farm anyway… at least… my half."

TWO MOONS OVER CEDAR HILL

Jorgé reached out for the Will before Stewart could pull it away and it ripped in half. Christina gasped. Stewart blindly lunged for the torn piece.

"It's not my right, Christina."

"Inheritance isn't a question of anyone's right. We're all just stewards here, Jorgé. Maybe we're slaves. Like moths to firelight, victims of our own worst instincts. Our time here is transitory."

Jorgé threw up his hands with a laugh. "I know that," then as if suddenly remembering every reason he had to celebrate, he grabbed Christina up into his arms and kissed her soundly on the mouth. "I see the big picture. I'm not so good at focusing on the parts."

"Well, this is all warm and fuzzy," Richard finally pulled them out of their family hug. "I'm sorry about your dog, Stewart. I'm sorry I'll have to be leaving."

Stewart slapped Richard on the shoulder. "Sorry the blast didn't turn up anything for you, ol' boy. I know you'd have enjoyed seeing a treasure unearthed."

Richard smiled amiably. "I'm sure it'll turn up someday, Stewart."

"Or it won't. It doesn't really matter. It's the myth that matters."

Richard shrugged. "I thought you were close out there." He gestured toward the front of the house at the same instant he hefted his suitcase.

Sofie Couch

"I didn't. I was always pretty certain the only thing in Grace Thompson's grave was a lead box filled with her ashes."

Richard stopped. "Ashes?"

"Yeah. Not many people were cremated back then. Messy business – cremation. But there was a kiln on the property, perfect incinerator for that sort of thing. Daddy dug it up long time ago and found a metal box of ashes, so I was pretty sure the only thing out there was her urn of ashes. I'd be truly amazed if there was anything out there in the family cemetery of value."

Richard's eyes darted in the direction of the journal that Christina was clutching to her chest. "Here. Look at this."

Richard held out his hand and it took Christina a moment to register what he was requesting. Hesitantly, she handed over the journal. Richard opened the book to a dog eared page and pressed his finger to an underlined passage.

"I go there every day, still not knowing if this grave on the hillside holds Salter's body or my family's legacy. No plain stone would suffice for my one true love. I have saved enough of my husband's generous allowance to purchase a stone carved with the emblem that was always dear to his heart – the two moons with the single star..."

TWO MOONS OVER CEDAR HILL

"There," Richard read. "She was buried beside her lover. There's something metal down there... if Stewart didn't blow it to kingdom come today. It must be the treasure."

Christina held out her hand for the journal. "Where'd you find this?" Richard handed it back over and she read with Jorgé reading over her shoulder. He strained his eyes, then finally pulled reading glasses from his breast pocket. Christina touched the corner of his glasses.

Christina sank to the floor and Jorgé, more slowly, knelt down beside her. Leaning against the door frame, they read.

"'At the graveyard marked by four cedar trees.'"

"But that was more than a hundred, fifty years ago," Richard supplied. "They would be long gone by now."

"Not necessarily," Jorgé countered. "Cedar is a primitive tree - very long-lived."

"It's a field of soybeans now. They were cut down."

"Where did you bury Beebo?" Stewart interrupted and everyone looked up at him.

"Stewart, I'm sorry. I should have let you see him one last time first, but, I was afraid... Tomato.... I buried him out behind the barn."

But Christina followed her brother's train of thought. "The same place we buried your barn cat when you were a kid."

Then Jorgé caught on. "Not in the family plot. The pets are buried in a separate place."

"And Grace Thompson wasn't mourning the loss of a lover of whom the family approved."

She and Jorgé looked at each other.

Jorgé spoke the words aloud. "It was forbidden. He was a second class citizen – someone with whom her blood could never mingle."

"A slave," Stewart supplied.

"What? I'm not following."

Everyone turned their attention to Richard.

"S.B – Salter Lyons. Slaves often took or were given the last name of the white family who owned them."

"And G.T., was Grace Thompson."

Stewart filled in the gaps. "Salter was given the task of burying the family treasure, but something happened. He buried it, but he died before he could mark its location."

"And Grace Thompson," Christina continued, pulling the medallion out of her blouse, "mourned over what she thought to be his grave – a fresh turned grave in the *slave* cemetery. A cemetery marked by four cedar trees."

TWO MOONS OVER CEDAR HILL

"Which, one hundred, fifty years later is grown into a cedar forest… on a hillside," Jorgé contributed.

All eyes turned in the direction of the southwest mountains and the estate's namesake, Cedar Hill.

"We've been looking in the wrong cemetery."

They were silent while they individually put together the pieces of a puzzle that stretched back one hundred, fifty years. Finally, Jorgé looked up at Stewart and extended his hand for a helping hand up.

"You'll grab your metal detector?"

"Yeah. And I'll call Annabelle. You grab the shovel." Stewart pulled up short. "Tomato."

"He's in school. Should we wait?" Christina only just began to feel the full impact. Tomato was her nephew and *just* her plain old nephew, thank goodness.

Stewart was shaking his head though. "No. I don't want to drag him through this – the excitement, then the let-down, if we don't turn up anything." He was thinking like a father.

Christina slipped her necklace inside the crew neck of her knit shirt and they all turned to leave.

Richard's eyes widened with the implication, then he rushed to follow.

Chapter 48

1864

No one missed him after a day, but by the end of the second day, a general distress call had gone up among the neighbors.

Salter was missing.

It did not occur to anyone that Salter might have runaway in search of a better life. More likely, some accident had befallen him.

It rained most of the first day, so the family did not leave the house. Jack Lyons came early in the morning with odd tidings and officially dashed any expectation of an engagement to Grace for the following spring. He had entered the house without knocking and sprang to Mrs. Thompson's side, asking her to be strong, then upon seeing Grace on the stairs, he left in much the same hurry.

Grace thought she understood. Salter had gone away as her mother had instructed and poor Jack perhaps thought Grace had gone away with him. She spent much of the day in her room and when she came out in the evening, her eyes were red rimmed and her face was pale. Her mother credited her her good sense for being upset over her break up with Jack Lyons.

By the second day, the rain had stopped and Mrs. Thompson was able to take her daily walk to

TWO MOONS OVER CEDAR HILL

the graveside of her late son, only when she came back, she was more upset than Grace had been.

"The grave is still. There is no fresh turned dirt." She screamed, half hysterically at Grace. "You go to River's Edge and demand to speak with Salter. Bring him here."

Grace paled. "And you and I both know he's not there, Mama."

"He must be there. Go Grace. He will tell me what he's done with it or I'll have him beaten this side of death until he'll wish he could cross over."

Grace ran, without the aid of a wrap, across the back yard, past the incomplete folly. She was in tears by the time she reached the smoke house, but she knew what she would find there.

A dark woman followed on her heels as Grace threw open the door.

"Where is he?"

The dark woman was already crying. "He's been gone now two days. Disappeared night before last."

Grace ran to the Lyons's house. It was larger than her own home, yet it was cold. As Jack had done, without knocking, she pushed through the front door. A woman servant rose from cleaning the fireplace in the parlor.

"Miss Grace!" She wiped irreparably dirty hands on the front of her apron.

"Mr. Jack. I need to see him."

And immediately, this woman began weeping large, silent tears. "He's not here, Miss." The woman's eyes darted toward the mantle where a letter was propped against the looking glass. It had Grace's name on it.

Hastily, Grace snatched it down and tore open the blue tinged envelope.

"What's it mean, Miss?" The weathered woman begged, but Grace did not answer.

Grace felt for the medallion between her breasts, then turned and left the house, leaving the front door open in her wake.

It was uncertain whether anyone ever closed the door behind her. Weeks later, notice was received that Jack Lyons's body had been found on the banks of the James River near Richmond. A male relative took over the brick yard. With the end of the war, those oppressed people who were once enslaved, left the farm taking with them what little they needed to survive, some moving for a warmer climate further south, others taking work where they could find it, a few staying on at the only home they had ever known.

Grace knew Salter must be dead. Her suspicions were confirmed when, months later she chanced upon the slave burial ground. It was marked by four young cedar trees planted at its four corners and she knew who must be buried in the freshest of the graves. The wind blew a few leaves from the mound and the ground had yet to grow a cover. Every day she would walk to the site, talking to Salter about their unborn child.

Before the year was up, her father, freed from prison arranged her marriage. He was a cousin on her father's side of the family, and with her modest allowance, she was eventually able to purchase a headstone. Her husband was a good man. He probably suspected she had never married the father of her child – a lost love – but he did not suspect the father's race as their child was born a dark haired beauty. Out of respect for her husband she did not have a name carved on Salter's gravestone. Instead, she had the simple piece of granite marked with the same symbol that was on her necklace – two moons and a star.

After a short life as a wife and mother, Grace Thompson was laid to rest in the "family" plot. Her husband, being a modern man, had her cremated and her remains buried in a fancy lead lined box. As a tribute to his devotion to her, he had a gravestone made. "Grace Thompson, 1848-1865." He took from her, the terra cotta medallion she had always worn about her neck and in its stead, had the same design engraved on her stone. He never knew of the matching stone in a cemetery not often frequented by his brethren.

Chapter 49

Present day

Past the smoke house, Christina glanced at the spot where she and Jorgé had first kissed and where they had last kissed. She held his arm and helped him to limp after Richard and Stewart who led the way.

"We really should put some ice on that."

Jorgé looked at her like she was crazy.

"Yeah. I mean when we get back."

He nodded. "Good." And kept limping, leaning heavily on the shovel.

Jorgé's keen eye knew they were in the right place when they arrived. He pointed in the direction of an ancient, dead Cedar. Some minor sleuthing found the detritus remains of two other stumps. Cedars had long since come and gone – their numbers being strangled out by deciduous trees that towered over them. It was the natural progression of timber growth – a lightning strike, then brush, then cedars, then deciduous trees. The leaf litter from the deciduous trees had kept the undergrowth sparse. The first stone found was no more than an out of place bit of slate that thrust unnaturally up, out of the ground. Everyone spread out, moving the leaf litter with feet and hands until Richard called out.

"I think I've found something." He pulled up a stone that was lying flat on the ground. It had been cleared of dirt in the not so distant past, its face clean of moss and dirt – just a few leaves.

"There." Christina pointed to the etched symbol – the two moons and star just visible.

"Well," Jorgé looked around at them. "I guess this is it."

Stewart grinned, smiled at Annabelle who was still looking bewildered by the news.

Mostly, Jorgé, with his injured ankle, dug, taking turns with Chita, Annabelle and Richard while Stewart leaned on his red-tipped cane. Christina moved more dirt than Richard. Annabelle was slowly fed the details of the slow discovery.

"…and it was Richard here," Stewart pointed over his shoulder at Richard who was nearly useless at digging, "found the clue in the old diary about the cemetery marked by four cedars – the great-grandaddies of the farm's namesake, Cedar Hill. By the way, Dick, what are you charging us for your labor?" Stewart asked Richard who was leaning on one of the only two shovels.

"I don't think I've ever performed this much manual labor in one sitting. What's the going rate?" He looked to Jorgé whom he classed in the manual labor bracket.

"The reward is the thrill of the hunt," Stewart supplied.

"I'm beginning to see the appeal."

Richard shoved the spade into the ground and stopped.

"Oh no." He went down on his hands and knees and rubbed at something. "Oh no."

Christina and Jorgé moved to the edge of the hole. Christina caught her breath.

"*Madre de Dio.*"

"What is it?" Stewart asked, straining to see with his ears rather than with eyes.

With reverence, Jorgé picked up what looked at first like a stone. Only when he turned it to face them, did Christina realize what they were looking at.

"It *is* a grave."

Stewart took the skull that was handed up out of the hole. "It's a grave, alright." Stewart ran a finger across the brittle skull, and a chunk of dirt fell from the one intact eye socket.

Richard sat back on his haunches, evident disappointment on his face.

"So that's the end of the trail?"

Jorgé gingerly prodded a rib bone that protruded from the dirt.

"It would seem," Christina supplied.

"It is a set-back, but I do believe we were on the right trail." Jorgé sat down on the edge of the hole.

"Maybe Grace Thompson *did* know he was buried here," Christina said.

TWO MOONS OVER CEDAR HILL

"Maybe Grace Thompson knew something more." Stewart spoke from the side of the hole. He held out his hand, cradling a mud encrusted piece of metal, the brilliant gold reflecting sunlight for those with visual appreciation.

"Look at this." Richard pulled at a bit of fabric, miraculously preserved by the unusual mineral content of the soil. He swept at the dirt below, then looked up with a grin. "There's something else down here – under the body."

Everyone craned over the hole to see as it was revealed. Now with some of the reserve of a true salvager Richard moved aside the bones, laying some on the ground outside the hole, laying some to the side within the hole until his hands had brushed clear the lid of a metal steamer trunk. Richard looked up for assurance that what they were doing was alright, then cleared the dirt from the entire surface of the pock marked metal chest.

With more caution than Christina would have imagined Richard capable of, she watched as he patiently dug at the dirt around the sides with square cornered precision, ensuring its easy removal, before lifting it out with Jorgé's help.

Richard reached for the latches.

"No. Not yet." Stewart stopped him.

"The hell with that." Richard pulled at the rusty latch. It snapped off in his hand.

"Patience, man. It ain't going nowhere… and Tomato should be here."

"I've waited… for years." Everyone turned to the person who spoke from a little distance and whose footsteps through crisp leaves had been muffled by their excitement. "I'm not waiting anymore." Treeny stepped out of the woods. She held the last of Jorgé's triple-packed firecrackers in one hand, her cigarette lighter in the other.

Jorgé was the first person sensible to the threat of the woman he thought he knew. He took a step toward her, then stopped when she struck the lighter threateningly.

"That chest is mine."

"Mother. Be sensible." Richard took another step toward his mother, but she made the same threat and Jorgé put out his hand to stop the younger man.

"Treeny… is your mother?"

Richard ignored Christina's question. "It's not ours, Mother. It never was."

"He promised me! Stew said he couldn't marry me. Their mother wouldn't give him a divorce," and she pointed the accusation and the explosive at Christina. Jorgé stepped between Christina and Treeny. "He said he'd make up for what I lacked by way of a name the day he found that treasure." Her voice shook.

TWO MOONS OVER CEDAR HILL

"Mother, you're not going to do anything this desperate for what's probably going to turn out to be of no value."

But she turned the threat of her cigarette lighter on her own son. "It's not just for me. It's for you too. This was to take the place of your never having a daddy. And Stew's promise to me predates those Wills by about twenty years."

"Stew Senior's other family!" It was Jorgé who put it all together. "That's where I know you from."

"You're 'Trinity'." Christina still had the tennis bracelet, but had long since disposed of the card that named the intended recipient.

Stewart nodded, squinting his eyes. "You? You scooped me on the colt?"

"The colt?" Richard looked harried and only turned his attention away from his mother for an instant, but in that instant, she put lighter to fuse and threw the giant firecracker.

Like a choreographed dance, they each flew into action, knowing their roles. Richard launched toward his mother. Annabelle threw her body at Stewart. Jorgé launched his body at the fizzing fuse and Christina swung her arms to grab Jorgé and pull him back just before the extra-strength firecracker blew up.

The explosion shook the ground under their feet. A rain of leaf litter showered down on them, but quickly settled. Jorgé pulled away from Christina and they both ran to stamp out the sparks that ignited the combustible detritus on the ground.

Treeny wept and Richard held her in his arms like a distraught child. Stewart crept out from under Annabelle, assuring himself with his hands, that she was unharmed.

"You knew?" It was Christina who finally found her voice. "You've known all about me… my family… all these years?" Her tone held accusation and her betrayal was focused on Richard.

Richard nodded, looking up from his mother's huddled body. "The property on the water – the shop – was the only thing I had. I always wanted to be one of Dad's *real* children – you and Stewart – were all he ever talked about, his obligations to you, his guilt. I also heard about the treasure – constantly."

"This treasure was promised to countless people," Jorgé said with a calm soothing tone. He took a step toward Richard and his mother while still casting cautious glances at the singed spot on the forest floor. "You, your mother, Stewart, generations past. The irony is, the ground reclaims everything eventually." He looked down at the bones at his feet. "Our time here is fleeting and our deeds will be measured by the amount of time it takes the earth to recover from the damage we've inflicted."

TWO MOONS OVER CEDAR HILL

"You were Daddy's other family." Christina stepped up beside Jorgé, but looked down at Richard and Treeny. "That makes you a part of our family. No one, none of us, would ever try to take from you what should be shared."

Richard looked from one to the other as though they were mad.

"She really wasn't trying to take anything that wasn't promised to her. She's not like that," Richard tried to excuse his mother's actions.

"Promised or not, it's not a matter of birthright, due, or inheritance." Stewart shrugged. "It's our history. Like it or not, it's who we are, where we came from and our future." He scowled. "I may not like it, but I guess, it's yours too." Christina and Jorgé both nodded, then looked to Richard.

"You people are crazy," but Richard's focus was on his mother who was still squatting in front of him and rocking on her haunches.

"Yeah, but we're your family, so you're stuck with us," Christina said.

The tension left Richard's shoulders. Jorgé moved to his side and together, they lifted Treeny from the ground, then led her back to the house followed by Christina, with Annabelle and Stewart bringing up the rear. They all kept glancing behind, assuring themselves that the treasure really was there.

Treeny was put to bed with Annabelle acting as her nurse. She had been sedated with a pill left over from Mayella's cache of prescription drugs.

And attention returned to the dirt encrusted chest.

"I'm standing here, in awe of you, Stewart." Richard watched him with new respect. "One latch is already broken off, man. At least, let's have a peek."

"Come on, Dad. Just a peek."

Stewart smiled at Tomato, brushed a glob of dirt from the trunk lid, ran his hand over the top with reverence, then slowly put his hand to the remaining latch and flipped it up.

TWO MOONS OVER CEDAR HILL

Chapter 50

October 23rd:

I have telephoned Christina and asked that she come home. I could not bring myself to tell her that I would not be able to extend my life until she arrives. I haven't the courage for that.

I have stolen from my child ten years of happiness that she might have spent with the man we both love. I can take no more from her. So I have left to Jorgé, my entire estate. He has remained faithful to her, so I am confident that this will settle any doubt I may have planted so many years ago. Christina will see that he loved her only — not me and not for the farm he might have gained through marrying either of us.

No one should have to suffer the existence I have led in waiting for a man who would never love me in return.

I cannot tell what the ramifications will be of my actions, but I feel in my heart that this rights several very old wrongs. Perhaps it ends a family history of matriarchal solitude — the sad fate of so many of my female ancestors.

Jorgé read the last entry in Mayella's journal, then passed the book to Christina.

A day later, Jorgé picked up a small metal box, he opened the lid and cast the burnt chips of bone into a grave on a hillside in the forest. The other bones that had, for so long, guarded over a treasure, now lay beside the ashes of another.

"G.T. plus S.L."

Jorgé closed the lid, tucked the box under his arm, and then reached for Christina's hand.

Christina reached to the necklace still around her neck and pulled out the clay fired medallion. "I'm sorry you had to lose something of your history in all of this."

Jorgé shrugged. "I found my future." He kissed her.

"Do you think it should be returned to its rightful owner?"

Jorgé covered the medallion in his hand, then pressed it to her heart. "It *has* been returned to its rightful owner." He reached to his own neck and pulled out the strip of leather that used to be on the necklace. He had retrieved it from the cigar box in the trash beside their bed. Raising it to his lips, he kissed it.

"And from one enslaved man, freed to the earth, to another, I won't forget whose sweat this bears and I'll be honored to wear it as if he were my family."

Christina hesitated a moment before allowing herself to be led away from the old burial site. Arm and arm, they made the trek back to the house.

"Your brother and Richard are disappointed you're not more involved in the cataloging of the family treasure."

TWO MOONS OVER CEDAR HILL

"It sounds as though he and Richard have finally found a common interest. And truth of it is, I don't think Stewart has had much thought for me lately. Not now that he has Tomato to share this adventure with, and Annabelle in his life again."

"And Stewart and Richard are like long lost friends – or at least companionable brothers who have overcome their sibling rivalry. I am surprised though. Richard's interest in the treasure does not seem mercenary as I would have expected. He is a genuine admirer of antiquities and history. Perhaps, like me, he's just been searching all this time for family."

When they reached the salt house, Jorgé slowed down, then stopped to look in the door. "I share much in common with Salter Lyons. Much of the undocumented migrant community shares a common bond with this man."

Christina ducked under his armpit and stood in the center of the main room. "It still has really good karma."

"It would make a warm home for two people who didn't mind close quarters."

"And the main house is getting crowded." Christina made herself comfortable on the hearth.

"It could use some plumbing... and electricity wouldn't hurt. You wouldn't miss your home?"

"This is home." She rose from the hearth and wrapped her arms around his waist.

Chapter 51

1865

Grace Thompson rocked in a chair and looked down on the beautiful face of her brown eyed child. She nursed at her breast and she traced the outline of her dark downy hair around her forehead. Behind her, the door opened and her husband stepped out onto the porch. The doctor was often on call, and he was on his way to Dragon where a family of six all suffered from a common illness.

He bent and kissed his wife, before kissing the child that was asleep at her breast.

Grace had found her smile again in the months following her confinement, then her marriage. She knew her husband probably suspected she was not a war widow, but he never questioned her and he accepted her child as his own. The baby's eyes were blue at birth, but they had quickly turned to the amber tinted brown. Her hair, though downy soft, would have a decided curl that would reappear in future generations and she would grow up to be strong, enriched by the diversity in her blood. And like her father, she would be a steward of this farm to the west of the bay and east of Cedar Hill.

TWO MOONS OVER CEDAR HILL

Credits and Acknowledgements:

Special thanks to the staff at the Albemarle County Historical Society in Charlottesville, Virginia.

I would also like to acknowledge my beta reader extraordinaire, Beate Boeker – a skilled writer whose opinion I greatly value. If Beate says, "fix it", I don't ask why. I just fix it.

Cover art by Sasa Jareb.

Sofie Couch

I hope you have enjoyed TWO MOONS OVER CEDAR HILL. This book has several "sister books" which you may enjoy as well.

MOONSHINE

Rivanna Rivers wants to find the father who left her saddled with the same name as a local tributary.
Matt Maddox wants to avoid going to jail, but that's hard to do when your family invites scandal, your wife turns up dead, and you produce moonshine to support your family.
Annabelle Freeman just wants to get through "back-to-school" night without anyone discovering that she buried her grandfather in the garden.
Independently, they learn they all have three things in common: family, moonshine, and murder.

ANGELS UNAWARES: Fall For Grace

The Grim Reaper can kill with a touch. Too bad for the girl he loves.
Grace Breeden sees dead people. But why then can't she see her late mother? "Blue guys", as Grace refers to them, roam the earth searching for their opportunity to transcend, but one particularly persistent blue guy is shadowing Grace, involving her in near misses that lead her to surmise that there's something a bit "grim" about this specter. Keeping her friends close and the Angel of Death closer, she tries to save her living family from the reaper, but someone, or something, is threatened by her gifts... and wants her dead.

TWO MOONS OVER CEDAR HILL

You can find these, and more books by Sofie Couch at Amazon, Kindle.com, and discerning booksellers everywhere!

Printed in Great Britain
by Amazon.co.uk, Ltd.,
Marston Gate.